DOUG HELD OUT
A COMB TO HER

"The entire time you were on the phone you were combing those curls of yours with your fingers. Just trying to be helpful."

Nicki could feel her cheeks getting hot. "I always do that when I'm thinking."

"Do tell." Doug leaned over the desk toward her as he slipped the comb back into his pocket. "It's kind of cute."

This was not at all the scenario Nicki had planned. She made an effort to take control. "You're a very quick student of law, Dr. MacNair, but I cannot and will not allow you to disrupt my class as you did today."

To her surprise, Doug smiled and leaned even closer to her. "So how about we go out to dinner, Counselor, and you set me straight?"

He tried to touch her hand, but she pulled it away in time. Unfortunately, before she could stop herself, she used it to fluff her curls.

Doug laughed. "At least I can see you're thinking about it...."

ABOUT THE AUTHOR

There's a saying in publishing circles that the second novel is always the most difficult. Not so with Chicago-area author Jeanne Triner. After completing her first novel, the highly acclaimed Superromance *By Any Other Name*, Jeanne took a well-deserved holiday in Kenya with her husband. Then it was back to the computer to create yet another winning Superromance. Like Nicki Devlin, the heroine of *Make No Mistake*, Jeanne has enjoyed a successful law career. And, like Nicki, Jeanne has the determination and devotion to beat the odds and achieve her dreams!

Books by Jeanne Triner

HARLEQUIN SUPERROMANCE
267—BY ANY OTHER NAME

Jeanne Triner

MAKE NO MISTAKE

Harlequin Books

TORONTO • NEW YORK • LONDON
AMSTERDAM • PARIS • SYDNEY • HAMBURG
STOCKHOLM • ATHENS • TOKYO • MILAN

Published August 1988

First printing June 1988

ISBN 0-373-70319-8

Printed in U.S.A.

To Connie
With special thanks for your expert advice.
Any credit for accuracy belongs to you.
Any blame for mistakes is mine.

CHAPTER ONE

"LADIES AND GENTLEMEN of the jury..." Nicki Devlin tried not to limp as she stepped around the lectern to approach the jury box. The last minutes of the closing argument were an important part of her case and no time to risk being accused of using her own misfortune to win the sympathy of the jury.

"Four years ago my client, Carol Stuart, took a break from her rigorous schedule to enjoy a camping vacation with her family. For the first time in years, she allowed herself to do some of the things that other sixteen-year-olds might do on a carefree summer day. She even took her brother's dare and climbed a tree."

Nicki looked over to see Carol listening intently. They were probably the only two people in this room who understood how few and far between those moments of adolescent foolishness were for a competitor in training.

"Only when the branch snapped beneath her did she remember that champion gymnasts shouldn't take such needless risks. Carol had had her share of injuries in practice, and she knew the minute she hit the ground that she had broken her arm."

Nicki squeezed her eyes closed briefly, remembering the many times she'd known, in the middle of a fall, that it was going to be worse than the others.

She took a deep breath before continuing. "As Carol's parents drove her to the emergency room of Hickman

General Hospital, she reviewed her situation. A broken bone would delay her training program, but it was not the end of the world. She'd been through it before, and she knew she should be sufficiently healed in plenty of time for her next major competition. That was four years and three operations ago. Today, Carol still has pain, her arm is a mass of scars, and all the doctors agree that she will never regain the full use of her right hand. Why is that?''

Nicki paused for emphasis and rested her hands on the jury rail. This was definitely one of those times she wished she weren't so short. It would be much more impressive if she could loom intimidatingly over the rail, rather than having it hit her just below the ribs. ''Carol Stuart has lost the vital function of her hand because the staff at Hickman General was negligent in the care they rendered her. The doctors there either didn't remember or didn't think it was necessary to check for compartment syndrome, bleeding and swelling in the muscles near a break that might cause pressure on the nerves, even though both Carol and her parents asked whether the test was advisable. Five hours later, after Carol was flown home to consult with her specialist, it was too late. She had already suffered irreversible nerve damage.''

Again Nicki paused. She rubbed her fingers up and down the palm and back of her own hand, studying it thoughtfully. She wasn't certain she was making the desired impression on the jury, but her own stomach was churning. She could still vividly recall the agony of hearing the words ''irreversible damage'' applied to her. She had been so sure that her life had come to an end. In many ways Carol had been stronger than Nicki had. She had faced up to her injury rather than wasting time, first with the denial, then with the bitterness. But Carol had someone else to blame for what had happened to her. The doctors were clearly at fault.

Nicki had only herself to blame. She had allowed her emotions to affect her performance, and it had cost her dearly. She clenched her hands and relaxed them again as she addressed the jury.

"Now some of you might be thinking that we are asking for a lot of money to compensate a young woman for decreased use of her hand. And if Carol Stuart were just any young woman, you might be right. This would still be a serious injury, an injury that demands compensation, but not the type of injury that destroys a person's life. But, until that day four years ago when she trusted the emergency room staff at Hickman General to care for her simple fracture, Carol Stuart was one of the top three gymnasts in the country. After all the years of training, all the years of sacrifice on the part of herself and of her family, Carol Stuart was on her way to the Olympics."

Nicki glanced pointedly at the distinguished, elderly attorney behind the defense table. "All during this trial my opponent has contended that there is no evidence that the plaintiff would have been successful in that competition." She pushed her fingers through her short, curly, blond hair, leaving the impression that she was confused by his argument. "Ladies and gentlemen, I have no intention of suggesting that my client would have won fame and fortune through her participation in the Olympics. I am merely going to point out that Carol Stuart was well on her way to successfully pursuing her life's goal and to request that, when the jury considers the question of what value to place upon Carol Stuart's pain and suffering, they be sure to ask themselves—" Nicki backed away from the rail to scan the whole jury at once "—how much is a dream worth?"

TWO HOURS LATER Nicki sank gratefully into the leather sofa in her office, tucked her stockinged feet under her and smiled at Carol. "Sit down and relax for a minute. Watching you bounce around is more exhausting than the trial was."

"I can't sit down. We won! Your law partner just told me the jury brought in the largest award ever given in a case that didn't involve permanent paralysis."

Nicki let her smile widen into a grin. "Yeah, that would excite Ron, all right. Personally, the high point of the whole trial for me is that this is the first time the press has reported on one of my cases without referring to me as 'a one-time Olympic hopeful.' I've finally graduated from failed athlete to successful attorney."

"Come on, Nicki. You've been a success from the beginning and don't pretend that you aren't just as happy about this verdict as I am. Now that the trial is over, I want you to know how much I appreciate everything you've done—and I don't mean just the legal stuff. I couldn't have gotten through this if you hadn't been there for me as a friend as well as a lawyer. When we started out, I was just grateful to have someone with your reputation and track record representing me. I had no idea how lucky I really was. Even if we'd lost, I would still have come out ahead, just because I got to know you."

"Bite your tongue, kiddo. We never talk about losing in this office, and that applies to friends as well as cases. Don't you dare lose touch now that you have your happy ending."

"How can you think I would do that? I intend to be an absolute pest." Carol plopped down onto the arm of the sofa. "Now, what's next for you—another confrontation with a medical malefactor?"

Nicki threw up her hands in mock horror. "Please, no. I need time to recover. Let me rest on my laurels for a while."

Carol shook her head. "If I've learned anything these past months, it's that Nicki Devlin doesn't rest, period. Whatever's next on your agenda, you'll throw yourself into it heart and soul—the curse of the trained athlete. In my case, since Mom's doing everything for Eric's and my wedding, I'm going to work on throwing myself into some serious rest and recreation. You should consider it."

"Funny you should mention that. I don't know if it qualifies as R and R, but I'm escaping from the courtroom into the classroom for a while. I'm going to teach a trial practice course and a seminar on handling malpractice cases at the state university in Riverdale, and I'm looking forward to getting out of Chicago and enjoying small-town campus life."

"Sounds great. Maybe you'll connect up with a cute professor."

"No thanks. I'll have enough on my hands. My kid sister's in grad school down there, and she's dating the 'cute professor' I'm replacing. She's put me on notice that I have to keep her entertained while he's off on sabbatical. I won't have time for anyone else."

Carol leaned over and gave Nicki a brief hug. "Just be sure you take some time for yourself. You deserve it. Now, I have to run. Thanks again for everything. I'll call in a week or so to see how you're doing down in the pastures of southern Illinois."

Nicki walked Carol to the door, then put on her boots, gathered her coat and gloves and stood for a minute at the office window looking out over Michigan Avenue to the icy, January lakefront.

She was genuinely fond of Carol and was glad the trial had ended successfully, but the victory left her as much tired as elated. Ever since her accident, she had been working toward making the courtroom the arena in which she satis-

fied her aching need to compete. When she'd graduated
from law school, she had sought out a firm that specialized
in personal injury cases and, because of her unique background and special rapport with athletes, had quickly established herself in the sports injury field. Her big break had
come when a senior partner, banking on her impact with the
jury, turned the high-profile *Ryan v. MacWilliam* case over
to her. Her victory made the national news and launched her
career. She left the firm with her reputation solidly established and opened her own partnership with Ron Foley.
Since then the work, and the successes, had been nonstop.

After handling several cases a year, Nicki knew she
needed a break. She had been pushing herself too hard
lately, and her instincts told her this was no different from
when she had been skiing competitively. She had to stay
alert for signs of burnout. Replacing her sister's boyfriend,
Blake Windham, for a semester, offered Nicki a welcome
change. She was looking forward to trying her hand at
teaching a bunch of eager law students to be top-notch trial
attorneys.

DR. DOUG MACNAIR STOPPED in the doorway at the front
of the lecture hall to straighten his tie. Much as he hated to
admit it, he was nervous. The empty chairs, ranged in
heighted ranks to almost surround the professor's lectern,
seemed intimidating. When Doug had arranged to audit this
law school class as a part of his campaign to establish a
medical malpractice risk management program at the hospital, his only concern had been to acquire as much information about malpractice trial law as possible so he could
teach medical personnel how to protect themselves against
lawsuits. He hadn't anticipated first-day-of-school jitters,
but they would be worth it if it helped to get his risk management proposal accepted by the hospital board.

A quick survey of the room told him that, with the exception of his best friend Dr. Paul Carlson and an attractive, young woman with curly hair who was sitting in the highest row at the back of the room, he was the first to arrive. He tucked his newspaper under his arm and put a hand in the pocket of his slacks, hoping to affect a suave yet casual air as he sauntered past the lectern to take a front row seat next to his friend. He pulled the desk arm of the chair into place, then slouched back and extended his legs, crossed at the ankles.

Paul never lifted his eyes from the thick, blue textbook he was studying. "Can it, Doug. The pink sport coat becomes you, but there isn't anyone here to appreciate your act."

"That so? What about the adorable mop-top sitting in the back row?"

"Are you kidding me? It's amazing her mother allowed her out without a sitter. She's a baby, MacNair. If your midlife crisis is going to cause you to persist in this ridiculous ladies' man routine, the least you could do is play with the big girls."

"I resent that. I'm only thirty-nine. What makes you think my desire to wear something other than hospital greens for a change and to develop some semblance of a social life is a midlife crisis?"

Paul shook his head and looked toward the ceiling. "Take your life expectancy and divide it by two. What's that tell you?"

"I'm an obstetrician, not a mathematician." Doug sat up straight, pushed his newspaper off the desk and used picking it up as an excuse to twist around for another look at the back of the room.

The woman was preoccupied with writing something on a legal pad, so he took a moment to study her. She was young all right, but hardly a baby. He'd guess twenty-nine or thirty. She just gave the impression of being younger because she was such a tiny little thing. That crazy mass of blond curls didn't do much to add sophistication, even with the aid of the tailored, navy-blue pin-striped suit. This was undoubtedly the kind of woman who grinned sheepishly instead of smiling, he told himself. Just as he was about to turn away, she looked up and caught him watching her. He gave an embarrassed shrug, and she smiled knowingly at him. "Wrong on that point, MacNair," he mumbled, as he took a deep breath and faced forward. "Nothing sheepish about that."

Paul arched an eyebrow. "It's been a long time since I've seen you blush."

"What do you suppose it means if the first time a woman smiles at you, you feel your heart flip over, your pulse start to race, and you can't breathe anymore?"

"Cardiac arrest?"

"This is serious, Paul. I think I'm in love."

"Take two aspirin and call me in the morning."

"My friend, the cliché." Doug sat back and began to hum "My Girl" as he flipped through the paper and watched the students coming into the classroom.

He was just beginning to tap out the rhythm on his desk when Paul sat upright and glared at him. "Will you stop with the concert already? Since I let you talk me into attending this class with you, the least you can do is let me take it seriously. I'm trying to study here."

"Study? Study what? This is the first day. You don't even know what the assignment is. Besides, we're only auditing. I doubt Blake is going to call on us."

"Honestly, MacNair, I don't know what you'd do if you didn't have me to keep you in touch with the real world. In the first place, this is law school not kindergarten. The assignments have been up on the bulletin board near the bookstore for a week."

"Bookstore?"

"Yes, bookstore. As in the place where one buys books."

"I thought we might share."

"Think again. Second, the hospital is not paying your tuition just so you can sit here and ogle female law students. You are supposed to be learning enough about a trial lawyer's approach to malpractice cases to be able to teach the rest of us poor abused doctor types how to prevent lawsuits."

"I know that. It was my idea. Remember?"

"Then you should do your homework. Third, Blake Windham isn't teaching the course this semester. He just got the chance to go to sunny California for six months to work on his book."

"I'll kill him. No way I'll sit through this course if Jennings is teaching it. That man thinks the only purpose for doctors is to provide someone for lawyers to sue." .

"It won't be Jennings. They brought in someone from outside. Blake recommended her."

"Her?"

"Ah-ha—I thought that might interest you. Nicole Devlin. I'm surprised you haven't heard about her. All the law students are ecstatic at getting the chance to work with her. She just won the Stuart case. You know, the one that was in the papers a couple of weeks ago—the gymnast with a stiff hand."

"Darn right I know. An old classmate of mine was one of the physicians on that case."

"Then he didn't learn as much in medical school as you did. The emergency room staff really botched that one."

Doug could feel himself getting mad. His own malpractice trial had been almost five years ago, but the hurt and anger it had caused him was as intense as if it had been yesterday. "Botched it? Isn't that an interesting position for another physician to take? Are doctors supposed to be infallible, Paul? No allowances for mistakes?"

"Sure we make mistakes, but if those doctors at Hickman had had the guts to recognize their mistake in the first place and had stopped playing God long enough to listen to the patient and her parents, that young lady would have had her shot at the Olympics."

"We don't know that."

"I suppose we don't, but apparently the jury thought they did, and I happen to agree with them. I read the transcript and Ms Devlin presented a very fair and convincing case."

"Don't you mean put on a good show?"

"No, I don't. And if you're going to be that bitter, you're going to be wasting your time here."

"I'm not bitter, but I do know what it's like to sit on the stand and try to explain what happened while some attorney interrupts you, leads you on and makes you talk in circles until he destroys your credibility in front of everybody. Those are the tactics lawyers, such as our substitute professor, use to win their cases. Believe me, I'd like nothing better than to turn the tables on her."

"Come on, Doug. You always tell the residents and interns to keep an open mind. We don't even know the lady." Paul paused and winked. "I hear she's great looking and, with all those contingency fees, she must be rolling in it. Could be just what you're looking for."

Doug acknowledged Paul's attempt to break the tension by trying to tease back. "No thanks. None of those competitive courtroom types for me. Besides, I'm already in love with curly-top back there." He cocked his head to the back of the room. "Remember?"

"So glad you're beginning to take love seriously."

"I've been serious about everything for too long now, don't you think? I'm ready to have a little fun." He grinned and rubbed his hands together. "And for the next hour I'm going to get my kicks by heckling one Ms Devlin, malpractice attorney extraordinaire."

Paul sighed. "If that's going to make you feel better about something that happened years ago then go ahead, but I suggest you proceed with caution. If she's as tough in the classroom as she's supposed to be in the courtroom, you might find yourself standing in the corner."

At the sound of the first class bell, Doug and Paul ceased their conversation, as did most of the students near them. Doug glanced around and saw that the room was almost full now. Most people were looking expectantly toward the door.

Nicki smiled to herself as she scanned the class from her seat at the back of the room. Brushing her fingers through her curls, she stood up stiffly. "You may all close your books and relax. Today we're just going to chat."

Thirty heads turned at once to look at her as she made her way down the steps to the front of the lecture hall. Mercifully, her leg felt good today. She could control the limp.

"Good afternoon. I'm Nicole Devlin. It will be my pleasure to teach this course this semester and your good fortune to take it. If you've been paying attention so far, you've already learned more about winning in the courtroom than most attorneys know after seveal years in practice...."

"Such as the importance of being arrogant?"

There was a collective gasp from the class but Nicki showed no reaction. She focused on the man in the deep rose blazer. He had looked so good-natured before—when she'd caught him watching her and had been rewarded by his embarrassed, crooked smile. But now, with his bushy eyebrows knit together and his cheek muscles hardened to smooth planes, he was clearly angry about something, and she had no desire to be the victim of that anger. She had only a moment to assess the situation and respond. Older, expensively dressed and hostile, undoubtedly one of the visiting doctors she'd noticed on the class roster, and given his thick reddish-brown hair and bronze complexion, he probably wasn't Dr. Carlson.

"Arrogant, Dr. MacNair?" He looked surprised. Good, she'd called it correctly. "Self-confidence and knowing how to press an advantage is not arrogance. Juries seldom find arrogance too endearing—which is why doctors often have problems with jury trials, I might add—but the confidence that you are in control at all times is critical to the presentation of your case."

"And you feel that you're in control as long as you can sneak up from behind?"

All of her mental warning signals were flashing. The man was on the attack, and he wasn't about to be put off too easily. So be it. She thrived on competition.

"Thank you, Dr. MacNair. Point two, don't hesitate to use the element of surprise to catch an opponent off guard. As long as you don't stab anyone in the back, there's nothing wrong with sneaking up from behind."

The class laughed nervously and Nicki smiled to ease the tension that was strung across the room. "Sometimes the smartest move is to stand back long enough to assess the situation and the other players. That's point three. Don't ever underestimate the opposition. Learn all you can about their style and their strategy so that—"

"What about learning all you can about the facts of the case? Do they mean anything to you or is it all just a game you play—spouting platitudes about justice and fair trials when you're really destroying someone's career and life for the sport of it?"

Several of the students groaned with annoyance, but Nicki simply leaned back against the blackboard, crossed her arms and, with a steady stare, appraised her opponent. She felt the corners of her mouth pull tight as she struggled to control her temper. Fortunately she'd developed a talent for doing just that. "I can see your point, Dr. MacNair, although I'd prefer if you had couched it more as a question than as an accusation. I'm sure there are some attorneys who consider our legal system to be a game, just as there are some bad and careless doctors. But for most of us, the facts of the case are the only things that matter. Because of the competitive nature of trial law, it is easy to lapse into the terminology that is used when discussing games, and many of those terms do apply—rules, strategy, calling the plays and, most of all, good sportsmanship. These are the things I hope to teach you during this semester."

She pushed herself away from the blackboard and handed a stack of course outlines to the man she assumed was the other doctor. "Dr. Carlson?" He nodded uncomfortably, as though embarrassed by or for his associate. "Take one and pass them on, please." MacNair himself looked only thoughtful. Perhaps her response had diffused his anger for the moment.

She had planned a short class and was able to complete her introductory lecture and make her comments about the format of the course without further incident.

"Thank you, Dr. MacNair, for helping me to illustrate my points so effectively, including the last one for today, which is to always keep the jury's attention. I'm sure we've managed to keep the class mesmerized." She offered him her hand and he took it with a hesitant smile. His grip was impersonal but firm and warm, and he held her fingers just a fraction longer than Nicki would have expected. She felt her heartbeat quicken for an instant as she narrowed her eyes at him. He acknowledged her questioning look with an almost imperceptible nod of his head, which left her to wonder whether he had shared her reaction or simply noted it.

He turned to face the class. "Don't forget sportsmanship. Even we arrogant doctors can be gracious in defeat."

The class applauded and Nicki laughed in spite of herself. This was going to be an interesting, but probably not relaxing, eighteen weeks.

As the students began to file out of the classroom, she again focused her attention on MacNair. "Since we finished early I assume that you have no conflicting appointments. I would like to see you in my office in a few minutes."

Dr. Carlson began to ease his tall frame out of his desk chair. "I tried to warn you, Doug. This is the part where she makes you stand in the corner. Go for it, Professor. He's gotten entirely too used to being teacher's pet."

Doug gave them both a disgusted glare, and Nicki laughed again. "Oh, we'll break him of that soon enough. Law school has a reputation for being a very humbling experience." When she left the room, she was struggling to keep her anger with her. She would need it if she were going to convince her troublesome student to behave himself. But try as she might, she could not shake the thought that Doug MacNair was a very nice name and the man who carried it had one terrific smile and a handshake that made her head spin—certainly not the kind of reaction Nicki was used to. She had grown up knowing the importance of keeping a clear head.

She turned down the hall that led to the faculty offices and quickened her step when she heard her phone ringing. She was still talking to her partner ten minutes later when Doug strolled in. He pulled a chair up to her desk, braced his elbows on the armrests, propped his chin on his hands and proceeded to stare at her. She turned her back to him and pretended to take notes as she listened to Ron flipping through papers on the other end of the line.

"The office looks like a tornado hit since you left, and I can't find the file right now, but I tell you, Nicki, this one is perfect for you."

"You think they're all perfect for me, Ron. How can your office possibly be a mess when I took all the work with me?"

"Come on, Nicki, be a nice girl and just check it out. Something very strange happened with this kid and the hospital is right around the corner from you, so it'll be convenient, and..."

Nicki glanced nervously back at Doug. "Listen, I can't talk right now, but I'll get back to you in a bit." She dropped the phone into the cradle, threw down her pencil with a flourish and turned to Doug.

"It's got to stop, MacNair."

"I couldn't agree more." He reached into his inner jacket pocket and held a comb out to her.

She stared blankly at him.

"I assure you it's clean." He leaned over the desk toward her.

"I don't remember asking. Hygiene isn't part of the curriculum."

"Just trying to be helpful. The entire time you were on the phone you were combing those curls of yours with your fingers."

Nicki could feel her cheeks get hot. "I always do that when I'm thinking."

"Do tell?" Doug nodded his head slightly as he slipped the comb back in his pocket. "It's kind of cute."

This was not at all the scenario Nicki had planned. She stood up in an effort to take control. "You're a very quick student, Dr. MacNair. I must admit you did take me by surprise."

He leaned back, rested his right foot on top of his left knee and put his hands behind his head. "Not quick enough, I'm afraid. I've underestimated my opponent, haven't I?"

"Definitely." She walked around the desk and stepped behind him, both to get herself a moment's reprieve from his piercing stare and to force him to change his relaxed position. He didn't move. "I cannot and will not allow you to disrupt my class as you did with your questions today."

"I thought that was what law school was all about—Socratic method—asking questions."

"It is. I, the scholarly professor, ask. You, the earnest student, answer."

"That's not fair."

"Life's not fair." Nicki had been on her feet, in heels, most of the day, and her leg was beginning to throb. She went back to the chair, closing her eyes with relief as she sat down. When she opened them again Doug was looming over the desk at her, resting tensely on the knuckles of his powerful hands, partial fists warning her that he was about to challenge.

"No, life isn't fair, Ms Devlin, but you're the one who can't accept that, aren't you?" He leaned closer, and she rolled her chair backward but wouldn't allow herself to look away. He gave her no chance to answer. "Sometimes a baby is born with a deformity. That's not fair. Sometimes someone has an operation that doesn't work out. That's not fair. And sometimes a pretty young woman suffers an injury that isn't fixed just right, and she's left with a limp that she can't cover up all the time. That's not fair, either. It's easy to see how that might make her bitter, how she might think that if she could make someone else pay, some doctor for example, that would make things more fair, but it won't, you know."

Nicki drew a sharp breath as she felt her chest muscles tighten. She narrowed her eyes and watched Doug push himself away from the desk and roll his shoulders in a visible attempt to relax. It was a struggle for her to control her initial flash of anger, but she knew the best way to counter his outburst was to remain calm. Better to take her turn at sitting back in the chair and observing him. To stop herself from running her fingers through her hair, she picked up a pencil and tapped it thoughtfully against her teeth.

To her surprise, Doug smiled at her. "I guess we both have an oral fixation. You eat pencils. I run off at the mouth. So what do you think. Do I have a future in courtroom rhetoric?"

She felt a wave of relief. Apparently his latest tirade was over. "Well, you certainly have the unpredictability element down cold, but the rest of the presentation needs work."

He sat on the edge of her desk, one leg over the corner, the gray flannel of his trousers pulled tight across his muscular thigh. She found his athletic build disturbingly attractive.

"Really? I would have thought presentation would be my strong point." The suggestive tone of his voice gave her the uncomfortable impression that he had been reading her thoughts.

"Sorry to disappoint you, but you have a lot to learn. Not the least of which is don't challenge the motivations of your witness unless you are positive you know all the facts. You called this one wrong, MacNair. I don't..." She stopped herself. She didn't owe him any painful explanations about her past.

He waited expectantly for her to go on, and when she didn't, he started to say something, paused, then leaned closer to her again. "So, how about we go out to dinner, Counselor, and you set me straight on the facts?"

He tried to touch her hand, but she pulled it away in time. Unfortunately, before she could stop herself, she used it to fluff her curls.

Doug laughed. "At least I can see you're thinking about it. What do you say?"

She reached out to finger the material of his ultrasuede jacket. "I say I make it a practice never to date men who dress better than I do."

"What if it's just my defense mechanism? If the clothes are flashy enough, you don't notice the slightly oversized nose, the lopsided smile, and the gray eyes that I've always thought were uninteresting until I realized they were exactly the same color as yours—so they must be stunning after all."

Nicki heard the compliment, but chose to ignore it. "I think you've made a mistake, Doctor. I'm not the right type of counselor to help you overcome your insecurities."

Doug shook his head and massaged his jawline. "You're good. I bet you never lose a case."

"I don't lose because I never take a case that doesn't deserve to be won on the facts."

"The facts as you see them."

"Of course."

"I guess that's fair."

"I always try to be, except in the classroom, as you've pointed out."

"If that were true, you'd go out with me and give me a chance to redeem myself."

"I'll do better than that. I'll just forgive you here and now. Given that glint in your eye, I think your hopes for redemption are slim at best."

"I'm crushed."

"I doubt it. Now if you'll excuse me, Dr. MacNair, I have a cocktail party to attend."

Doug snapped his fingers as he left his perch on the desk and stood directly in front of her. "Hot dog, the cocktail party. I forgot all about it."

Nicki raised her eyes slowly. He wasn't particulary tall—a little under six feet perhaps. But as she looked up at his broad shoulders, she felt positively tiny by comparison. It was disconcerting, and she refused to allow herself that response. She had already lost a beat in her comeback. "Did I just hear you say 'hot dog'?"

He nodded innocently.

"I could have sworn you were a younger man than that."

She gasped as Doug caught her hand and clasped her fingers to the side of his neck. "The jugular is right here. Use a knife next time. It hurts less."

She could feel his pulse beating against her palm. "Another insecurity?"

"I'm loaded with them. The unfortunate by-product of having known too many cruel and heartless women." He winked at her and brushed his lips over her fingertips before letting go of her hand. "The good news is you still have a chance to make it all better. I'm going to the cocktail party too."

Nicki had never encountered anyone this skillful at keeping her off balance. She couldn't tell whether he was trying to show her that he was sensitive, or sensual, or fringing on insane, and she didn't even want to let herself ponder the question of why he was trying to show her anything at all.

"Not as my guest you aren't. It's only for faculty members."

"That's me, curly-top. I'm the law school's liaison to the medical school."

"Impressive title. What's it supposed to mean?"

"Nothing impressive about it. As you well know, law students and professors often need to call upon the medical school to provide someone to play the role of 'medical expert' or 'pathologist' for mock trials. We do them a favor and the young doctors in training benefit from a chance to practice what it would be like to have to take the stand. In return, the law school sends over people to lecture on how to set up a small business, file tax returns and make insurance claims. I coordinate all of that, so you see, every time you want a medical student to play expert witness for one of your sessions, you have to come to me."

"Terrific."

"I thought that's how you'd feel. I just hope I won't be having one of my bad days when you contact me. Senility is a real problem at my age."

"Do you accept apologies?"

"Yes, if they're sincere."

Nicki leaned back in her chair and struck a thoughtful pose. "Let's see. Can I sincerely tell the man that I'm sorry for pointing out that, when enthused, he lapses into a vocabulary that is reminiscent of the Mouseketeers?" She shook her head vigorously. "Nope. I don't think I can." She leaned forward and addressed Doug. "Sorry, I guess I'll just have to try to catch you during a lucid moment."

He shrugged dejectedly. "Whew. The kid strikes out again. Like I said, you are good."

"The best. See you at the party, Doctor. I've got a few phone calls to make first." He shoved his hands in his pockets as he started to leave. "Oh and, Doug—" he turned expectantly ''—behave yourself in class from now on. It's hard enough for a person of my physical stature to get the students' respect.''

His delightful, crooked grin reappeared. ''Why is it I don't believe that for a minute?''

CHAPTER TWO

As NICKI DROVE HOME to change for the cocktail party, she mentally reviewed the details of her second phone conversation with her law partner. Ron Foley had been a classmate of the original attorney on this new case and was feeling pretty proud of himself for finding a client for Nicki to handle while she was supposedly on "vacation" from the office for a few months.

That was always the way with Ron. He was terrific when it came to public relations, but terrible in the courtroom. When they were first starting out that had worked well for Nicki. She had hated doing the entertaining and marketing that had been necessary to bring new business to their fledgling partnership, and she had liked the idea that Ron let her keep full control of the casework. Now, however, most of their clients came to them because of her impressive record of courtroom victories and, lately, Ron was not even holding up his end of the business. It was a problem that Nicki would have to confront sooner or later. At least he ran the office, he was someone to talk to about her strategy for their cases and he was, after all, related to her mother's present husband.

He was also right that this case was just the type she found the most interesting and challenging. Ian Dorchester had been a talented young swimmer and diver. A juvenile diabetic, he had neglected to take his insulin prior to a high school swimming competition and had collapsed during the meet. He was taken to the hospital in diabetic coma, a serious condition, but nothing unusual. Treatment should have been fairly routine. Yet, due to some apparent complication, Ian went into cardiac arrest and, although he survived, now suffered from reduced muscle coordination and epilepsy. His days as a competitor were over.

No one seemed to know what had caused Ian's heart attack. If Nicki took the case it would be up to her to determine if one of the hospital staff was at fault before she decided if there were grounds to file a suit.

Normally Nicki enjoyed the investigative process, but something about this case made her uncomfortable. Perhaps it was only that the original attorney had withdrawn so quickly and offered no explanation for his resignation other than incompatibility with the client.

If she were honest with herself, Nicki also had to admit that, although she had often tried cases involving doctors who practiced in the area where she lived—doctors whom she saw at charitable and social functions—this time she was concerned about taking a case in the small university town where she was teaching.

Just the thought of having to face Doug when she went to the hospital to take depositions made her cringe. Even though he wasn't personally involved, he would certainly know everyone who was. She'd witnessed examples of his anger already, and she could just picture the disgust on his face as he accused her of trying to destroy the careers of his associates.

It disturbed her that she was so concerned about doing something that Doug might not approve of. She hardly even knew him, and she had promised herself a long time ago that she would never again make any career decisions based on what she thought other people expected from her. Yet, as soon as she met an attractive man who sparked her interest, she was ready to forget both the promise and the lesson that had led her to make it.

She pulled into a parking space behind her apartment, then raked her fingers through her hair. Doug was certainly right about one thing; she needed to acquire a comb. But that was where his influence on her life would stop. She would decide whether or not to take the Dorchester case based not on personal concerns, but on facts, just as she'd always done before she had met Dr. Doug MacNair.

Nicki glanced up at the window of the third floor apartment that Blake Windham was letting her use while she filled in for him. It had been the perfect arrangement for both of them. He had hated to leave it unoccupied and Nicki had needed a furnished place to stay that didn't require a lease. It was a typical bachelor's pad, but that didn't bother Nicki since she'd never much cared where she lived. All her waking hours were spent at the office anyway.

She winced as she saw a light flicker on in the kitchen, signaling that her sister Sarah had come by earlier than expected to feed the cat. Since Nicki had originally intended to go directly to the cocktail party from the law school, she had asked Sarah, who had a garden apartment in the same building, to see to Elmo's needs. Now, Nicki knew her unscheduled clothing change would not go unnoticed, and her younger sister would immediately want to know if there was a man involved. It was tempting to get back in the car and follow her first plan.

As much as she dreaded facing Sarah's cross-examination, Nicki felt a surge of affection when she thought of her sister. In spite of the seven-year age difference, they had grown up to be both family and best friends to each other. When their stepfather had walked out and their mother had had a breakdown, Nicki had been seventeen and had cared for ten-year-old Sarah until their mother had fully recovered. Now Nicki and Sarah had left their family home in Aspen and come to Illinois. Although they kept in touch with their mother and her new husband, professional and school commitments meant that visits were less frequent than any of them would have wished, so again the sisters relied on each other. Nicki's work schedule didn't allow her much personal life, but she always had time to call or see Sarah. And on the rare occasion that she took a vacation, Nicki timed it to coincide with her sister's school holidays.

Sarah often expressed her gratitude to Nicki for using money from her trust fund, and later her law practice, to put her through college and now grad school, but Nicki assured her that she had repaid the debt many times over, simply by providing someone for Nicki to talk to. As a young girl, Nicki hadn't made many friends. She had been too busy training and competing. As an adult, she hadn't made many more, perhaps for the same reason. She needed Sarah's support and companionship every bit as much as Sarah needed hers.

Over the past year, however, Sarah had begun working as a research assistant for Blake Windham, and within a couple of months, had fallen in love with him. Nicki had had reservations about the romance because Blake was much older and more experienced than Sarah, but after meeting him and finding him to be attractive, intelligent, and for all appearances, quite nice, she had finally decided that she had no right to advise Sarah on that aspect of her life.

If only her sister had felt the same way about Nicki. Sarah had always been the more gregarious and socially aware of the two sisters and had often advised Nicki on such matters. But since Sarah and Blake had become a couple, Sarah had expanded on her role as Nicki's social consultant until, by her own admission, she had decided to launch an all-out campaign to find a "great guy like Blake" for Nicki. Unfortunately, she chose to ignore Nicki's frequent and heartfelt protests that she was perfectly happy as she was.

After her accident, Nicki had used the same single-minded concentration that she had developed as an athlete to structure a new life for herself. Aware that she was not the type of person to succeed on many fronts at once, she'd chosen to give all of her energy to the thing that would provide her with the most satisfaction—her career. Law enabled her to make her own decisions, to compete only when she wanted to, and to satisfy her personal desire to help others without having to become emotionally involved with anyone. For once she was in complete control of her life, and if the price for that control was to spend her evenings alone, she was more than willing to pay it.

Until ten years ago, Nicki had always been surrounded by people. She'd never known what it was to be alone, but she'd been so terribly lonely. Everyone had plans to stake their claim on a part of Nicole Devlin, and she had tried to give them all what they wanted. In the end there had been nothing left for Nicki herself except her dreams—dreams that had vanished all too quickly when she awoke in the hospital after her last race. Today, she needed something more solid to hang on to. She would not risk releasing her grip on the woman she had become, especially not to comply with her sister's romantic notions about playing matchmaker.

Nicki's hopes for a hasty retreat were dashed when Sarah's tousled, burnt-orange curls appeared at the window. She spied Nicki immediately and began to wave with her characteristic enthusiasm. Nicki sighed as she waved back and headed for the building. At least Sarah would have no reason for suspecting that there was an attractive, well-dressed doctor in Nicki's malpractice trial seminar.

She opened the apartment door to find Sarah sitting in the living room waiting for her.

"Hi-ya, big sister. What did you think of Doug Mac-Nair?"

Nicki groaned inwardly. Clearly Sarah had discussed the class list with Blake. "Arrogant, overbearing and quite possibly crazy."

"And the most outrageously gorgeous man you've ever seen in your life."

"He's outrageous all right." Nicki tossed her briefcase and coat on a nearby chair. "Next time you talk to Blake tell him he should have warned me there was going to be a behavioral problem in the class. The good doctor tried to sabotage my first lecture."

Sarah grinned. "But he didn't get away with it. Right?"

"Right."

"That's my sis. You've never lost one yet. Poor Doug. I guess I should have warned him." Sarah pushed herself off the sofa with a sigh and flounced into the kitchen.

"Hey, whose side are you on?" Nicki followed her and stood leaning against the refrigerator while Sarah opened a can of cat food.

"I always stick with the handsome man."

"Is that any way for my only sibling to talk? Let's not forget who is doing whom a favor. If I hadn't put my practice on hold and rushed down here to fill in for your friend Blake, he wouldn't have been able to go to California to work on his book."

Sarah cast her a disgusted, sidelong look. "Remind me to be eternally grateful as I cross-stitch my way through Saturday nights." She stooped to put cat food in Elmo's bowl. "You know, I've been dutifully feeding this beast of yours every night for a week now and I've never seen him. Is this some cruel game? See Sarah feed her sister's imaginary cat?"

"The food is always gone isn't it?"

"Yes, but you're such a lousy cook I might be able to explain that."

"My little sister is not in a good mood. You know Elmo is just shy."

"Maybe he should see a counselor. Someone to help him deal with his insecurities."

Nicki smiled to herself, remembering Doug's speech about his numerous insecurities. "That's what I suggested for Dr. MacNair."

"You said that to Doug MacNair?" Sarah looked horrified. "The man is the closest thing to a mythical god we'll ever see walking the face of the earth, and you tell him he needs a shrink. What did he say?"

"As I recall, he said 'hot dog.'" Nicki turned and went to her bedroom to search for something slinky, yet tasteful, to wear. As she expected, Sarah was only one step behind her.

"We're not talking about the same man here, Nicki. I'm thinking of Dr. Doug MacNair—dignified, conservative, dedicated beyond belief, has obviously never looked in a mirror or would be too conceited to be bearable and never says more than two words in a social context."

Nicki shoved her suit aside and began to drag dresses out of the closet. "'Hot dog' is two words, and apparently he's looked in a mirror since you last saw him." She held a green knit under her chin and turned expectantly to Sarah who gave her a thumbs-down sign. She threw the garment on the floor and reached for another.

Sarah bent down to gather up the discarded clothing. "Oh goody. This could get interesting. Are you sure he didn't disrupt more than your lecture? Is this my sister, originator of the business-suits-go-anywhere school of fashion, looking for a dress to wear to a faculty cocktail party?"

"It's my first function here. I want to make a good impression."

"Sure, sure." Sarah picked up another rejected garment. "Could it be I'm witnessing the embryonic stages of a romance?"

Nicki felt her cheeks grow warm. "Hardly. That would imply future development and I'm not interested."

"Come on, Nicki, just because Chris was a jerk doesn't mean you should give up on men. That was just one bad experience."

"And what about our loving stepfather?"

"Okay, two bad experiences."

"Listen, Sarah, I've been out on many more dates than you have in the last few years."

"Sure you have, and you've left early with a headache so many times they're all taking up a collection to pay for a brain scan. Those guys were losers."

"Would you care to retract your opening argument—something about 'just one bad experience'?"

"I would not. You know very well that you never go out with anyone you could be the least bit interested in. You have lots of friendly little dinner dates, but the minute you think there's a chance someone could sweep you off your feet, you run."

"And, apparently, no one ever tries to stop me. I can't run too fast—bum leg, you know." She burrowed deeper into the closet hoping to avoid further teasing. At the sound of Sarah's shriek, she tried to back up, only to find her way blocked by all the dresses and coats she'd pushed past earlier. When she finally managed to free herself from the tangled arms of her wardrobe, Sarah grabbed her and buried her face against Nicki's shoulder. Nicki held her protectively. "What's the matter, baby? What happened?"

Sarah refused to look up. "I don't know. I threw your clothes on the bed and all of a sudden the whole pile moved. Then something brushed against my legs, only—I couldn't see anything."

Nicki exerted her best effort not to laugh, but failed. Sarah glared at her.

"Sorry, little sister. First encounters with Elmo are often pretty spooky."

"That was Elmo? That was the animal I've cared for so conscientiously while you're off playing Perry Mason until all hours of the night? That was the sweet little ball of fur you wrote all those affectionate letters about, your sole companion when you can't make it home for the holidays?"

Nicki just nodded her head.

"Yeah. Well, I've got news for you, Elmo," Sarah yelled in the general direction of the bed. "If we ever meet face-to-face, you're dead meat." She stomped out of the room and a moment later the apartment vibrated with the slamming of the door.

"Never has learned to control her temper," Nicki mumbled as she knelt down and tapped the floor with her fingers. A large, orange tabby cat emerged from under the bed and brushed against her hand. "Thanks for the diversion, kitty. Sarah can be a bit of a nuisance." *Embryonic romance, indeed.* She picked Elmo up and gave him a hug. "If Mama's a smart lady, she'll stick with you, fur-face, and forget about the sexy doctor."

Despite her firm intentions, Doug was still on her mind twenty minutes later. She was brushing on her mascara, when she came to the disconcerting realization that her eyes *were* exactly the same color as his. She'd always thought of the color as boring, somber gray, but on him it was an ever-varying mix of hard, angry steel, soft, sensuous suede and just a glint of quicksilver mischief.

DOUG'S EYES DARTED to the doorway of the cocktail lounge for what must have been the hundredth time that evening. At last he was rewarded for his vigilance. Nicki had arrived. She slipped off her black wool cape and stepped up to the coat check window. Her simple gray silk sheath hugged her figure in all the right places, tastefully accentuating every curve. Crimson heels and jewelry added just the right touch of festivity. He glanced affectionately at her rumpled curls. What a fascinating blend of professional sophistication and young girl freshness she was.

"Doug, are you listening?"

He dragged his attention away from the vision in gray and focused on the chubby, bald man who was head of pathology at the hospital. Doug had assumed he would be the only member of the medical community at this function, but apparently the law school had invited everyone who had ever given a guest lecture to the law students.

"Of course I'm listening, Stanley. How could I help but be fascinated by a discussion of why a hospital's claim for expenses against a bankrupt estate should take priority?"

Doug glanced back at Nicki as she brushed the light dusting of snow from her hair with her fingers. The nonchalance of the gesture touched him. Every other woman who had come in had rushed immediately to the powder room to repair the damage done to their flawless coiffures by the elements of nature. No such nonsense for Nicki.

"So what do you think?" Stanley rested his hand on Doug's arm.

"First us, then the undertaker, then the starving wife and children." Doug stepped back and flicked the back of his hand against his sleeve to eradicate Stanley's finger marks from the suede. "There's no room for maudlin compassion where fiscal matters are concerned."

Stanley quickly closed the space that Doug's backward step had put between them and rested his hand on Doug's arm again. "I couldn't agree more. Our society should not, no, cannot allow death to absolve one's self of one's responsibilities...."

Doug tuned Stanley out as he scanned the room seeking Nicki. When he heard the sound of her unforgettable, lilting laugh, he became even more impatient with his talkative companion. The only person he'd come here to see was standing somewhere behind him, laughing, and he was shackled with Stanley, who clearly spent most of his waking hours talking to corpses about matters of great social import.

"So if a man has made no provision for his family that's simply unfortunate for them, is what I say. What do you think, Doug?"

He had been on good behavior for about as long as he could stand. "I think that your patients, may they rest in peace, must be fascinated by your amazing insights." As Doug hoped, Stanley broke into a fit of giggles, then turned to share the joke with the man standing next to him. Doug took the opportunity to escape to the bar.

As soon as he was certain that Stanley had found someone else to inflict himself upon, Doug walked over to the group of people Nicki was talking to and slipped into the circle beside her. He handed her a glass of white wine and was rewarded with her brilliant smile.

"Thank you. How did you know this is just what I wanted?"

"Lucky for you it is." He returned the smile. "The only choices are wine and beer. The beer is warm and I think the red wine must have come to us directly from the chemistry lab—the experiment failed.''

She took a sip of her drink then peeked up at him over the edge of the glass. "Yum. I love grapes with vinegar, don't you?"

He swept the glass out of her hand, setting it on the table behind them with the other discards and stared into her eyes with melodramatic attentiveness. "How disillusioning. I should have thought such lips as yours would impart a dash of sweetness to anything they touched."

She raised her eyes toward the ceiling and shook her head. "Listen, Doug, before you get too carried away here, I think it's only fair to warn you that I also saw the late-night movie last evening and the sentiment, while lovely to be sure, sounds a tad familiar."

He tried to look wounded. "So original poetry doesn't come easy to me. I was only trying to pay you a sincere and heartfelt compliment."

"Really? I would have never guessed." He noticed her mouth tighten slightly. "You'll find I don't shake easily, Doctor. After five years of dealing with defense attorneys who'll try anything to get the cute little lady lawyer all upset, I've become a bit wary."

"I can understand that, and I have to admit I was hoping to take you off guard. So this time I'll play fair and warn you in advance. This is a compliment. That dress looks fantastic on you, and it matches our eyes perfectly."

She grinned. "Yes it does, doesn't it?"

Just as he was about to ask her to join him for a more palatable drink elsewhere, Stanley came up behind him with one of the hospital's emergency room physicians in tow.

"Hey, Doug. You'll never guess what Allen just told me."

"You've got that right. I won't guess. So if you want me to know, you're just going to have to tell me." He felt a wave of disappointment wash over him as Nicki turned to talk to the woman standing on her other side. Having finally been rewarded with a grin, he had hoped she would agree to go for a drink. Now he'd have to start over. "This had better be pretty important, Stanley."

"Do you remember all the hoopla about that swimmer kid, the one who had the heart attack in the E.R.?"

"Vaguely. Dorchester wasn't it?" Nicki stopped talking and glanced over her shoulder at him then turned away again, but he could tell she was still listening.

"That's the one. Well, apparently, the kid's attorney dumped the case, so it looks like there won't be any suit after all."

"How do you figure that? They'll just hire someone else."

"Why should they if the first guy didn't find anything wrong?"

Doug felt the muscles at the back of his neck tighten. "Don't be naive, Stanley. What makes you think there has to be something wrong? All that's required is a less than perfect result, something short of the anticipated medical miracle. Then the patient runs out and keeps hiring different attorneys to conduct fishing expeditions until they find someone to blame." It had always angered Doug that the woman who had sued him had gone to three attorneys before she finally found one who thought he could find a reason to file a case. "Eventually one of those lawyers will get some poor physician on the hook and play with him until the insurance company drops enough money on the patient to get him to cut the line."

He turned to see Nicki openly listening to him. This was hardly going to help him make an impression on her, but right now he was too upset to stop himself. "Yes indeed, it's one terrific system of justice we've got working for us. Isn't it, Ms Devlin?"

"The system is far from perfect, but I've yet to come across a better one. Perhaps you have."

"Well, something has got to change. Members of the medical profession have to protect themselves from an increasingly greedy legal profession."

"I'd be happy to give you some advice on that front."

"Such as?"

She took his arm and led him into a corner near the bar. "Such as, I know one member of the medical profession who could go a long way toward protecting himself from serious bodily injury at the hands of some member of the legal profession if he would lower his voice. You're outnumbered fifty to one, Doug, and more than half of these people are drunk on warm beer and cheap wine. They might not take kindly to being called greedy by a man who paid more for this sport coat alone than many of them make in a month."

Doug looked around the room in confusion. "I'm not talking about these lawyers. I know all of these people. They are the teachers, the legal scholars, the ones who are struggling to maintain the standard of legal ethics. I'm talking about the ambulance chasers, the high fee blackmailers, the courtroom piranha...."

"I take it then, Dr. MacNair, that you are talking about me."

One look at the taut lines around her mouth and at the corners of her eyes told him that she was every bit as capable of intense anger as he was, and he had no doubt it was time for him to back down. "Who me? Talking about you? No, uh-uh, absolutely not. In fact, I haven't said a word in the last twenty minutes."

"If only we could have been so lucky." She shook her head then turned on her heel and made her way through the crowd to the ladies room.

"Looks as though Doug the Debonair has struck out again."

Doug turned to find Paul standing behind him. "A temporary setback."

"Keep it up and you'll set yourself back a century or two. I missed most of it, but from what I heard, that was a pretty stupid thing to say. What did you expect her to do? Applaud?"

"Why not? When the brilliant Dr. Doug MacNair speaks everyone always applauds." He sighed. "I hate to admit it, Paul, but I think I may have met my match."

"Well, I hope so. You've been insufferable for far too long."

"What are you doing here anyway? Since when have you had an affiliation with the law school?"

"Since a dear friend of mine got me to sign up for the Risk Management Committee and talked me into auditing a trial practice course so he wouldn't have to buy his own book. But, never fear, I wasn't invited to this exclusive shindig. I just came to find you."

Doug tried to fight the instantaneous twinge of apprehension. "Is there something wrong at the office—trouble with a patient?" He began to reach for his car keys.

"Relax. If it were important I'd have beeped you. After eight years of sharing the same office suite I'd think you could give me some credit for common sense. Besides, I thought you were supposed to be on a big campaign to loosen up. So far, the new Dr. MacNair is behind in the polls."

Doug grinned, knowing he'd been caught. "Right. I'm cool. I'm calm. I'm curious. What's up?"

"Remember my buddy, Michael Gaylord, the dentist who bought into that glitzy new club?"

Doug nodded.

"Well, opening night is tonight and I was going to get a group together to go. He'll be real depressed if there isn't a good turnout, and when he's depressed his hands shake. I've got an appointment with him next week so moral support is in my own best interest."

"Don't expect me to help you. I'd like nothing better than to see that tongue of yours drilled down to size."

"You could ask Ms Devlin."

The thought of holding Nicki in his arms for a slow dance made Doug warm all over. He had no trouble imagining exactly how she would feel, how she would smell, how she would move against him. He shook his head slightly and tried to focus his attention back on his friend. "Okay. When and where?"

Paul gave him the details then promised to stop by the office to check their messages before going to the club.

As Doug waited for Nicki to return to the bar area, he tried to sort out his confused emotions. She was attractive and she was certainly intelligent and witty—reasons enough for him to want to go out with her. But, she was also a successful malpractice attorney who negotiated large settlements and won record-breaking verdicts for her clients. Although he knew he had no right to feel betrayed by her career, a part of him felt just that. Yet when he let his thoughts drift back to what it would be like to dance with her, the betrayal didn't seem to matter anymore.

It was almost twenty minutes later when Nicki finally decided she had done as much socializing as was possible within the confines of the rest room. She was going to have to go back to the party. Her only hope was that Doug had left.

As soon as she stepped through the door into the main room, he was beside her. "Well, that sure took long enough. What do you women do in there anyway?"

She arched an eyebrow at him.

"Can we pretend I didn't ask that?" he pleaded as his cheeks began to color.

Grown men weren't supposed to be that adorable, were they? "My what a lovely shade. Now your eyes match my dress and your complexion matches my shoes. Too bad we're not the same size."

To her surprise, Doug just shook his head and laughed. "A lesser man might be threatened by you, Ms Devlin, but you'll find that I, like you, don't shake easily. How about we take some time to find out what else we have in common? You might even become rather attached to me."

She had no doubt that that was a very real possibility, and not one she wanted to risk. "Dr. MacNair, in light of your earlier references to piranha, have you ever heard the phrase 'A woman without a man is like a fish without a bicycle'?"

"Yes."

"Well, that should give you a pretty clear picture of how I feel about getting attached to you right now."

She saw his eyes twinkle. "I'm asking you to go dancing, not biking. Some friends of mine are on their way to a disco. I thought we might join them."

Nicki felt as though she'd just had the wind knocked out of her. She couldn't remember when anyone had last asked her to dance. Apparently her limp had worked to warn people away from that, and it had been just as well. Leave it to MacNair to ignore the obvious and stumble into painful territory. "No thank you." Her voice sounded harsh even to her. "I'm afraid I have a lot of work to do this evening."

He reached out to touch her shoulder. "Is something wrong?"

She ducked out from under his hand. "No. Of course not. I just remembered some important business I need to attend to."

"Since we're exchanging pithy quotations have you ever heard, 'All work and no play. . .'?"

"I've heard it. I like being dull. Good night, Doug. Have fun." She turned away and walked up to the coat check.

A few minutes later she stepped outside into the gently falling snow. As she stood at the traffic light waiting to cross the street, she lifted her face to the sky and let the snowflakes brush against her cheeks. There was some truth in what she'd said. Sometimes she did like being dull. It was a pleasant change.

By the time she'd turned twenty it had seemed like she had lived through enough to fill several lifetimes. She'd started training when she was eight and had never let up, never stopped getting better, never stopped competing, until her accident. She'd traveled all over the world, set aside a sizable trust fund for her future and developed a mature-beyond-her-years demeanor—common in young athletes who had grown up facing television cameras and journalists and who couldn't afford for anyone to know how frightened they really were.

Back then she'd never stopped to just enjoy the feel of the snow against her skin. Snow had been serious business. She'd spent hours analyzing its composition each day. How icy? How much powder? How fast? But she'd never learned that no two snowflakes were alike until Sarah had told her.

The light changed and Nicki crossed the street and got into her car. She should probably have stayed at the party longer, but it seemed as though the only way to avoid Doug was to go home. Or, as Sarah would put it, to run away. Nicki didn't deny it. She'd developed quite a talent for discouraging smooth-talking, well-dressed, handsome men. Doug was just a little more tenacious than most.

CHAPTER THREE

NICKI GLANCED BRIEFLY at the clock on the wall of her law school office. It had taken her almost a week to set up this appointment with Ian Dorchester and his parents, and now that they were here, it seemed unlikely that Ian would be given an opportunity to say anything if Nicki didn't intervene.

She tapped the top of her pencil impatiently against her teeth as she listened to Mrs. Dorchester's soliloquy about what a promising future Ian had had until this terrible thing happened. Finally, Nicki sat forward. "Mrs. Dorchester, I think we might be missing the point. Surely no one will deny this has all been a tragedy, but that, in and of itself, does not give us grounds for a lawsuit. Right now we can't begin to know whether Ian's heart attack was caused by medical negligence or by fate."

"That hardly seems the appropriate attitude for someone who is supposed to be representing our interests," Mr. Dorchester shot back. "Don't you care about what has happened to us?"

"I care very much about what has happened to Ian." She paused to let her emphasis of "Ian" over "us" sink in. "I also care about the truth. I have never filed a suit unless I was confident there was malpractice involved, and I don't intend to now. If you would rather look for another attorney, you are certainly free to do so. I'm sure there are any number of lawyers who believe there are always grounds for a suit if a patient isn't happy with the results of medical care. I am not one of them.''

"But we were told you were one of the best malpractice attorneys in the business.''

Nicki nodded. ''I am. If it turns out that a physician was negligent in treating Ian, we'll file a suit, we'll go to trial and we'll win. But I won't file a groundless lawsuit just to try to force an insurance settlement. That's not the way I do business. So the decision is yours. Talk it over while I go find us something to drink.''

On her way to the faculty lounge, Nicki did battle with her instincts, which told her to walk away from this one. Ian's parents were entirely too eager to take action. And since they had opened the meeting by telling her that she was not to discuss the case with the previous attorney, she couldn't help but feel that they were hiding something.

The only reason she was still considering taking the case, was Ian himself. He had not said a word since he'd arrived. Even when Nicki had directed her questions specifically to him, he would just shrug and look at his parents, who were always ready to jump in with the answer.

As she had watched the sullen teenager, Nicki recognized the symptoms of the same guilt and despair she had experienced herself. She knew how it felt to bear the burden of having let everybody down. He could never hope to deliver what undoubtedly had been expected of him ever since his special talent as a swimmer and diver had been discovered. If she got involved in this case, Nicki hoped she could also spend some time with Ian, helping him to get his own life back into perspective and to accept that athletics weren't everything. That was a difficult lesson to learn alone.

As soon as Nicki returned to the office with the coffee and soft drinks, Mrs. Dorchester started talking. ''I hope we didn't say anything to offend you, Ms Devlin. We would like for you to represent us. It's just that we're very upset and anxious about everything that has happened during the last year."

Nicki nodded. "I can understand that. And it's not a matter of my being offended. But it is important for you to know the way I work. This is going to be a long, arduous process, so we're better off getting as many problems as possible behind us before we begin it."

As she talked, she walked around the small office handing out beverages. She knew Ian had noticed her limp earlier, and she could tell he was watching her now. Rather than being embarrassed by that, she found herself thinking that it was good for him to realize he wasn't the only one who had problems. She returned to her desk chair.

"Well, Ian, why don't you tell me everything you remember about what happened?" Raising a hand to forestall Mrs. Dorchester's automatic response, Nicki leaned toward the boy and waited.

"I don't remember anything. I didn't take my insulin so I passed out. The next thing I knew, I was a cripple."

There was no mistaking the bitterness in his voice. "Oh, hardly that, Ian. From what I can see, your dysfunction is less severe than my own, and I certainly don't think of myself as a cripple."

"What you think is up to you. All I know is I can't dive anymore. That's how I judge for myself."

"I'm sure it is—right now anyway." She settled back in her chair so she could still see his parents while directing her questions to him. "Why didn't you take your insulin that day?"

"I forgot." Ian glanced nervously at his mother. "I didn't want ..."

"He means he went on a camping trip and forgot to take it with him," Mrs. Dorchester continued.

Nicki kept her attention on Ian. "Is that what you meant?"

"Of course it's what he meant. I just told you that." Mrs. Dorchester walked over to her son and put a protective hand on his shoulder.

With a disgusted sigh, Nicki broke eye contact with Ian and pulled her chair close to the desk again. "All I really need today are the facts, so it looks as though the most efficient thing to do is let you tell them, Mrs. Dorchester. But I should warn you, if we pursue this matter, it is Ian, not you, who will have to get on the stand and tell the judge and jury what happened. As his attorney, I would like to give him as many opportunities as possible to practice telling that story."

"I don't see any need for you to question him like that. It sounds so accusatory."

"Not nearly as accusatory as the defense counsel is going to sound. We're back to the same problem again. If I'm going to represent Ian, you have to trust me."

Mrs. Dorchester returned to her seat. "I'm sorry. But he's gone through so much already."

And he'll be going through so much more, Nicki thought. "Okay, now would one of you like to tell me the events that led up to Ian's trip to the emergency room?" She wasn't surprised at all when it was Mrs. Dorchester who began to speak.

"It was spring break. We had just moved here in the fall because the high school had such a good swimming team, so Ian was very excited when three other boys asked him to go along on a camping trip the weekend before the Easter swimming meet." She glanced at Ian before continuing. "He's never had much time for friends and it was important to him. Well, it was the first time he'd gone away like that since the diabetes was diagnosed. He packed in a hurry and forgot to take his insulin with him. I know I should have reminded him, but I was at work when he left.''

''Couldn't he have gotten some once they reached their location?''

''Yes, he doesn't even need a prescription to get the insulin itself, but you know how boys are. One of the fathers would have had to make a special trip into town to find a drugstore, and the other boys would have asked questions. He didn't want to be different, and since they were only away one night, he didn't think it would be too serious providing he took an injection as soon as he got home. Unfortunately, they had car trouble and made it back to town just in time for the meet, so they drove directly to the school. His father and I both work, and we had planned to get to the meet just in time for the diving. That is—was—Ian's specialty, although he swam in other events as well. By the time we arrived, the ambulance had taken him to the emergency room and they had already done this to him.'' Mrs. Dorchester gestured in Ian's general direction and began to cry.

Nicki glanced at Ian, then back to the sobbing woman and finally down at her notes. She knew that as a result of his heart attack, Ian suffered from reduced motor coordination, which slowed his reflexes, and that he had developed epilepsy. But sitting there, he looked like any other teenager who was more than a little uncomfortable with what was going on around him. Nicki couldn't help but feel that his mother's dramatics did him a great disservice. No wonder he thought of himself as a cripple.

''Mr. Dorchester, I know that neither of you have any idea what went on at the hospital, but I wonder if the previous attorney had already begun his own investigation.''

''I believe that he had.''

"Good. Then would you have any objection to contacting him yourself and asking if he would let us see the results of that investigation?"

The man stood abruptly. "I'd have a great number of objections. Mr. Cooper's approach to the case was totally incompatible with what we would have expected from our attorney. We do not want your investigation hampered or influenced by his prejudices."

Nicki was taken aback by the vehemence with which he spoke. "I will certainly abide by your wishes, but I'd like to point out that this would be a costly decision on your part. You will be paying me to cover some of the same ground that Mr. Cooper has already explored."

"We are aware of that and that's the way we want it."

"Fine. Then I'll ask you to sign some medical records release forms, and I'll start lining up experts to help me review those records." As the Dorchesters packed up their copies of the various forms, put on coats and prepared to leave, Nicki stepped over to talk to Ian. "Didn't your doctor warn you that the need for insulin increases when you are under stress?"

"Sure."

"Then why did you go in and compete when you knew your insulin level was already low?"

Ian shrugged. "Because the stress from competing is nothing like the stress from not competing, but I don't suppose you'd understand that."

He slipped on his jacket and walked away before Nicki had the chance to tell him that she understood only too well.

ON FRIDAY, Nicki rounded the corner near her classroom to see Doug pacing the hallway. He had a fierce scowl on his face, and her heart sank when she realized that, although she had not seen him since the cocktail party, his hostility was clearly directed toward her.

He stepped into her path. "Well, congratulations, Ms Devlin. Maybe 'piranha' doesn't apply in your case, but I am glad you took a break from ambulance chasing to come teach your class."

Normally, Nicki countered an opponent's attack with one of her own. But with Doug, none of her responses were ever the normal ones. No matter how angry he'd tried to sound, his eyes showed not anger, but disappointment, as though he felt she'd let him down.

Nicki had never dealt well with the idea that she might have disappointed anyone, and Doug was no exception. She leaned against the radiator and looked up at him. "So tell me, what have I done now?" Her voice sounded miraculously steady, given how queasy she felt.

"How long did it take you to track down the Dorchesters once you overheard my conversation with Stanley at the party? Did you go after them as soon as you shut me down? Was that the urgent business you had to attend to?"

He was standing so close to her that she could smell the damp wool of his topcoat. Her mind registered that it must be snowing again then darted back to Doug's looming presence.

"I had already been called about the Dorchester case before the cocktail party. In fact, when you walked into my office Friday afternoon, I was discussing it with my partner."

"Right. They why were you eavesdropping on my conversation at the party?"

"I was 'eavesdropping' because I heard you mention a name I was familiar with. And as I recall, Doctor, you were not having a conversation. You were making a speech. You can't deny that it was your intention for me to hear every word you said, whether I wanted to or not. Can you?''

Doug just looked at her then shook his head. ''I'm doing it again. Someday I may learn to ask for explanations before I get angry. No, actually I'll never change.'' Finally he sighed heavily. ''Doesn't being right all the time ever get boring?''

''Yes, but then, dull and boring go rather well together, don't you think?''

''Extremely well. Who would have thought the mixture could yield someone who is nothing short of amazing?''

Nicki laughed. ''Thank you, but I'm afraid that, although quite short, I'm anything but amazing. What I am is hardworking and methodical. That's why I'm so good at what I do. And that is why I don't have to go looking for clients. They come to me.'' She stepped forward as the class bell rang. ''Now if you'll let me get in there and teach this class, you might get to learn something about legal investigations, or 'fishing expeditions,' as you call them.''

''Aren't you afraid to reveal the tricks of the trade to the opposition?''

''If I had any tricks, I probably would be. Good lawyers don't do magic.''

Doug closed his fingers over her arm to keep her from walking away. She just stared at his hand for a moment, trying to understand the warm ache that washed over her at such a simple touch.

''Neither do good doctors, Nicki.''

The sound of his voice broke her spell. ''Believe it or not, I know that—maybe even better than you do.''

DOUG LISTENED INTENTLY during the class as Nicki discussed the importance of the investigative stages of a case, explaining that one did not file a lawsuit until he or she was certain there were grounds for doing so. He watched her as she paced thoughtfully back and forth at the front of the room, running her fingers through her hair at regular intervals, and he wrestled with the realization that the more he learned about her, the more he liked her.

The first time he'd seen her, he'd found her to be physically attractive, but given what she did for a living, he'd thought it would be fairly easy to dismiss her—until she had taken him on during that first class session. It was rare for him to lose a verbal sparring match, and he'd lost more than once to the incomparable Ms Devlin. He smiled to himself. She was a challenge.

He couldn't deny that his prejudice against personal injury attorneys was the product of his own bad experience. But that didn't make it any easier for him to accept a member of the enemy camp as an honest and forthright professional who considered her work every bit as much of a service to society as his own. He kept thinking he was going to be able to catch her at something he could point to as being fundamentally unfair, or at least cause for debate. But every time he thought he had her cornered, she escaped, and not by slipping around him, but by confronting him head-on. Surprisingly enough, he found himself pleased by her victories.

She paced in front of his seat, paused, then turned. The scent of her perfume wisped past him. She had a lot of nerve saying she didn't do magic, then strolling around in front of him smelling like a spring meadow, punctuating her sentences with a sweep of her hand here and a toss of her head there, and greeting every student's question with a nod and a smile and sometimes even a bit of a laugh.

As she made assignments for the next session, Doug settled on his strategy for getting a chance to learn more about the enchanting Ms Devlin. Either he'd end up hopelessly hooked, a rather exciting thought, or he'd find out she wasn't what she seemed and her spell would be broken.

As Nicki walked across the parking lot, she had to stop to remember where she had put her car. There was no way to distinguish one snow-covered mound from another. She brushed off the door handle and tried to ease into the front seat without causing an avalanche from the roof. After turning on the ignition, she began to search diligently for the snow scraper. Apparently Sarah had been the last one to use it because there was no sign of it in any of Nicki's usual storage spots. Finally, she crawled inelegantly into the back seat only to find the missing scraper tossed recklessly into the furthest corner of the hatchback trunk space.

Just as she stretched over the seat to retrieve it, a large swatch of snow disappeared from the window in front of her, letting in light from the street lamp. She stopped mid-motion and looked up to see Doug peering in at her with a big grin on his face. She caught her breath. Maybe there were women who could see Doug MacNair smile and not have their hearts skip a beat, but she sure wasn't one of them. Of course, appearance wasn't everything. In fact, appearance might not be anything, but there was no point in denying it; when it came to simple physical attraction, this man was her idea of perfection. Unfortunately, he had certainly caught her at a less than perfect moment.

Vowing never to let Sarah borrow the car again, she attempted to turn around in the back seat. The awkward maneuvering required by the limited space was compounded by the conviction that her skirt was hitched up to a most unladylike height. Silently cursing her audience, Nicki was finally forced to effect her escape by opening the back door, only to be rewarded with a lapful of snow.

Doug, adding insult to injury, began brushing her off with unnecessary enthusiasm.

"That's quite all right, Doctor. I think I can handle it."

"No problem. This is a full-service operation." He turned to finish scraping the side window.

"Yes, well, you've been more than thorough." She looked at the freshly cleaned windshield. "Am I expected to tip?"

"I'd say you've already tipped quite enough, thank you."

She felt her cheeks grow warm at the confirmation that he had, indeed, witnessed most of her acrobatics. "I couldn't find the snow scraper."

"So I guessed. You don't seem the type to try cartwheels in a Nissan without a good reason."

"And you don't seem the type to enjoy cleaning snow off other people's vehicles."

"Always ready to help a lady in distress."

"Noble, but I wasn't in distress—until you showed up."

He shrugged. "Probably not, but I was." He pointed to a battered Ford pickup. "My own jalopy is a little touchy in the winter and won't start."

She glanced over at the truck then back to him. His fitted camel topcoat hugged his broad shoulders and hung open so she could make out the outline of his thighs. A dark brown cashmere scarf was draped carelessly around his neck and flapped against his chest in the breeze. He stripped off his leather gloves, which were now stained dark from the melting snow, and shoved them in his pocket. Then he brushed away the snowflakes that had been clinging to his long, dark eyelashes. Damp and glistening from the snow, they made his eyes sparkle even more than usual.

"Well?"

Clearly he was expecting some reply from her, but it took Nicki a moment to remember the topic under discussion.

"Well, perhaps you should take some money out of your clothing budget and replace that clunker. It doesn't fit your image."

"Maybe, but that won't help me today. You're staying at Blake's place aren't you?"

Nicki nodded.

"I live just around the corner from there."

"It's a nice neighborhood."

"Come on, Nicki, I was hoping for a ride."

"Sorry, but I'm not going home. I'm meeting some students at Pizza Palace, which is on the other side of town." She glanced at her watch. "And I'm already late."

"I think it's in terribly poor taste to start fraternizing with students so early in the semester. Looks like I'm going to have to come along to protect you from accusations of playing favorites."

"No chance. I don't even know who's going to be there. They're interviewing me for an article in the law school's student paper."

"Even more reason to take me with you. You'll want a witness in case they misquote you."

"I never let the press back me into a corner."

"Okay, if I can't appeal to your own self-interest, perhaps I can engage your humanitarian instincts. I'm hungry. I haven't eaten a thing all day."

"I hear the hamburgers at that place across the street are great."

"Yes, but pizza is one of my three favorite things in the world."

Nicki sighed heavily and opened the passenger door with a flourish. "Get in, Doug. I don't have time to argue about this."

"Don't you want to know what my other favorite things are?"

She picked up the suggestive slide in his voice. "Absolutely not."

"Not ever?"

"No." He did have a knack for getting his way, she thought, as she walked around to the driver's side and got in.

"I'd love to know all about your favorite things." His husky whisper sent a tingle down her spine.

"Silence is real high on my list."

"Fits right in with dull and boring, huh?"

"I'm extremely consistent."

"I'm glad you go to extremes about something."

"Was that a put-down?" She glanced at him and looked back to the road.

"That was deep despair. I'm not very good at all this 'man on the make' razzle-dazzle to begin with, and you can be a severe blow to the old ego."

"Are you a man on the make?"

"No. Not really. Unless you count wanting to make friends."

She would have loved to believe that all he wanted was her friendship, but it didn't seem likely. "Then I'd suggest you cut the razzle entirely and rely on your own natural charm for the dazzle."

"You think I have natural charm?"

"As much as I hate to admit it, yes, I do."

"Hot dog."

She shook her head. "Even as he speaks, he proves my point. You are unique, Doug."

"So are you. See?" He patted her knee casually. "Even by being unique we have something in common."

Nicki hoped he hadn't noticed her grip tighten on the steering wheel at his brief touch. "I'm attempting to drive in a blizzard right now, so I really can't give that last statement my full attention. But I suspect that it made no sense."

"Sure it did. Trust me."

"When Hades freezes over, MacNair."

Doug slipped a handkerchief out of his pocket and reached over to wipe the steam off the windshield. "That might be sooner than you think if this weather continues. This is the sixth consecutive day we've had heavy snowfall. It's getting tiresome."

"Not for me. I love it. It's so cleansing. The air smells fresh, and everything gray and ugly is camouflaged by glistening, white crystals. How can you get tired of anything so beautiful?"

"Typical for me. I get consumed by the work aspect—in this case the shoveling—and I let that overwhelm my ability to appreciate things. I'm trying to change, though. The new me is beginning to enjoy more." He folded the handkerchief and returned it to his pocket. They rode in silence for a while. "You surprise me a little, Nicki. I wouldn't have thought you took the time to notice anything that wasn't related to law, and certainly not something as inconsequential as snow."

Nicki maneuvered the car into a parking space and opened her door. "Law is very important to me. It's the way I make my living. But snow was my life." She pulled her collar up against the wind and walked toward the restaurant.

Doug took a moment before following her. He suspected that her cryptic statement was in response to her perception that he had accused her of being too fixated on her career. Since she had no way of knowing that he, too, had spent years ignoring everything around him except his medical practice, she had misinterpreted what he'd thought was a show of understanding.

In the restaurant, he saw her approach a table already occupied by six young people. Coming up behind her just in time to pull out her chair, he bent down to whisper in her ear. "Sorry. I didn't say what you heard."

"No apology necessary," she whispered back. "All I heard was the truth."

He took the seat next to her and, after being introduced to the law students, was perfectly happy to sit back and watch her relate to them. She seemed to be equally as comfortable sharing a pitcher of beer and deciding pizza toppings as expounding on the responsibilities of the legal community to society at large. She had some very definite opinions on the necessity to modify the court system to control what she saw as abuses, and Doug was impressed that she obviously had given a lot of thought to issues that most people just took for granted.

On a personal level, he was surprised to learn that she had been serious when commenting on her height in relation to keeping respect in the courtroom and the classroom. She confessed that when it came to making an impression on a jury, she had found herself at a severe disadvantage as a young, petite, soft-spoken woman. Many of her male opponents were not above attempting to embarrass her personally in order to make her appear inept. As a result, she had taken special instruction to teach her to project her voice and sound more forceful, acting lessons to teach her the effective use of body language, even courses on power dressing to help her appear more mature and in control.

Doug had to smile as he watched the way she rested her chin on her hands and cocked her head to one side when she was listening, peeking out from under the mane of disorderly curls that framed her face. Whatever she'd done to "toughen up" as she called it, she certainly hadn't sacrificed all of the delightful, enthusiastic young girl to the austere businesswoman yet. It was possible she thought she had, or at least that she wanted to give that impression to others, but Doug wasn't buying it. He'd spent too many years using an aura of professionalism to hide from his own social insecurities not to recognize the behavior in someone else.

By the end of the meal he had no doubts that the Nicole Devlin who had trained so hard to become an extraordinary attorney had succeeded. But he was more interested in the part of Nicole that made her an extraordinary woman.

IN THE CAR ON THE WAY HOME, Nicki glanced sideways, trying to gauge Doug's mood. His uncharacteristic quiet made her wonder if she had said something to make him angry again. Finally, she couldn't stand it anymore. "Is something wrong?"

"Ah-ha. Just as I thought. You lied to me. You don't like silence, after all."

"I do so. But it doesn't seem like your usual style."

"I have a lot of different styles. I call this one contemplative. What do you think?"

"It's kind of scary. What were you contemplating?"

"You, and how little I know about you."

"How much can you expect to know after a few hours together?"

"That's what bothers me. I thought I knew all I needed or wanted to know before I even met you."

"Oh that's right. The ambulance chasing, courtroom piranha out to destroy innocent doctors for personal vengeance. Not very flattering."

"No. Not to either one of us. Are you really as ethical as you sounded, talking to those kids back there?"

"I hope so."

"You were pretty impressive."

She arched an eyebrow. "What was it that impressed you so? Could it have been my insistence that we take the democratic approach and vote on whether to get anchovies on the pizza or not? Or was it my forthright and, unfortunately, truthful announcement that I cannot be held responsible for my actions after more than two beers?"

"Both. Along with just about every other word you said." He turned to face her. "You're uncomfortable with compliments, aren't you?"

"I love compliments. I just don't happen to think that being ethical warrants one. It is, after all, the expected standard of conduct."

"You can't be that naive."

"I'd like to be."

"And here I thought you were a cynic."

"I am, in the original sense of the word. The Greek Cynics believed that virtue was the only good and its essence lay in self-control and independence. Sounds pretty dull and boring, don't you think?"

"Sounds pretty hard to live by."

"Not really, but speaking of 'live by.' Where exactly do you live?"

"You can just drop me off at your place. I can walk from there."

"That's crazy. It's late, the sidewalks are icy, and I've got the car out anyway. I might as well take you home."

"No! I mean I need the fresh air. Really."

Nicki shrugged. "Okay. Have it your way, as usual." She pulled into her parking space and they walked to the door of her apartment building. "What are you going to do about your car?"

"I'll call Paul or something. Unless, of course, you'd like to help me."

"Sorry. You should know I can't. I have a meeting with one of your residents, remember?"

"Right. Rehearsal for examination of an expert witness. Where are you practicing?"

"Here. She lives somewhere nearby so it'll be easier than going to the law school."

"What time?"

"Nine. Why?"

"Oh, no reason. Just making sure you have a bona fide excuse for not giving me a lift."

"Do I?"

"Sounds like it. Too bad."

"You don't look like you think it's too bad."

"I hide my disappointment well. Thanks for tonight."

He touched her chin gently and studied her with a silent question in his eyes. Nicki felt her heart begin to beat more rapidly as she realized if she made the slightest move in his direction he would kiss her good-night. She took a step backward instead. "No thanks necessary. You paid your own way."

"But you provided the entertainment."

"I've never thought of myself as particularly entertaining."

"Then you do yourself a disservice. You're an interesting woman, Nicole Devlin. I can hardly wait to get to know you better."

"What makes you think you'll get the chance?"

"I'm a man who makes my own chances. Good night, Nicki." He turned and started down the sidewalk.

She continued to watch him and chuckled to herself as she noticed that for every three steps he took he skated for one, just like a little boy skidding home from school. Doug must have been taking his new approach to enjoyment seriously.

He certainly seemed to take a great deal of pleasure in even the simplest things. And, in spite of herself, Nicki took pleasure in knowing that Doug MacNair found her both interesting and entertaining.

CHAPTER FOUR

AT EIGHT-THIRTY the next morning, Nicki was not ready to face the day. She had been much too restless to sleep last night and, after tossing and turning for several hours, had finally gotten up to work. She had hoped that making some progress on the brief Ron had asked her to write for him would put her mind at ease, but even though her work went well she still hadn't relaxed enough to consider going back to bed.

Her thoughts kept drifting to Doug and his negative reaction to malpractice attorneys. It annoyed her that he was so closed-minded about the need for patients to have legal recourse against bad doctors, but it was also reassuring. As long as he had such strong feelings on the issue, he probably wouldn't be too diligent in pursuing her, and the sooner he tired of that game, the better off she'd be. She found him entirely too attractive, and it was becoming increasingly difficult for her to remember to keep her distance.

Eventually she had fallen asleep at her desk. When she awoke, her leg was throbbing, she had a stiff neck, and she felt anything but rested. A glance at her watch had told her that she had less than half an hour before Stephanie Henderson, a psychiatry resident, arrived to practice the demonstration.

After starting a pot of coffee, Nicki ran to the shower and had just managed to towel dry her hair and throw on a pair of jeans and a pink sweatshirt before the doorbell rang. She took another swipe at her hair, groaned at her disheveled reflection in the mirror and ran to the front hall without taking time to find her shoes. The damp towel still in her hand, she opened the door ready to launch into a string of excuses for her appearance. "Hi, I'm Nicole Dev—"

"Morning, curly-top. I brought donuts, but I hope you have coffee."

Caught completely off guard, Nicki couldn't ignore the flash of pleasure that raced through her at the sight of the undeniably attractive and definitely male figure leaning against her door frame. She marshaled her resistance. "Stephanie I presume."

His answering grin revealed a hint of suppressed, boyish mischief, but there was nothing boyish about the glint of desire she saw in his eyes as he took a lazy visual journey from her wet curls to her bare feet, pausing a long moment to read the designer's logo on her sweatshirt. She felt herself blush.

The grin gave way to a knowing smile. "I must say, I rather like your morning look. A tad unprofessional, to be sure, but cute."

"Doug, what do you think you're doing here? This is supposed to be a work session not a coffee klatch."

"Stephanie called me this morning. She's ill and I couldn't find anyone to replace her on such short notice so I decided to do the demo with you."

"Sorry, but you don't qualify. The topic is supposed to be working with medical experts not questioning hostile witnesses."

"When have I ever been hostile to you?"

"Are you kidding? You know full well anytime the subject of trial practice comes up you turn purple with rage."

"You're safe today. Purple would clash with my outfit." He opened his brown leather aviator jacket to reveal a red-

and-white checked flannel shirt, pulled tautly across his broad chest and open just low enough to show a dusting of brown curls. She trailed her eyes down to the snug, faded jeans that hugged his thighs—magnificent, muscular, powerful thighs that would undoubtedly be rock hard to her touch.

"Well?"

Nicki jerked her head up at the sound of his voice. "I'm thinking," she mumbled.

"You're gawking, but that's fine with me. How is my natural charm today? Still intact even when I'm wearing jeans and no tie?"

To hide her embarrassment, she grabbed the donut bag out of his hands and headed for the kitchen. "Let's get some coffee. I hate dealing with the unpredictable on an empty stomach."

"Me? Unpredictable?" He followed her, leaned against the counter and assumed an innocent expression. "I'll have you know, most of my friends think of me as a staid, conservative, quiet kind of guy."

"Then either your friends have all the social awareness of moles or your membership in the Screen Actors Guild is up for renewal." She handed him two mugs of black coffee, turned him around and pointed him back to the living room. "I believe you took it black last night. Right?"

He stopped dead in his tracks and sighed contentedly. "The fact that you noticed how I take my coffee must signify something meaningful."

"It signifies that the table was crowded and, since no one was using the cream and sugar, I moved them to another table."

He slumped down onto the couch. "You have a devastating knack for squelching a guy's romantic notions."

"Thank you. I work hard at it." She set the donuts down in front of him. "Let me get my notes and we'll start going over the demonstration." She barely made it across the room before Doug was beside her again. He never allowed her to escape from the tingling awareness that all she had to do was reach out and she could touch him.

He bent down and picked up something from beside the desk. "You know, everywhere I look I see signs of a cat in residence—litter box, cat dish, and this mutilated ball of fluff that probably started life as a catnip mouse." He dangled the soft gray blob in front of her by what was left of its tail. "But I have yet to see any signs of the beast who was capable of committing this act of violence."

Nicki laughed. "For that I'm afraid I'll have to invite you into my bedroom." She half surprised herself by giving him the most flirtatious "come hither" look she could muster as she took him by the arm and led him to the bedroom door. "You see that lump under the bedspread? That's Elmo. He doesn't like visitors."

Doug walked closer to the bed. "So the poor little guy just hides? What would happen if I took a peek at him?"

Nicki shrugged. "Maybe nothing." Doug knelt on the floor at the foot of the bed. "And then again, maybe he'll attack."

Doug cocked his head, leaned back on his heels and stared at her for a moment, then began to lift the bedspread. "Don't bother to bluff. No guard cat would keep me out of your bed if that's where I wanted to be." He winked briefly and ducked under the cover then out again as the lump began to move. "Whoa there, fellah, that's a good kitty. You just stay calm." Doug was back on his feet and standing beside Nicki before she had time to say a word. "I thought you said cat, not tiger. That's the most enormous domestic feline I've ever seen.'' His eyes were open just a bit wider than usual.

Nicki caught her breath against the slight tightening in her chest. Doug would certainly be much less of a threat if he didn't have the ability to be so irresistibly cute. Where was the conceit, the machismo, the false bravado that made it so easy for her to write most men off? He obviously thought it was funny to play at being the rake, but he never maintained the facade for very long. She simply could not muster the necessary protective state of mind when dealing with someone who said ''hot dog,'' skated on the ice and was willing to admit that he was intimidated by a large house cat. ''Oh come now, Doug, you can't possibly be frightened of Elmo.''

''What a deceptively sweet name for such a vicious looking beast. How did you come up with that, anyway?'' He snapped his fingers. ''Wait, I've got it. He's bright orange so he's named after St. Elmo's fire.''

''Nope. He's shy, so he's named after a shy orthopedic surgeon.''

Doug looked surprised. ''No kidding? Would that be Elmo Vandercamp? How in the world did you meet him? Last I heard he was living in Colorado.''

Nicki cursed herself silently for attempting to explain Elmo's name. If she admitted that Dr. Vandercamp had actually treated her, Doug would have a lot of questions that she didn't feel like answering right now. ''I grew up in Colorado. He's become sort of a friend of the family.'' Keeping her tone light, she changed the subject. ''Shouldn't we get back to our coffee before it's too cold to drink?''

Doug assessed her silently for a moment, then apparently decided not to pursue the matter any further. ''Right— coffee.'' He gave a nervous backward glance toward the bed. ''So long, Elmo. It was a real pleasure meeting you.''

Doug had just brought the mugs of coffee in from the kitchen and taken his first sip when Sarah Bernard came in the front door without knocking.

"Hi, Nicki—" she paused and raised an eyebrow "—and Doug. I didn't mean to interrupt anything. I figured you'd be at the office by now, and Blake wanted me to send some of his books to him."

Doug glanced at Nicki but she didn't seem the least bit suprised.

"You aren't interrupting anything, Sarah. Doug and I are just working on a demonstration that we'll be doing for the class in a couple of weeks. I put all of Blake's stuff in the guest room."

Sarah wandered down the hall and Doug shook his head at Nicki in amazement. "Don't you think that's a little tacky?"

"No. Blake told me I could move whatever I wanted to."

"I don't mean that. Doesn't it bother you that he has left his girlfriend with a key to your apartment, and she comes and goes as she pleases without so much as a call ahead or a knock?"

Nicki narrowed her eyes in confusion for a moment, then laughed. "I thought you and Blake were friends."

"Not really. Blake is more a business associate than anything else. He consults for the hospital."

Nicki just nodded, then got up and called down the hallway. "Hey, Sarah, could you come back here a second, please?" When Sarah reappeared, Nicki slipped her arm around the young woman's waist. "Doug MacNair, I'd like you to meet my sister, Sarah Bernard."

Doug stood up to shake Sarah's hand. "Sisters? Now why didn't I know that?"

"Could it be because no one told you?" Nicki asked.

"Or because we are nothing at all alike?" Sarah piped in. "I have red hair, she's blond. I have blue eyes, she has dynamite gray ones." She cocked her head. "That are actually a heck of a lot like yours. I'm medium build she's minuscule. I'm bouncy, bubbly and great to be with, she's dull and boring." She grinned Nicki's grin and began to comb her fingers through her disorderly curls.

Doug rubbed his chin thoughtfully. "No, that's not it. It's something much more significant."

"Such as?" Nicki's voice sounded wary.

"Such as, you have different last names." He was taken aback by the dark cloud that settled over Nicki's features. He had meant his comment to be humorous. These days it wasn't all that unusual for people who were related to have different names. But one look at her face told him that, for her, this was definitely not a laughing matter.

He cursed himself silently. Just because Nicki didn't seem to be the least bit intimidated by him was no excuse for him to feel he could always say whatever came to mind. He wondered if she had a painful divorce in her background. "Sorry. That wasn't meant as a question, just an observation."

"Nicki's a little sensitive on that issue—as you can undoubtedly see," Sarah stated, with a sideways glance toward her sister. "Our father died when we were kids. Mom remarried and we took our stepfather's name. When they divorced, I was too young to bother to change again, but Nicki went back to Devlin. She hated him. He—"

"Sarah, that's quite enough. I don't think Dr. MacNair needs a complete family history. Do you?"

Doug winced at the harshness in Nicki's voice. He watched Sarah's expression flash from stunned, to hurt, and when her jaw tightened in anger, he took an instinctive step backward in a futile attempt to remove himself from the scene.

"No, no, of course not. Pardon me for venturing onto sacred ground."

The two women stared at each other as though neither was quite sure what to do about a hostility that had taken them both by surprise.

Doug held his breath. He knew there was no way for him to ease the tension.

Tears welled up in Sarah's eyes, and she clenched her hands into tight fists. "You know, Nicki, it may have been your accident and your broken bones, but darn it, just because your scars are the ones that show doesn't give you a right to act like you own all the heartaches. You weren't the only one hurt."

Nicki stiffened visibly and turned so pale that, for a moment, Doug thought she might faint. She slipped her fingers into the curls above her temples, closed her eyes and rubbed the sides of her head as though she were unable to understand what was happening. Before he could go to her, Sarah rushed past him and threw her arms around Nicki's neck in an obviously desperate hug.

"I'm sorry, Sis. God, I'm sorry. I didn't mean it."

They clung to each other for a long time. Finally, Nicki pushed back her sister's tousled bangs and planted an affectionate kiss on her forehead. "It's okay, baby."

"I really didn't mean it," Sarah sobbed.

"Shhh. It's okay. Let's just forget it."

Sarah shook her head. "I don't want to forget it. I want to remember exactly what it feels like to know I've hurt you, because I don't ever want it to happen again." She backed away and sniffed. "Blake and I are arguing and I just... Oh, never mind. That's no excuse. I was terrible."

"We both were. I had no right to jump on you like that."
Sarah started to say something else, but Nicki interrupted.
"How about we talk more about it later? We do have company right now. You know?"

The young woman spun around and faced Doug.
"Brother, when I screw up I sure do a thorough job of it.
I'm sorry, Doug. Believe me, we aren't usually like this."

Doug just nodded and tried to give her what he hoped
would be a reassuring smile.

Sarah blushed brightly as she backed to the door. "I'll get
Blake's books later. You guys have a good session, if that's
possible after this fiasco."

The door clicked shut and, without a word, Nicki walked
over to the desk and began flipping through file folders,
making it clear that she had no intention of discussing what
had happened.

For lack of anything better to do, Doug sat down and
took an enormous gulp of coffee. It was cold. He closed his
eyes and swallowed quickly then seized the opportunity to
lighten the mood. "Nicki, do you like ice coffee in the winter or should I go reheat this?"

"I never like ice coffee. Can I trust you near the stove?"

"Sure, I'm a great cook."

"Well, that makes one of us. You handle the coffee." She
rubbed the back of her neck. "I'm getting some aspirin."

"I've got a better idea." He stepped behind her and slid
his hands along the satin smooth skin at the sides of her
neck. She tensed for an instant and he thought she might
pull away, but when he began to gently knead the tight
muscles at the tops of her shoulders, he felt her relax.

"How's this?" he asked, controlling a surge of satisfaction at the idea that she could be comfortable with his touch.

"Fishing again? You know it feels terrific."

"Um-hm." She was the one who felt terrific, he thought—soft, warm and delightfully fragile. "Did you get much sleep last night?"

"A nap at my desk, but I'm used to that." She tipped her head back against his hands with an easy familiarity that made him want to wrap his arms around her.

"You work too hard, you know?"

"I work as hard as I have to."

Doug shook his head. "No. You work as hard as you think everyone expects you to." He felt her begin to tense again but couldn't resist probing. "Is that how you try to pay everyone back for all the hurts they've had to bear?"

She started to pull away but stopped herself. As usual, Doug marveled at her self-control.

"I didn't realize psychology was your field, Doctor."

"It isn't, but I've done a lot of self-analysis. When you're ready, you will too. You're too smart not to figure out what you're doing to yourself."

She lifted her shoulders in a languid stretch and slowly moved away from him, but he'd been watching closely enough to realize that her motions were carefully executed to create the impression of casual indifference.

"Yes, but not smart enough to figure out what I've done with the blasted file. I think I left my briefcase in the other room. Would you get the coffee while I check for it?"

The minute Nicki closed the bedroom door behind her, she put her hand on her neck. Her skin still felt warm where Doug's fingers had been. In spite of that warming touch of his, he had no right to think he could step in and start telling her how to change her life.

When she turned around, she expected to see the familiar lump under the covers. Instead, Elmo was sitting on the bed blinking at her sagely. "I know. You think I work too hard, too." She sat next to him and scratched his head as he purred his assent. "That's easy for you to say, but if I spent all my time at home cuddling you, who would pay the bills and keep you in cat food?"

She picked up her briefcase from beside the bed and quickly located the missing file. Then, unwilling to face Doug just yet, she flopped back against the pillows and stared at the ceiling. She couldn't remember when she had last felt this exhausted. She had no doubt that Doug was right in saying that her work load was taking a toll, but it was the argument with Sarah and having Doug witness it that had left her absolutely drained.

Doug knew nothing of the circumstances surrounding her accident, yet he certainly hadn't missed that Sarah's attack had exposed Nicki's most vulnerable side. And as much as she hated to admit it, he had come entirely too close to seeing her confront the painful connection between her guilt and her need to achieve. "An astute man our Doctor MacNair," she mumbled to Elmo.

She had decided years ago what she had to do to feel good about herself, and she knew the sacrifices that would be required. Her emotional response to Doug was disorienting enough in and of itself. She would not allow him to bait her into questioning her underlying goals.

Standing up, she blew the cat hair off the manila folder she was carrying and raked her fingers through her curls before opening the door. For the time being, her only goal was to finish this rehearsal and get Doug out of her apartment.

She no sooner walked back into the living room than Doug was by her side, brandishing a donut. "Here, eat this before you fade away. You're tiny enough as it is without starving yourself."

"Doug, would you do something for me?"

He bowed theatrically. "Your slightest wish..."

"Go find a place to sit down and stay there for at least five minutes straight, so I can think."

"Am I distracting you?"

"Driving me to distraction is more like it."

He chuckled as he settled on the sofa. Nicki took a chair as far away as possible and turned it to face him. She was certain that he didn't believe her for a minute when she explained that it would best approximate a courtroom setting.

The first half hour of the rehearsal went well. Doug considered each of her questions carefully and gave clear and thorough answers. But as she guided her examination through the introductory information and on to the specifics of the case she had chosen for the demonstration, the instincts that served her so well in the courtroom flashed an alert. The witness was beginning to view her as the enemy.

With each new question Doug's body language telegraphed his increasing tension. He no longer lounged against the back of the sofa, right ankle crossed on his left knee. Instead, he leaned toward her, feet planted firmly on the floor, elbows resting on flexed thighs. His tone became hard and his answers clipped, each one punctuated by alternately clenching his hands into tight fists and making accusatory stabs in her direction with his index finger. The lines around his eyes deepened and the corners of his mouth tightened with bitterness until she could no longer ignore his obvious and increasing anger.

"Is something wrong, Dr. MacNair?"

"Yes, Ms Devlin, something is wrong. How long are we going to continue this?"

Nicki glanced at her watch. "I guess we can stop anytime. The whole idea of the rehearsal was to put the supposedly inexperienced medical student at ease. You clearly don't need that kind of coaching."

"No, Ms Trial Attorney, I don't. Unfortunately, I can't claim to be inexperienced in courtroom drama. However, based on my recollections, today's script seems somewhat inaccurate."

"Now wait a minute, Doug. I told you that interviewing hostile witnesses was not on the agenda today. What is your problem?"

"My problem, as you put it, is that you are trying to set me up by asking me polite questions, listening patiently to my answers, accepting what I say, and responding with more polite questions. When do your young lawyers get to observe the techniques of asking leading, ambiguous questions and contradicting the answers with examples dredged from out-of-date medical books? How will they learn to distract the jury from the facts by accusing the witness of being inept, ill-informed, and too interested in making money to care about a patient's welfare? Don't you think you should let them see what really happens to doctors in the courtroom?"

Nicki slammed her legal pad down on the end table and stood up. "Listen, MacNair, I don't know how long you thought I was going to be a good little girl and hold my temper while you took potshots at me and at a profession I represent and respect, but your time has run out. I was not a part of whatever bad experience you had, but I've been in a lot more courtrooms than you have. It's my job. I take it seriously. I do it well, and I pursue my chosen career not to destroy people, but to provide advocacy for those whose lives have been irreparably damaged by another's negligence. Sounds corny, but it's a concept for which I would think an intelligent and compassionate person might have some glimmer of understanding."

"Do you expect me to believe that you always conduct yourself so politely in the courtroom?"

"Always? No, of course not. I conduct myself as the situation mandates."

"And if you weren't trying to impress me, what would our situation mandate?"

"Don't flatter yourself. Impressing you was the last thing on my mind. There was no basis on which I could challenge your testimony. The quickest way to discredit myself would be to try to refute an expert who obviously knows much more about the subject than I do. I asked you questions. You answered honestly and succinctly, and you were presenting information the jury had a right to hear."

"Sure. And how many attorneys do you think feel that way?"

"All the good ones, but does it matter? How many doctors do you think would get on the stand and answer questions as openly as you did? Yet you don't hear me attacking you because you seem to be more willing to play fair than some of your peers, do you?"

"No."

"Would you like it better if I were one of those stereotypical sleazy lawyers that always plays the bad guy on television?"

"Of course not. Although that would certainly make you a lot easier for me to deal with."

Nicki took a deep breath to regain her composure. "I wasn't aware you felt you had to 'deal' with me. What am I doing that makes it so difficult?"

Doug rested his head in his hands. When he looked up his eyes were filled more with confusion than bitterness. "Not *have* to deal with you, Nicki—want to. And I'm afraid you aren't doing anything but being yourself."

"Well that's hardly something I can change too easily."

"I should hope not. You're wonderful."

"I thought I was difficult."

"That's just it. You're so wonderful it makes you difficult to deal with."

"You're crazy." She had made the mistake of pacing too close to him during the course of the argument. Now he stood up, placed his hands on her shoulders and forced her to face him. "Listen, Nicki, I'm sorry. I really am. But it's very hard for me to square who and what you are, or seem to be, with what you do for a living."

"But that's so unfair. You can't condemn an entire profession because of the undesirable conduct of a few."

"Isn't that what you do?"

"No, it isn't, Doug. And for some reason I can't begin to understand, it's very important to me to get you to believe that."

He slipped his arm casually over her shoulder. "You could begin working on convincing me over lunch. I want to make amends for letting my Mr. Hyde persona emerge."

She ducked away, slightly unsettled by Doug's easy journey from storm to calm. "Sorry, Dr. Jeckyl, I have to work."

"You also have to eat." He walked toward her again.

"I have leftover pizza to finish up."

"Save it."

As he moved beside her, the apartment suddenly felt incredibly warm and much too small for the two of them. Anything was better than staying in such close quarters with him. "Okay."

Her assent must have shocked him because, miraculously, he took a step back. "Do you mean it? Really? Okay?"

"Yes."

He gave her a pleased, crooked grin and his eyes flashed excitedly.

"Wait," she interjected before he could say anything. "Allow me—hot dog!"

"You got it."

Nicki was on her way to get their coats when the phone rang. She grimaced, hoping it wasn't Ron with more work for her. "Hello."

"Hi, Nicki, Sarah. Are you still speaking to me?"

"Of course."

"Well, just to show you that I'm always thinking about you, I was reading the local paper and I saw an ad for the new outpatient facility at the hospital. As part of the promotional campaign, they're giving a tour of the clinic and the emergency room this afternoon. I thought you might be interested in an off-the-record peek behind the scenes."

"You bet I'm interested. When does it start?"

"Let's see. It says noon. That only gives you half an hour to get over there. Are you still tied up with the sexy doctor?"

"I'll make it. Thanks, Sarah." Nicki hung up before her sister could press for details and turned to confront Doug with the change of plans.

Mirroring his earlier entrance, he was lounging against the front door frame, waiting expectantly.

"Doug, I hate to miss your attempt to make up for your vile behavior, but I'm afraid I'll have to take a rain check on lunch—duty calls."

"What about your duty to me? I spent a long morning slaving away here as a favor to you and I don't even get lunch."

Nicki slipped on her coat. "I really am sorry, but this can't be helped."

"I'm starving and I can't even get to a restaurant without a car."

"You're always starving. Listen, I have to run. There's pizza and beer in the fridge. Help yourself. Just lock up when you leave."

"Nicki, someday you're going to have to learn to say no to the demands people are always making on your personal life."

"I'm trying, Doug. After all, look how often I say no to you. Enjoy your lunch."

Doug stepped aside as Nicki breezed out, half slamming the door behind her. With a disgruntled shrug he made his way to the kitchen. He had just finished slipping the pizza in the oven to heat when, out of the corner of his eye, he saw something move. He turned to see Elmo peeking around the edge of the kitchen counter.

"Well, hi there, fellah. Did you think the coast was clear when you heard the door close?"

The cat eyed him warily but didn't run, and Doug made no attempt to approach him. Instead he opened his beer and stared back at the big, green eyes. After a couple of minutes, Doug gave up. "Okay, you win. I blinked first. How about a victory toast?" He poured a splash of beer in the cat's bowl and stood back. Elmo didn't even hesitate before running to his dish to see what was being offered. After the first tentative lick, he settled down to such concentrated drinking that he never even looked up when Doug knelt beside him and began to scratch his neck.

By the time lunch was ready, Elmo was perched on a stool at the breakfast bar contentedly washing his face. Doug sat down next to him and munched on a slice of pizza. "So what do you say, pal? Do you think you could put in a good word for me with your mistress? She has yet to realize what a great guy I am, but now that you and I have gotten to know each other, you could vouch for me." Doug examined his half-empty beer bottle. He really hadn't had enough to drink to justify sitting here asking for a character reference from a cat—not even a cat named after a surgeon. Maybe Nicki was right. He was going crazy and he couldn't help but feel that she was the one who was driving him to it.

ON HER WAY to the hospital, Nicki told herself she should consider herself lucky to have gotten away without having to have lunch with Doug. So why did she feel so disappointed? He was arrogant, insulting and always looking for something to argue about. She smiled to herself. He was also handsome, interesting, and fringed on adorable when he was admitting he was wrong. The way he talked to her, the way he moved around her, the way he touched her so casually, all made it obvious that he was perfectly comfortable when they were together. And that kind of relationship was a new experience for her.

Nicki was used to being at ease, relaxed, even funny around men. She'd never much cared what impression she left as a woman as long as they respected her as a professional. Doug, on the other hand, had no respect at all for her profession, yet she still found herself wanting him to have a good opinion of her. In fact, if she'd stop kidding herself, she'd have to admit that she wanted more than that. She wanted him to like her, to keep asking her out, to keep finding reasons to be near her. She jerked her thoughts to a halt as a warm tingle of anticipation washed over her at the memory of his touch.

She pulled into a parking space in the hospital lot and chastised herself for allowing Doug to interfere with her professional life even when he wasn't around. She should have spent the last twenty minutes thinking about what she wanted to learn and accomplish during her emergency room tour, not fantasizing about one gray-eyed Casanova. She had far too many responsibilities right now to allow herself the luxury of a romantic interlude.

CHAPTER FIVE

THE NURSE who was playing the role of tour guide was a chatty, motherly type who was clearly proud of the hospital's facilities. Although a tour like this could hardly serve as a substitute for the detailed investigation Nicki would have to do later, she knew that it could provide a valuable overview of the organization of the hospital where Ian had had his attack. If she were alert she might even be able to pick up some clues that would be less easy for her to uncover once she was known as the enemy.

The guide led them into the new health club and explained that the hospital was interested in combining what had previously been post-injury or illness rehabilitation with general health maintenance and sports medicine. Nicki made a mental note. That information might help her if she ever got to the point of talking settlement on Ian's case. If the hospital were trying to solicit memberships in its club and to market sports medicine as a service, it might be more hesitant to go to trial and garner unfavorable publicity over a malpractice case involving a promising young athlete.

She listened intently to the detailed description of all the elaborate sports paraphernalia in the gym and reminded herself that she'd done nothing yet about finding a place to work out. This certainly looked like an ideal facility.

The tour moved on to the emergency room, which was mercifully devoid of patients. The guide pointed out some of the more impressive equipment, explained the value of improved technology in medical care, then introduced several of the emergency room nurses, saying they would probably be willing to answer questions. Nicki's attention was immediately caught by the name Margaret Orb, whom she knew had been on duty the afternoon that Ian had been brought to the emergency room.

As other members of the group began to ask general questions, Nicki worked her way over to Margaret, who was busy adjusting a complex looking machine.

"That's some device. What does it do?"

The woman looked up and smiled shyly. Nicki was surprised at how young she appeared. For some reason she had expected anyone who dealt with the day-to-day stress of working in an emergency room to be older and harder than this girl.

"It's nothing too intimidating. Just your basic cardiac monitor. Attach these to the patient, turn it on and see how the old ticker is doing."

Nicki grinned. Shy or not, here was someone who undoubtedly had a natural talent for putting a patient at ease. "What, no complicated medical terms to dazzle me? How disillusioning."

This time Margaret's smile was a bit more self-assured. "Most of that medical mumbo jumbo just scares folks. I think it helps if someone explains things to you in terms you can understand. Don't you?"

"I do indeed, but I wouldn't think that would be a very popular opinion among your peers."

"You'd be surprised. The medical profession is finally beginning to recognize the importance of being approachable. A few years ago, a tour like the one you're on would have been unheard-of. Now it's routine."

"Don't the nurses hate having to lead the troops around and answer questions when there's other work to do?"

"Are you kidding? We love it. It's a wonderful change to be able to explain what goes on here to people who aren't already bleeding or in pain. It's kind of difficult to wax eloquent about our excellent medical services when we're worried whether someone will live long enough to hear the whole speech."

"Well, as far as I know, I've got a pretty long life expectancy so why don't you give me the speech? Just what does go on here? What happens to a patient from the time he comes in the door?"

"Wow, that's a pretty tall order. Every case is different. For example, you didn't say how he came in the door—on a stretcher, on his own, walking with the help of friends."

"Let's say on a stretcher."

"Conscious?"

"No."

"Accident? Heart attack? Or don't we know?"

"Let's say we don't know."

"Okay. First, we'd make sure he was breathing and was going to continue to do so. Then we'd take him to one of those cubicles over there and the doctor or resident on duty would start trying to figure out what was wrong."

"Now let's say we know our unconscious patient is a diabetic."

Margaret stiffened visibly. "We'd run the necessary tests and prepare to treat him for diabetic coma." Her voice sounded tight and her words slow and measured.

Nicki pretended not to notice the obvious change of tone. "What kind of tests, and what does the treatment for diabetic coma entail?"

Instead of answering, Margaret looked at her watch. "I'm sorry, but I just remembered I'm late for an appointment. There are pamphlets about the treatment of diabetics available in the medical services office." Then she turned and almost ran out of the room.

Nicki rejoined the tour on the way to view the CAT scanner. Her conversation with Margaret Orb had left her troubled. Her first response to the young nurse had been so favorable that she never would have suspected Margaret could have been a party to any negligence, but her reaction to Nicki's question about diabetes had been extreme. Nicki wondered if everyone at the hospital had been warned not to discuss anything that might refer to the case, or if Margaret, in particular, had something to hide.

At the conclusion of the tour, the guide led the group to the cafeteria for coffee. When Nicki walked into the room, she saw Margaret sitting at a table with a handsome, young doctor and talking in a very agitated manner.

Acting on a hunch, she walked up to the nurse who had been guiding them. "Excuse me, but I see Margaret Orb over there. It was such a pleasure meeting and talking with her in the emergency room. She seems so dedicated to what she is doing. Is that her husband?"

The nurse glanced over her shoulder toward Margaret's table and clucked derisively. "No, dear, that's one of our senior residents, Dr. Norman Gregory, and he's no one's husband."

As Nicki had suspected, Margaret was talking to the resident who had cared for Ian in the emergency room. Norman reached over and took Margaret's hand. "Well, they do make an attractive couple."

The tour guide rolled her eyes to the ceiling and shook her head. "Honey, Norm Gregory has got half of the women at this hospital believing they're his one and only. He's a real expert at juggling the ladies. I don't know when he finds time to practice medicine."

As Margaret and Norman walked out of the cafeteria, Nicki shifted her position so she was blocked from view by the coffee machine. "Is he a good doctor?"

"Who knows?" The nurse shrugged. "He does what he's expected to do and no one complains. When he's practicing on his own we'll see if he can charm his patients as well as he can charm his girlfriends."

Taking her coffee to an empty table, Nicki sat down and pulled out her notepad. The second nurse's willingness to gossip about Dr. Gregory made her think the hospital staff, as a whole, had not been warned about the Dorchester investigation. If they had, no one would have said anything to a stranger that might have cast a bad light on any of the personnel who had treated Ian.

Now she was even more certain that Margaret's response had been suspect. In addition, once upset, she had gone directly to Norman to tell him what had happened. Was that because she had needed an understanding ear or because she thought that he would have an interest in learning that someone was in the hospital asking about Ian?

Nicki felt a sympathetic twinge for the shy, young nurse. She was just the type of woman who would be vulnerable to the practiced charms of the handsome, womanizing doctor. She was probably thrilled that he would even bother to notice her. That was certainly a feeling that Nicki could understand. She had been through it all herself when she was seventeen. Had Margaret, like Nicki, been so honored to have the attentions of a successful, attractive man that she had been willing to take a risk with her own career to comply with his wishes? Nicki sighed deeply. People did such foolish things in the name of love.

She took a sip of her coffee and began to list everything she had learned about the hospital and its personnel while on the tour.

When Nicki threw her pencil down half an hour later, she looked up to see Paul Carlson striding toward her.

"Hi, teach." He smiled broadly as he sat down at her table. "Is there no limit to what an unscrupulous attorney will do to get secret information on the enemy? I saw you being herded from the CAT scanner to the cafeteria. You should be ashamed of yourself—taking a public tour."

Nicki slipped her notepad back in her purse. "Are you joking, or bringing me a message from Doug?"

"I'm joking."

"But Doug wouldn't see the humor in it?"

"No, I'm afraid not." Paul sat forward and wrapped both hands around his coffee cup. "I'll tell you a little secret about our friend Doug. He had a malpractice lawsuit filed against him several years ago."

"No kidding? Really? Who could have ever guessed such a thing?"

A smile lit Paul's eyes then died out. "I suppose it is pretty obvious, but the whole thing shook him badly. Doug's a damn good obstetrician, and he's never really gotten over what he thinks was a bum rap."

"Let me guess. Doug had to make a judgment call on a patient's treatment. He made a perfectly reasonable decision, but the result was something less than perfect. The patient filed a suit and the amount was small enough that the insurance company decided not to fight it. They paid up and Doug lost his chance to be vindicated. Am I close?"

"On the button."

"I wish I could say that kind of thing didn't happen very often, but you and I both know better. I'm sorry Doug has been so hurt by it."

"Unfortunately he took it as a personal attack and, even though he hadn't done anything wrong, he felt as though he'd failed. As he saw it, the legal system had gotten the better of him. He thought he'd let down everyone who had been counting on him to be invincible, and for Doug, that really meant everyone."

"Invincible in everyone's eyes is a pretty heavy burden." Even as she said it, Nicki could recall the weight of carrying her own youthful ideas of responsibility.

"Don't I know it, but that was typical for Doug. He was the eldest kid in a big family and the only one to finish college before his father died. He took it upon himself to see that all of his brothers and sisters got the same chance he'd had. So there he was, going to med school, working an extra job, and just generally trying to be everything both financially and emotionally to his family, his friends and his patients. You can imagine what he must have been like."

Nicki shook her head. "No, Paul, I'm afraid I can't. I know only too well what it's like to lead that driven type of life, but I can't really imagine Doug MacNair doing it."

"That's because he hasn't given you a peek at the real Doug MacNair yet. He's going through an 'I too can be a social animal' phase."

"Reaction to the lawsuit?"

"No, that was years ago. Reaction to getting older and realizing that when he goes home at night he's lonely."

"That's the price we pay for our careers."

"I don't want to believe that. And thank God, Doug doesn't either anymore. He was really obsessive. If Doug worked only half as hard as he used to, he'd still be one of the best Ob's in the business. But there has to be some balance—like when we were in college. He was always the number one student but he also managed to be a character—the original wild and crazy guy." Paul chuckled. "We almost lost him for a while there."

"Well, the patient sure seems to have bounced right back. He's definitely a character."

"Yeah, he is isn't he?" Paul's satisfied smile faded. "But don't let all the nutty stuff fool you, Nicki. Doug is also one of the most sensitive and caring people you'll ever get a chance to meet, and a very good buddy of mine."

"That sounds suspiciously like a protective warning."

"Not a warning. Just information I think you ought to have."

"Why?"

"Because he obviously has a crush on his teacher, and I know how easily he can be hurt."

"Let him down gently, huh?"

"If you must." Paul shrugged. "But why let him down at all?"

"Maybe I bruise easily, too."

He said nothing for a moment then gave her a short nod. "Fair enough. But we can all still be friends, can't we?"

"Sure."

"Great. Then how about a movie tonight?"

"Really, Dr. Carlson, I thought you had Doug's interests at heart."

"I do. He's coming too."

"I see. Which one of us is playing the role of chaperon?"

"Wait a minute here. I think I'd better start over. I am going to a movie tonight with Doug and a female psychiatry resident who is sort of a friend of ours. I thought you might like to join us."

"I'm inclined to say no, but I'm intrigued. What does 'sort of a friend' mean?"

"Just that. Stephanie used to live next door to me when I was in high school and she was still in diapers, or close to it. She looked me up when she came here for her residency and we all pal around."

"Stephanie?" Nicki didn't even try to hide the suspicion in her tone.

"Right?" Paul eyed her curiously. "Stephanie Henderson. Do you know her?"

"Not really." She tapped her pencil on the table in a sharp, staccato rhythm. "How is she feeling, by the way?"

"Fine, I guess. I just talked to her a few minutes ago. Why?"

"No reason." So Doug the unpredictable had struck again. "Listen, Paul, I've changed my inclination. I'd love to come tonight." Two could play at this game. "But do me a favor, will you? Pick me up before you get Doug. I'd like to see the look on his face when he finds out I'm there."

"I'd like to oblige, but that'll be a little difficult. Doug is driving."

"Not tonight he isn't. His car is out of commission."

"Oh?" Paul began to grin. "Which one?"

"He has more than one car?"

"Three, if you don't count the old junker he keeps promising to get towed out of the law school lot."

"I see." Her agitated tapping became a loud steady thumping.

"From the look on your face, I think I'm beginning to see, too. Doug's in trouble, isn't he?"

"No, Paul." Nicki stood abruptly and stuffed her pencil in her purse. "Doug is not *in* trouble. Doug *is* trouble."

Paul winked. "We'll see you at seven then?"

"I wouldn't miss it for the world." She turned and walked out of the cafeteria with as much self-control as she could muster while seeing red.

Nicki stormed into her apartment and threw her purse on the sofa. She couldn't stand the idea that Doug had succeeded in outsmarting her to get his own way. "He couldn't find anyone else to fill in on such short notice, my eye."

Sarah appeared in the hallway with an armload of books. "Are you talking to me?"

"No, I am not talking to you," Nicki snapped. "I'm talking to the gods of revenge."

"Um. Heady stuff. What do they say?"

"They say one Dr. Doug MacNair should be drawn and quartered, that's what."

"Yuck. Too much blood and gore—and illegal. There must be a better way. I mean, why ruin such a perfect physical specimen?"

Nicki went to the refrigerator and took out a beer. "Any suggestions?"

"Several, but then most of them are probably illegal too." Sarah set the books down and got a beer for herself. "By the way, what has he done?"

"He lied to me." Nicki sat on the rocking chair and began to rock vigorously.

"Are we executing people for that now?" Sarah flopped down on the sofa.

"We ought to be." Nicki twisted the cap off the bottle and took a swallow. "Where does Doug live?"

"Where all the rich folk live, across town on the ridge. Why do you . . . ?" Sarah's eyes grew wide and she began to sit up slowly. "Don't look now, Sis, but the beast is on the prowl."

Nicki jumped as Elmo bounded onto her lap and rubbed the side of his face against the hand in which she held the beer bottle. "Well, well, this is certainly something new and different. Hello, boy. Haven't you noticed we have a guest?" He blinked at her with sleepy eyes before curling his body into a tight ring and going to sleep.

Sarah shook her head in amazement. "Strange animal. Say, how about we go get a burger tonight? We could do with a long talk, and you can fill me in on Doug's latest exploits."

"Sorry. Unless it's something important to you, I have plans."

"You have plans?" Sarah cocked her head skeptically. "What kind of plans? Working on briefs until midnight and then taking a break to write a couple of law journal articles?"

"I happen to be going to a movie."

"A movie? Interesting. I didn't realize *How To Make Effective Use of Your Law Library* was playing in this neighborhood. Want company?"

"I have company, thanks."

"Did you hear that, Elmo? She has company. And who do we think the lucky companion might be? Hmm?"

Nicki took another drink of beer and said nothing.

"Who? Nicki, I want to know who managed to talk you into taking a night off to go to a movie for what might be the first time in ten years."

"Paul Carlson."

"And who else?"

"I told you."

"Baloney. Paul Carlson would never move in on Doug's territory."

"Doug's territory!" Nicki jumped to her feet, catching Elmo and dumping him unceremoniously back onto the chair as she did so. "I am not and never will be Doug's territory. Whatever gave you a stupid idea like that?"

"You're mad at him aren't you?"

"Mad at him? I want to murder him. What does that have to do with this?"

"Think about it. When is the last time you cared enough about what a man thought or said or did to get angry at him?'' Sarah gathered up her books and strolled to the door. "Face it, Sis, you're hooked. Have a good time tonight."

Nicki stood there staring at the front door. Sarah had to be out of her mind. Nicki certainly wasn't this furious with Doug because she cared about him. On the contrary, this last stunt of his had convinced her that he had absolutely no redeeming social value. Undoubtedly, he thought that his harmless little fabrications were cute or clever. Well she didn't find lying, in any of its guises, the least bit appealing, and she could hardly wait to tell him that this evening when he began his inevitable litany of creative excuses.

Her gaze fell on the stack of mail beside the door. Sarah must have brought it in when she came by for the books. She began to sort through it. Several bills, a letter from Ron asking for some research that would take the better part of her free time next week to finish, and a folded label from a cat food can—probably a reminder from Sarah that the supply was running low.

She unfolded it and read the nearly illegible scribble on the back. Only a man of medicine had writing this bad.

Dear Nicole,
Had lunch this afternoon with a witty and charming young physician named MacNair. Seems to be a capital fellow and someone you ought to try to get to know better. In my opinion he could really liven things up around here, which would be beneficial for both of us.
                                                              Elmo

Nicki laughed out loud before she turned to look at her snoozing feline. "I don't know what kind of benefits you hoped to derive, but I've already had my share of witty and charming men like your Dr. MacNair, and I know him quite well enough, thank you." She bent over to study Elmo more closely. "Don't you dare smile at me like that, fur-face. You're as bad as Sarah and I refuse to fall prey to this conspiracy. Can't you understand? He tricked me. The man is a cad."

Nicki sighed heavily before trudging off to the bedroom to begin another exhaustive search of her closet. How was one supposed to dress for a movie date with a cad?

CHAPTER SIX

NICKI SMILED SWEETLY as she slipped into the front seat of Doug's BMW that evening. "Goodness, Doug, you must have had a busy afternoon—a new car complete with license plates, vehicle sticker and parking permit for the hospital lot—I'm impressed."

She twisted around to greet Paul and the pretty, dark-haired woman sitting next to him in the back seat. "And you must be Stephanie. So nice to meet you at last. I do hope you're feeling up to the evening. What was it you had, a twenty-four-minute bug?"

Stephanie burst out laughing. "I'm afraid my only bug is sitting next to you. Doug asked me to show a new resident around the hospital. He said it couldn't wait and that he'd call you and cancel our appointment."

"Oh, he did better than that. Since he lives just around the corner, he delivered the message in person."

Paul leaned forward and tapped Doug on the shoulder. "That's my boy. As long as you're going to dig yourself into a hole, there is no point in stopping before it's a full-fledged grave."

Doug just shrugged in his usual offhand fashion. "I told you I make my own chances." He flashed his brilliant grin and began to whistle some fifties tune that Nicki couldn't quite remember the name of.

She scowled at him and turned to stare stonily out the side window. She'd thought he'd be at least a little embarrassed and had been hoping for abjectly apologetic, but no such luck. Apparently lying came so easily to him that it wasn't something he concerned himself about. As soon as Doug parked the car, Nicki hopped out and, with a wink, attached herself to Stephanie's arm, pretending to be engaged in a very serious and very personal discussion. She managed to continue her charade until they were standing in the theater lobby, then she felt Doug's hands close gently over her shoulders.

"Okay, Nicki, I'm sorry. It was a stupid thing to do, but I really was desperate, you know? And I had a long cold walk in your neighborhood last night before I was finally able to catch a cab. Haven't I suffered enough?"

"Life at hard labor wouldn't be enough."

He looked genuinely wounded. "You aren't the least bit flattered that I would go through so much trouble just to spend some time with you?"

"Definitely not." She had allowed herself to be flattered by a man's attentions once before and Chris hadn't been nearly as skillful as Doug was.

"Does this mean you aren't going to sit next to me, share my popcorn, and let me nuzzle your neck when the house lights go down?"

"Yep, that's what it means." She tried to ignore the tingle that raced down her spine at the thought of his lips against the sensitive skin of her neck.

"Not even if I beg?" He was on his knees before she could say a word. Several astonished bystanders began to whisper nervously.

She could feel her cheeks getting hot. "Oh, for heaven's sake, get up, Doug. I'll sit with you and eat popcorn, but absolutely no nuzzling. Is that clear?"

He refused to move.

Nicki looked to Paul and Stephanie, but they just shook their heads helplessly. "Doug! Get up!"

"I'm thinking about it. Sounds like a lousy compromise to me. How about I give up the popcorn and hold out for the nuzzling?"

"No way. The popcorn is the highlight of the entire movie experience."

He stood up. "Yeah, you're right. Extra large or super jumbo?"

"Super jumbo, lots of butter, ton of salt."

"You got it."

As Doug and Paul walked to the concession stand, Nicki looked at Stephanie and rolled her eyes. "You're a psychiatrist. Can't you do anything to help him?"

Stephanie laughed. "Actually, it appears as though he's already helped himself. When I came here a couple of years ago I was sure he was on his way to a breakdown, but he's finally learned to make some time for himself." She glanced over at Paul. "I wish everyone could see the light."

Nicki followed her gaze. "I thought Paul was the expert. Just this afternoon he was telling he how happy he was that Doug had learned to relax."

"He's an expert all right. When it comes to everyone else he's Mr. Awareness, but for himself, he can't see what's right in front of him."

"What's in front of him or who's in front of him?"

Stephanie shook her head sadly. "That too. It shows, huh?"

"I'd say so. Does he date other women?"

"Are you kidding? He works and that's all he does. When he's got a minute to spare he calls up his old buddies Doug and Steph and we do a Three Musketeers routine."

Nicki put a finger to her lips. "Shhh. They're on their way." She raised her voice slightly. "So, have the reviews for this been any good?"

Doug waved the popcorn enticingly under her nose. "Nope. You know the reviewers always hate a love story, but my sister cried through the whole last half and that's enough of a recommendation for me."

"I don't believe it. Is this a man who actually admits to liking sappy movies? What will that do to your macho image?"

"I just spent ten minutes on my knees begging a five-foot-two-inch, curly-topped tyrant to share my popcorn. I think my macho image suffered irreparable injury at that point. So I might as well admit it. I love a good love story, the mushier the better."

Nicki grabbed a handful of buttery kernels. "Well, I've got to say this for you, MacNair. You do have good taste."

He grinned mischievously and slipped an arm around her waist. "I certainly do."

She fought the urge to lean against him as they started down the aisle. Stephanie stopped at a row of seats, and when they all nodded their approval, stepped in and took the fourth seat down. Paul moved to the side and with a gentlemanly sweep of his hand tried to usher Nicki and Doug into the next two seats but Nicki grabbed Doug's arm, forcing him to hang back. "Go ahead, Paul. I'm one of those people who gets up twenty times during a flick so we should take the aisle." As he stepped in front of her, she gave Stephanie a thumb's-up sign.

"What was that all about?" Doug whispered, his warm breath tickling her hear.

She tightened her grip on his forearm as a cue that he should be quiet. "Don't be dense, Doctor." They settled into their seats.

"Gotcha." He whispered again. This time she felt his lips brush against her hair.

"Was that a nuzzle?"

He grinned. "No. This is a nuzzle."

She managed to get her hand up to her neck in time to halt his advance. "I thought we had a deal."

"I lied."

"Again? That's what got you into trouble in the first place. Behave, or I'm going to leave."

He turned forward in his seat. "Okay you win, as usual. I was just trying to set the appropriate mood. Don't you remember how great it was when we were back in high school, going to Saturday night movies? The girl was always trying to watch the film, the guy was always trying to get her to make out. The sweet agony of the frustration was so intense it was almost as good as the real thing." He chuckled. "Of course, no one knew that then because no one had had the real thing."

Nicki felt a poignant twinge at the reminder of the youth she'd never had. "No, Doug, I'm afraid I don't remember what that was like. I didn't date much when I was a teenager."

He looked surprised. "Are you kidding? Why not? I would have thought the guys would have been tripping over each other to ask you out."

"Let's just say I had other things on my mind."

"What other things? Don't tell me you were a workaholic even then."

"Look, Doug, I didn't go to high school like other kids. Okay? Now pay attention. The feature is starting."

DOUG STARED BLEAKLY at the screen through much of the movie. He'd known about her limp, known there was some painful story involving her stepfather, known that she was reluctant to talk about herself, but he hadn't let any of that stop him from questioning her and pressuring her about how hard she worked. What did he expect her to do—throw up her hands and tell him he was right; she'd been hiding behind her work but was ready to forget it all and start a relationship with him? Yes, that was exactly what he wanted.

He looked over at her profile just as she reached up to brush away a tear. His heart wrenched and he almost asked her what was wrong before he realized that most of the patrons around them were snuffling too. He smiled softly to himself. It had been a long time since he'd been more interested in the woman he was with than in the film he'd come to see.

He slipped his hand into the popcorn to find hers was already there. But before he could take hold of her fingers, she pulled back abruptly and waited for him to serve himself first. Why was she so determined to deny the attraction between them?

He thought about her comment that she hadn't dated much in her youth, then shrugged it off. Her high school years had been a long time ago. Certainly someone who was as clever and poised as Nicki Devlin could not still be in doubt of her ability to handle a man. Of course, if she were at all like he was during his own years as an overachiever, maybe she'd never allowed herself the time to test her social skills. He put the empty popcorn box on the floor and settled back in his seat. If she'd give him half a chance, he'd be more than willing to help her rectify that.

AFTER THE MOVIE, the four of them strolled down the street to a bar that Paul had suggested. When Doug reached out and took her hand while they walked, Nicki was not sure what to do. It seemed like an innocent enough sign of affection, but when she looked over at Stephanie and saw that the young woman had her hands in her coat pockets, Nicki slipped her fingers out of Doug's warm grasp.

While watching the movie, she had convinced herself that she was perfectly willing to become friends with Doug and his cohorts. She liked them and they were fun to be with. But she did not want to leave Doug with the impression that she would allow things to go any further. Unfortunately, she was at a loss when it came to knowing where to draw the appropriate line. She hadn't had any more experience at friendship then she'd had at romance.

Her attraction to Doug only made matters worse. It felt right to hold hands with him as they watched a movie or walked down the street, to lean against him as they stood in line. But those were impulses that she would have to fight. They were the warning signs for the same mistake she'd made with Chris. She had been so anxious to feel that warm, emotional rush that came with demonstrating her affection for someone that she hadn't realized how vulnerable it made her.

Chris had known, though. He had understood how desperately she was reaching out to find someone whom she could love and who she thought loved her, and he had used that desperation. Her devotion to him had been so pathetically obvious that he'd known all he had to do to manipulate her to his own advantage was to play the game, and that had been easy for him. Their supposed romance had provided him with the favorable press that had eluded him during most of his career and given him the chance to do lucrative endorsements with his sweet, young fiancée. And in the end, he got a willing, if inexperienced, lover who was perfectly happy to let him control her just the way everyone else had controlled her in the past.

Nicki hadn't realized until it was too late, how much of herself she would be willing to give once she'd made a com-

mitment to someone. And if she let herself get carried away
with Doug, the whole process would begin again. She would
not be able to limit her involvement to a few dates or a brief
affair. Whether he knew it or not, whether he wanted it or
not, she would begin to make irreversible decisions in her
life with his interests and feelings in mind. Then, when it was
over, she would have lost both him and her chance to
achieve her own goals, and he probably wouldn't even be
aware of what had happened.

Well, not this time. This time she would restrict herself to
trying to make a friend. For her, that was frightening
enough.

Mirroring Stephanie, she shoved her fists firmly in her
pockets and tried to push away the recollection of how even
the brief moment of Doug's fingers grasping hers had made
her feel warm and secure on this blustery winter evening.
That false sense of security was precisely what she was trying
to avoid.

As she picked up her pace to keep up with Doug's longer
stride, she dredged her mind for some appropriately casual
topic of conversation. "So, what did you think of the film?
Did it live up to your expectations?"

"I'll say. It was a real tearjerker. But I wish they'd have
left out the scene where the heroine goes through the miracle of childbirth. I can't stand the sight of blood."

"Reassuring to hear from an obstetrician. Do your patients know about this?"

"That's different. That's what I do for a living. I don't
want to have to deal with it when I'm supposed to be relaxing."

"My, you are protective of your private time, aren't
you?"

"Somebody has to be. If I left it up to everyone else I'd
be on call twenty-four hours a day."

Nicki withheld further comment until they were all seated and had ordered a pitcher of beer. Then she turned to Stephanie. "How do you feel about the pressures put on you by your profession? Do you resent not having more time to yourself?"

"Sure, sometimes. But there are other times when it's exhilarating to be totally caught up in what you're doing. It's very satisfying to think that you are helping someone. It's also devastating to realize that you are failing."

"Certainly you don't consider a patient's failure to get well a personal failure, do you?" Nicki asked.

"Not always, no, but more often than I should." Stephanie winked at Doug. "One of the most brilliant and successful physicians I know says that, in a way, we're just like athletes. We spend years training in our specialty and with each patient we enter a new competition against their sickness and their pain. If we fail it's like losing an important race. There's no chance to start over or run it again."

Paul filled four steins from the pitcher and passed them out. "When did I ever say that?"

"Not you, Paul, Doug. It's part of his lecture to new interns. He gave me a personalized version of it not too long ago."

Paul looked stunned, then waved his hand as if to dismiss the concept. "Doug just regrets the fact that he's always been an egghead instead of an athlete, so he's trying to make medicine sound macho."

The uncharacteristic edge in Paul's voice told Nicki that his comment was more than a tease, but Stephanie seemed oblivious to it as she leaned over and punched him playfully in the shoulder. "Don't be a poor sport, Paul. It's a terrific analogy. You're just jealous because you didn't come up with it first." She cupped her hands around her beer mug. "By the way, Doug, I never thanked you for our little talk. You said some things I needed to hear."

Paul rocked his chair back to rest on two legs and cleared his throat. "Excuse me, are Nicki and I intruding on a private conversation, or do you intend to let us in on the brilliant Doctor Doug's words of wisdom?"

Doug's eyes narrowed slightly as he studied his friend. "My, aren't you in a sociable mood tonight? You know darn well Steph was having a rough time a few months back. You were busy so I gave her a pep talk. Okay?"

Stephanie almost choked on her beer. "Pep talk?" she spluttered. "You told me I was being an oversensitive, self-important wimp."

"You were." Doug turned to Nicki. "She came in and told me how discouraged she was about some patients who weren't responding to treatment and I gave her my athlete comparison. Then she yelled at me. She couldn't believe I had the nerve to compare a hardworking, dedicated psychiatrist, concerned only with her patient's needs, to an egocentric, glory-seeking sports freak who was driven by nothing more noble than a desire for personal fame and satisfaction."

Even though she wasn't surprised by Stephanie's response, Nicki felt a flash of anger at the unattractive characterization of an athlete, but she withheld her comments.

Stephanie rolled her eyes. "I was pretty pompous. I had just decided I had new insight into the medical profession. As physicians, we were subject to undue stress because we always had to deal with other people's expectations. After all, patients come to us expecting to get well. When we can't cure them we have to carry around all the guilt for failing both them and ourselves."

"Sounds pretty obvious." Paul let his chair fall forward with a thump. "How did you manage to argue with that, Doug?"

"I didn't argue. I just went back to the athlete comparison to impress upon her that a physician's obligation is not all that unique. When you start talking about the obligation to live up to other people's expectations, it seems to me that athletes have a corner on the market. Think about what it must be like to be an Olympic contender."

Nicki drew a sharp breath as Doug paused for a swallow of beer. She had no reason to believe that he was toying with her. Since she hadn't actually competed in the Olympics, it had been years since the man on the street had recognized her as a onetime Olympic hopeful, and her name change had made it even easier to remain anonymous. Doug certainly wasn't acting as though he knew who she was. In fact, he wasn't even looking at her, but the scenario was getting a little too close to the truth.

"One day no one knows you exist. You are just a young kid consumed by your personal desire to be best. As you train harder and get better, all your friends and family and teammates start expecting great things of you. Then it's an Olympic year and you're thrust into the limelight as a possible medal winner. Now your training and your talent belong to everyone. You are everybody's hero or heroine, unless, of course, you lose. In that case you are a failure, not just to yourself but to a whole country. That's got to be tough."

Nicki listened in amazement. "You sound as though you've been through it."

He shook his head. "Not really, but we all have our successes and failures and disappointments. Doctors sure don't have the corner on the obligation market, right Steph?"

The young woman blushed but made no attempt to answer.

"Ease up, Doug," Paul interrupted. "Your annoying tendency to harangue is emerging. You don't have to give her the whole lecture again. She already said you were brilliant. Besides, given time and another stein of beer, I, too, can come up with something inspired."

Doug laughed. "Don't bother, buddy. What I said wasn't all that profound. Stephanie was just going through one of those highly driven phases that all new doctors deal with from time to time, and I wanted to remind her to keep things in perspective. We're always going to win some and lose some, and the only way to do our job is to not allow ourselves to become depressed by things we cannot change."

Nicki just shook her head. "You three are really something. Paul thinks Doug is too dedicated, Doug thinks Stephanie is too driven, and Stephanie thinks Paul is too obsessive. It sounds like some disease that's raging rampant in the medical profession."

"Your diagnosis may be right, but you've incorrectly limited the class of carriers. You've got one of the worst cases I've ever seen."

"I suppose I should be upset by that, Doug, but I view it as a good sign. I wouldn't have thought you'd ever admit that you could have anything in common with a malpractice attorney."

"Now that is a blatantly unfair accusation. If you'll think back, you'll recall that from the first day we met, I've been trying to get you to admit that we are a lot alike."

"Oh, right. I remember. We both have gray eyes."

Stephanie leaned closer to Nicki. "My gosh, you do. I've never seen anyone with eyes the color of Doug's before. I thought they were absolutely unique."

Nicki was sure she was the only one who noticed the slight tightening of Paul's cheek muscles before he put one hand over his eyes.

"Okay now, test question for Stephanie. Since you seem to notice the color of handsome men's eyes, what color are mine?"

When Nicki saw Doug was about to say something, she put her finger to her lips and shook her head slightly.

"Well, let's see." Stephanie hesitated. "Maybe I can get in a lucky guess. Your name is Swedish and you're blond so blue sounds like a good shot." At Paul's dejected sigh, she relented. "I'm kidding. You're eyes are brown, Paul, an unusual, warm, dark brown."

He grinned broadly and started to lower his hand but Nicki reached up to hold it in place. "No peeking yet. Take your own challenge. Guess what color Stephanie's are."

"I don't have to guess. I've been getting lost in those dreamy blue eyes of hers for years, but I haven't had the good sense to admit it."

Nicki let his hand go and laughed out loud at the stunned look on Stephanie's face. "Good job, Paul. You both pass with flying colors. I think this calls for a celebration."

"Me too," said Stephanie, shaking her head in disbelief. "Pardon the pun, but this has been a rather eye-opening experience. Why don't we go by Gaylord's club and dance the night away?"

"No!" Nicki's sharp response caused the other three to turn and look at her. "I mean, I really don't have the energy for dancing tonight. If you wouldn't mind, could you just drop me off at home?"

"Oh, no, you don't." Doug shook his head. "If you're not going, I'm not going. I got stuck there with these guys after you brushed me off last Friday and I couldn't walk for three days. They wear me out."

Stephanie looked disappointed. "That's okay. We'll do it some other time."

"Now wait a minute." Nicki held up her hand. "Just because Doug and I don't have the stamina to keep up, it shouldn't stop you two. Why don't you go on your own?"

Paul seemed happy to accept that suggestion as he finished the last of his beer and stood up. "It's a funny thing. Here Doug and I are exactly the same age and yet I'm in my prime and he's getting feeble. Would you mind taking us to my place to pick up my car?"

Nicki was relieved to hear that the edge had gone out of Paul's voice and he was teasing Doug as usual.

She and Stephanie elected to wait inside the door to the bar while Doug and Paul jogged back to the theater to get Doug's car.

Stephanie appraised Nicki through narrowed eyes then shook her head. "Nope, even knowing what I know now, I would never peg you as a matchmaker."

"Who me?" Nicki tried to look shocked. "I know nothing about such things."

"I'm sure. First we have the scuffle for seats at the show, then your revealing eye quiz, and now pretending you're too tired to dance so we can be alone."

Nicki swallowed her urge to confess that her refusal to accompany them had nothing to do with an interest in furthering their romance.

Stephanie rested her hand on Nicki's arm. "Well, whether you admit it or not, I just want you to know I appreciate it."

"Don't thank me. He was obviously already interested."

"And I was oblivious to it. He has always given me a hard time about dating the guys at the hospital, but I thought he was joking."

"Maybe he was. Who knows when he decided he wanted to be more than your big brother? Speaking of guys at the hospital, how are you on the gossip line? I took a tour there today and saw a very handsome resident named Norman Gregory. He looked like a definite possibility for some lucky single girl.''

"Ah, yes, gorgeous Gregory. Believe me, no woman who gets tied up with him and his ego is going to be lucky. He—"

"Wait a minute, Steph. If Doug heard me right now he'd have every right to say I was just another sleazy attorney.''

"What are you talking about?"

"I can't believe I just tried to pump a friend for information. Dr. Gregory might be involved in a case I'm investigating. So, if you don't want to talk about him or think it wouldn't be fair because you have been involved with the guy or something, just forget I asked.''

"Fortunately, I've been spared that annoyance. He confines his attentions to the nurses because he thinks they are easier to impress.''

"Are they?"

"For the most part, no. Usually the nurses who have been around for a while know a lot more than he does about both medicine and life. There are always a few vulnerable ones though.''

"Like Margaret Orb?"

"You have been doing some homework, I see. Precisely like Margaret. He's terrible to her, yet she stays devoted to him.''

"That's a shame.''

"Yes, it is. And thanks for the warning about your investigation, although I couldn't reveal any secrets anyway. I happen to think Norman is a class-A jerk, but I have no reason to question his ability as a physician.''

"At this point, neither do I. And, believe it or not, I'd just as soon it stayed that way.''

"That doesn't sound like it's in your client's best interest."

"On the contrary. If my client has been damaged by someone else's negligence, of course I want him to be compensated. But from the standpoint of avoiding emotional stress and putting a tragedy behind him as quickly as possible, I'd like nothing better than to tell him that he just got an unlucky break."

"I'm beginning to understand why Doug likes you. I'll admit I was surprised at first. Given your backgrounds, you two sounded like oil and water to me."

"We are. In fact, when it comes to my profession, an oil fire is a bit more like it."

They had been so busy talking they didn't notice that Doug had pulled up to the curb until Paul opened the hallway door and stepped in. "Allow me, ladies." He offered them each an arm. "Hang on. It's really slick out there."

Nicki started to shake her head but he stopped her. "Come on, help me make Doug a little jealous. After all, he did get the best of me tonight."

"And how do you figure that?" Stephanie asked.

"I hadn't planned on being tricked into making my intentions known this early in our relationship."

Stephanie gave him a dirty look. "May I point out that we have known each other twenty years. And by the way, I still don't know your intentions."

After much teasing and laughing, they finally dropped Paul and Stephanie off, and Nicki was convinced that whatever problem had existed between Doug and Paul must have been resolved when the two of them had walked back to the theater to get the car. "I take it you boys talked?"

Doug nodded. "We did. I apologized for being slow to realize what was going on. And he admitted that he hadn't figured it out himself before tonight. He's lived with my tendency to make insightful speeches—harangue as he calls it—for years, so when he realized how much it annoyed him that I had been waxing eloquent to Stephanie when he wasn't around, he knew things were more complicated than they seemed." Doug sighed heavily. "It looks like the Three Musketeers are at an end, and I'll have a lot of lonely evenings if I don't find someone new to pal around with."

He started to turn onto the main street heading toward Nicki's house, then stopped. "Got any ideas who might fill the position?"

"No."

"I was afraid of that." He completed the turn, then stopped again. "You know, it really is too early to call it an evening. Do you suppose you'd consider coming back to my place for a nightcap?"

He looked so forlorn that Nicki couldn't stop herself. "Sure. Why not?"

He just smiled as he backed the car into a driveway to change directions.

Why not, indeed? she wondered. She could think of a million reasons "why not" and only one reason "why." She wanted to spend some time alone with Doug.

CHAPTER SEVEN

AS SOON AS THEY ENTERED Doug's home, Nicki's attention was drawn to the glass wall on the far side of the living room. "You don't strike me as the type to need your own greenhouse."

Doug laughed. "That's for sure. I can't even grow dandelions successfully. But whoever originally built this house had a different orientation. The solarium is two stories high and runs the length of the living room and dining room."

"It's beautiful."

"It is that. It's also a pain to maintain. Fortunately I have a sister who is into gardening and she keeps it green in there somehow." He rested his hands on Nicki's shoulders. "Let me take your coat and get us some drinks. I'm thinking Kahlua and coffee, how about you?"

"That sounds good, thanks." She slipped off her jacket and Doug hung it in the hall closet.

"Back in a jiffy. Feel free to explore." He wandered off toward the kitchen.

Taking him up on his suggestion, she did peek into some of the doorways on the first floor. The house was large and the decor tasteful but impersonal—as though he didn't spend much time there. The only exception was his study, which was dominated by a collection of antique medical instruments.

Wandering back to the greenhouse, she stepped through the French doors into the large room and was instantly entranced. She was still there, standing under an enormous potted palm and staring silently into Doug's vast backyard, when she felt his presence.

He came up beside her and handed her a steaming mug of coffee laced with Kahlua. "I never realized this room could be so spectacular until I saw you in it."

She turned and smiled. "That's nice, Doug. Thank you, but I'm afraid the room is spectacular in it's own right. What a marvelous illusion—surrounded on three sides by snow-covered fields and pine branches dripping icicles—while we lean against a palm tree and sip after-dinner drinks."

"It is nice, isn't it? I appreciate the snow most when I don't have to get cold to enjoy it. A friend once took me to Colorado to ski in March—that was the greatest thing—to snowplow wearing cut-offs."

The painful reminder of something lost carried Nicki back to another time. She too had loved spring skiing best. The conditions were never very good but it was exhilarating to speed down a mountain in shorts and a T-shirt, feeling the wind rushing against her skin.

Her body had moved as she willed it back then—no limits, no caution, no pain.

She brought her thoughts back to the present. "Do you still ski?"

"A little. I was never very good at it. I do some cross-country though."

Nicki smiled. "Ah yes, the perfect choice for someone who wants to stay warm while playing in the snow." She directed her attention outside again. "It would be wonderful to stand out here when it was actually snowing—in the middle of a snowstorm, yet protected."

"I bet it would be, but I'm embarrassed to confess I've never tried it."

Nicki shivered a bit and he slipped his arm around her. "I'm afraid I don't heat this room as well as I should. Let's go back inside, and I promise I'll take care of that problem before you come the next time."

Wondering why it was that the idea of a next time sounded so right to her, she allowed him to lead her into the living room.

After they were seated, she could think of nothing to say until she remembered his collection. "I was in your study for a moment. Given how you like to keep your business and personal lives separate, you have a pretty strange hobby."

"Former hobby."

"What made you start it in the first place?"

"Not what, who. My sister, the plant nut, talked me into it." He shook his head and laughed. "Poor Tina. She thought I was entirely too fixated on medicine and kept nagging me to get a hobby, something new to get involved in. She was crushed when she learned that even my attempt to find a diversion took me right back to medicine."

"Why did you give it up?"

"I just lost interest. It's already one of the best collections of its kind. I'm thinking of donating it to the medical school."

Nicki took a sip of her coffee and watched him over the rim of the cup. "Doug, was it the malpractice suit that ruined your enthusiasm for medicine?"

"I'm still as enthusiastic about medicine as I ever was. I just realized I had to slow down a little. I didn't want to keep going in high gear for a few more years then burn out and lose interest entirely, like all the other former superstars out there who are just marking time. I'd rather keep making contributions to the profession until I'm ready to retire."

"Good, I'm glad. I'd hate to think that you let one bad experience destroy everything for you."

"Oh, I won't say it hasn't left some scars. That's what you attorneys never take into consideration. You think it's basically just between you and the insurance company's lawyer—find something that works out financially for the two of you—forget what the doctor is going through."

Nicki started to respond, but Doug held up a hand to stop her. "Wait a minute. Let me rephrase that. How about, many lawyers don't bother to consider what the doctor is going through. Is that a little less accusatory?"

"A lot less, and thank you. I talked to Paul earlier today, and I understand how awful it must be to know that you weren't at fault and not be allowed to prove it."

"The baby wasn't perfect."

"But did you do anything to cause that?"

He got up and began to pace. "Now that is the key question isn't it? There were times during the four years that nightmare went on when I didn't care whether I won or lost the case, I just wanted someone to answer that blasted question. It becomes very hard not to doubt yourself. Now that I've had time to put it all in perspective, I guess the only thing I did wrong was to try too hard to give the patient what she wanted."

"In what way?"

"I got called to fill in for a physician who was on vacation. When I suggested that we might have to do a cesarean section, the patient became very upset. She was adamant about wanting natural childbirth. I explained to her that there were risks both for her and the baby if we waited too long. She said she understood." He pulled his hand through his hair. "I listed all the possibilities over and over again, but she still wanted to hold on as long as possible."

"Did you document that conversation?"

"Of course. That one and the others. We made every decision together after I explained the options and the risks.

But you know as well as I do that all that documentation is worthless. The patient contended she was out of her mind with pain at the time, didn't remember anything I said and couldn't have made any kind of decision.''

"Is that possible?"

"No. I ran some tests and asked some questions every time we talked to be sure that she knew what was happening. I recorded that information too, but her attorney argued that my records were self-serving and may have been altered after the fact."

Nicki nodded. "Oh yes, I've seen that happen. If your records can hurt you, then they are evidence. But if they indicate you are blameless, they are inadmissible."

"That's right. Anyway, I monitored the fetus and we stayed right on the line the whole time. Nothing happened to indicate the necessity for an immediate cesarean so I made my decisions with the mother's desires in mind."

"And something went wrong?"

Doug shrugged. "Yes and no. The mother did deliver vaginally after a twenty-hour labor. Not easy, to be sure, but not unusual. The baby appeared to be normal at birth. A few months later it became obvious that the child had some problems. Whether they resulted from the troubles with the delivery or not, there's no way to know. It's not impossible that they did, but it's also not too probable."

"So what made the parents sue?"

"Need for money, I think. The father disappeared shortly after the baby was born. The mother went to stay with a sister who had an attorney friend. He put her in touch with some of his buddies, but even then she went through three lawyers before she finally found one who agreed to file a suit."

"I don't get it. It sounds like you had a strong defense. Why did the insurance company settle?"

"The usual—good business decision. Right before the case went to the jury, the patient's attorney offered to settle for a very small amount of money. Since my insurer's attorney thought that my testimony had sounded confused and unconvincing, the company decided not to risk it with the jury."

"So that's where all the hostility came from this morning. The patient's attorney played some word games with you and made you look like you didn't know what you were talking about?"

"You bet he did, but I was actually more angry with the insurance company's lawyer. He never gave me any warning as to what was going to happen when I got on the stand. Sometimes I think he'd already decided they were going to settle and didn't care how the trial went."

"That's not at all unlikely. It's too bad that happens in so many of these cases. If the jury were given a chance to look at all the facts and were told that they had to decide if anyone was actually negligent, I think the doctors would win most of the time. Then maybe there wouldn't be so many capricious suits filed just to get a few thousand dollars."

"Well, I sure as hell would never go along with a settlement again. If I have to hire my own lawyer and fight without the help of my malpractice insurer, that's what I'll do. Let the attorneys work for their big fees for a change."

"And what if the medical personnel really are guilty of malpractice? Should the plaintiff still have to go through the long, arduous process of fighting? Wouldn't it be more fair to have everyone just admit what happened and agree to settle?"

"No, because I don't buy the public's definition of malpractice. People aren't willing to concede that physicians are just human beings. We are going to make some mistakes, just like everyone else. Yet you think you have a right to destroy us for those mistakes."

"No one wants to destroy anyone, Doug. But when a doctor does act negligently the legal system has to provide a method to compensate the victims of that negligence."

"Good. Then let the legal system do its job. Take it to court and fight it through to the end."

"I do, whenever I get the chance, but I work for my clients. If the client wants to accept a settlement I can't very well turn it down just because I'd rather fight to the bitter end, can I?"

He shook his head thoughtfully. "No, of course not. I know how all this must sound, but I'm really not blaming you, Nicki. I just have some strong feelings on the subject and I can't help spouting off."

"Your 'annoying tendency to harangue'?"

He smiled. "I guess so. But I don't want to fight about it. Can we declare a truce?"

"Fine by me. I didn't consider myself at war."

"Good. I've had a nice time this evening and I don't want to wreck it. I'll need good memories to keep with me when my ship pulls out tomorrow."

Nicki arched an eyebrow. "My goodness, that sounds like you *are* headed for combat."

"In a way. I'm going to one those rigorous week-long medical association meetings. You know the type. Held on a cruise ship in the Caribbean. Two hours of nonstop learning sessions every morning from seven to nine then a full afternoon of water sports and sightseeing."

"Yes, I know the type—exhausting."

"Actually, I am dreading it. I'm one of the speakers, so I will have to be on good behavior. If I go off on one of my tangents aboard ship, they might throw me to the sharks."

"Life is tough. Leaving the piranha behind only to face the sharks. Poor baby."

"Baby?"

"It's nothing, Doug. Just a casual term of affection that I use with Sarah all the time."

"Affection? Did you say affection?"

"Did I? I don't think so. Must have been a slip of the tongue. I meant affliction. Whenever Sarah leaves me feeling as though she is an affliction I have to bear, I call her baby." Nicki glanced at her watch. "It's getting late and I have a lot of work to do tomorrow. Do you suppose you could take me home?"

He sat down beside her, took her coffee cup, set it on the table and held her hand between both of his. "Is it so hard for you to admit that you are becoming rather fond of me?"

"Yes." She met his eyes briefly then glanced away. "Yes it is."

He regarded her thoughtfully for a minute. "Okay, then I'll just have to accept that." He stood up with a sigh. "I'm a very patient man."

On the drive back to Nicki's, Doug tried to keep a light banter going, but he kept thinking of their earlier conversation. He felt good that she had been so understanding when he had discussed his malpractice case with her and even better that he had managed to keep enough perspective to realize when he was attacking her or her profession unfairly. He hadn't been quite able to stop himself, but at least he had known when an apology was in order. There might be hope for them yet.

He smiled. In an endearingly backhanded way, she had even managed to admit that she liked him. That was certainly a start. Unfortunately, he didn't know where to go from there. Until he understood why she was so afraid to acknowledge their mutual attraction, anything he did might complicate rather than advance the relationship.

He looked over at her as she stared thoughtfully out of the car window. This blasted medical conference was coming at a bad time. He hated the idea of going away for a week and leaving her alone to contemplate what was going on between them. Given the way she was sitting pressed against the door, she was probably already having doubts.

He reached out to trace his thumb down her cheek. "Don't tell me we went dancing after all."

"What do you mean?"

"You know. Two steps forward, one step back. I hope we're at least making that much progress."

"We can't tell if we've made progress unless we know our goal. Do we have one?"

"I do, but I can't speak for you." He pulled the car up to the curb in front of her building.

"Unfortunately, neither can I." She opened the door and stepped out. Just as they climbed the last step to the front door of the apartment building, Nicki's foot slipped and she grabbed for the doorknob to catch her balance. As she did so, she scraped her finger on a loose screw protruding from the doorjamb.

"Damn." She stuck the injured knuckle in her mouth to stifle a few other expletives. "I've noticed that screw sticking out every day for a week now. This is what I get for not seeing that it got fixed."

"Oh, oh. Does this mean that you are going to sue the landlord?"

"Give me a break, Doug," she spat out while still holding her wounded finger between her teeth. "I'm in serious pain here."

"Poor baby." He took hold of her hand and pulled it toward him, then grinned impishly. "Just a well-recognized term of affection. Now, let me see. Oh my, this does look serious. Fortunately for you, you have a man of medicine present, ready and willing to administer that classic all-purpose remedy—a kiss to make it better.''

Nicki laughed as he bent intently over her fingers, but the laughter faded at the first gentle brush of his lips across the back of her hand. The tip of his tongue traced a tender circle around each of her knuckles in turn, until he planted a final, lingering kiss on the scratch.

When he raised his head to look at her, the flash of silver in his eyes told her that his attempt at a tease had backfired on him as well as her. "That should adequately cure the immediate injury." His voice sounded hoarse and his casual grin flickered out as his hand slid to her waist. "But being a responsible and thorough physician, I feel it's my obligation to treat the whole patient."

Nicki's mind told her to back away, but she couldn't make herself move. She felt as though she were watching the action on a stage, anxious to know what would happen next, but helpless to affect the outcome. She tried to respond, to take control again. "The patient is doing just fine, Doctor."

"Perhaps, but the physician is hurting," he murmured as he pulled her close. "And I'm afraid I have no choice but to heal myself."

As the firm muscles of his thighs pressed urgently against hers, Nicki reached up to bury her fingers in his hair. His hand cupped the back of her neck, and she felt the whisper of his breath against her cheek. She closed her eyes and waited. An instant, surely his hesitation had only lasted an instant, but that was too long now. Just as at the start of a race, every one of her muscles was tense and ready. This was the right moment. Heart thumping, Nicki strained to close the remaining distance between them.

Then he was there. His lips against hers—first gentle, then firm, then hungry. The rush of release at his touch was like the wind tearing at her hair as she sped down a mountain. She rocked against him, swayed with him, her body responding, anticipating her instinctive needs as though, once again, negotiating a course dotted with flags and obstructions.

It was the warmth of him that brought her back to reality. She had never associated this dizzying sensation of exhilaration with warmth before. And she'd certainly never associated it with being held, caressed, protected by someone else. It had always been an insular experience, just her alone against the mountain and the snow. But now Doug was very much a part of everything she was feeling. She pulled her head back and hoped that he would release her, but as soon as he did she found herself clinging to him again.

He held her against his chest and stroked her hair. "You're shivering, curly-top. You'd better go in before you catch a cold."

She nodded but didn't move.

"I mean it. Doctor's orders. I want you healthy when I get back." He opened the door and nudged her into the hallway. "Go on, now. I'm not going to walk you up because if I get that close to your apartment, I won't be able to make myself leave."

She stepped into the hall and looked at the keys in her hand. Doug rumpled her hair, kissed her on top of the head and began to close the door. "Go upstairs, Nicki. I'm not going to drive away until I see the lights come on in your window."

As the door clicked shut she came to her senses and climbed the stairs to her apartment. She snapped on the lights then walked to the window to watch Doug pull away.

As soon as he was out of sight she began to shiver again. Funny that it wasn't the cold that made her shiver but the warmth. And the knowledge that something as simple as a good-night kiss had thawed a part of her that had remained frozen and numb for so many years.

BY THE END OF THE SCHOOL DAY on Monday, Nicki was already restless. After spending an hour staring blankly at yet another file that Ron had sent her, she decided she needed a diversion to take her thoughts off Doug. Remembering her resolve to get back into her weight-lifting regime, she drove over to the hospital's sports and fitness center. As she walked through the facility to familiarize herself with the equipment, she was surprised to see Ian Dorchester leaning against the wall in the back corner of the weight room. He was still dressed in his street clothes and clearly had no intention of working out. He simply stood there, mouth drawn in a bleak line, shoulders hunched, unconsciously tensing his muscles in sync with the movements of a young man who was lifting weights on the other side of the room.

Nicki could well remember the desolation of knowing that her once perfect body would never be that again. She walked toward him, hoping she could provide some encouragement. But as soon as he saw her, he pushed himself away from the wall and ducked into the men's locker room, letting the door swing shut behind him. Nicki called out to him to no avail.

"Odd," she mumbled as she retraced her steps to the membership office. Why should Ian want to avoid her? Again she felt a twinge of uneasiness about the lawsuit. It certainly appeared as though her client had something to hide.

While she was filling out her membership forms, she inquired about Ian and learned that he had joined a few months ago and came around often. But no one had ever seen him use any of the equipment. Again she felt a stab of pity for him, and wished he would let her help.

Nicki's thoughts were still on Ian when she returned home a short while later. As she always did, Nicki went immediately to her answering machine, noted there were messages and hit Play. Sarah wondered if she had plans for dinner— too late for that now. Ron was express-mailing a couple more files. "Wonderful, partner," she muttered. "We certainly wouldn't want you to start doing some of the work yourself."

As the next message began amid ear-piercing feedback and static, Nicki picked up Elmo and sat down on the sofa. "Curly-top, where are you? Do you know what it's costing me to talk ship-to-shore to a machine?" She stopped petting the cat midstroke and caught her breath. It made no sense that just hearing his voice should have this effect on her. "A man has a right to expect his girl to stay home and sulk while he's at sea. Hope you're getting a lot of work done. See you soon."

"His girl? Honestly, Elmo, can you believe him? We've never even had a real date." Nicki smiled to herself as she hit the rewind button to play the tape again. Of course, they had shared a very real kiss.

As she listened to the laughter in his tone and pictured the mischievous grin he was undoubtedly wearing as he left his message, uncertainty began to creep over her. She may have thought of what they'd shared as a real kiss, but that didn't necessarily mean Doug had felt the same way. Maybe heart-shattering first kisses were part of the game to him, just like trying to set the appropriate mood at the movie. And, as she'd told him then, she didn't have enough experience to know how to play along.

"Mama takes these things entirely too seriously, kitty," she said as she scratched the furry orange head.

The phone began to ring and she lunged for it.

"Nicki? Carol Stuart here. How are you doing?"

She swallowed her disappointment. "Good, Carol, real good. And you?"

"Miserable. Eric has gone down to Florida to play golf with the guys. He says it's his last big fling before the wedding. Do you have plans for the weekend?"

Did she have plans for the weekend? She wasn't sure. Maybe Doug would come by. She stopped herself. "The usual, a lot of work, but nothing definite. Why?"

"I was hoping to persuade you to teach me cross-country skiing."

"Okay, sure. I'd like that."

"Terrific. Do you have any place in mind?"

"If you don't mind coming down this way I do. An old teammate of mine has a lodge just the other side of the Indiana border near some beautiful trails."

"Sounds perfect and I don't mind the drive."

"I'll take care of the details. You just show up here bright and early Saturday morning."

Carol continued to talk about Eric and her upcoming wedding, but Nicki couldn't concentrate. Doug had told her he'd wanted her healthy when he got back. He had left a phone message telling her he'd see her soon. He'd probably meant this weekend, but she was not about to start structuring her activities just to be available for him. If she said no to Carol and he didn't call, she'd feel like a fool.

"Are you still there?"

Nicki dragged her attention back to the conversation. "Yes, of course."

"So—how is the new client? I stopped by your office to sign those papers you sent, and Ron said you had started another great case."

"Ron exaggerates. I'm working with an injured athlete, but we haven't even decided if he has grounds for a suit yet."

"Any hope?"

Nicki understood Carol's question immediately. "Not really. He'll swim again but not as a competitor."

"I see." Carol paused. "How are his spirits? Is he going to be okay?"

"I'm not sure." The image of a forlorn Ian leaning against the wall in the gym flashed before her. "He's taking it pretty hard."

"That's too bad." Another pause. "Damn. It's amazing how it still hits you in the gut after all this time isn't it?"

"Yes, it sure is. I hope I can help him, but I don't think he trusts me."

"Does he know who you are?"

"I doubt it."

"And, of course, you haven't told him."

"That's not as simple as you think. What do I say? 'You don't remember me, kid, but I used to be great,' sounds like an old boxing movie."

"Give him a copy of the book."

"I should have never agreed to that book. I hate that book."

"I know you do, but I don't know why. It sure turned my life around. *To Dance No More* says everything there is to say about courage."

"*To Dance No More* is a glamorized account of a conceited, bad-tempered young woman who simply had to learn to stop feeling sorry for herself. Unfortunately it has earned both the author and myself undeserved recognition. Thank heaven it's finally out of print. I only hope I have all the remaining copies safely hidden away in my office. Remind me to invite you to the bonfire.''

"Okay, okay, let's drop it. But it seems to me that you're being selfish, Nicki. If there's a chance it might help him, why not let him read it?''

"I'll think about it. Now I'd better go feed my starving cat. I'll see you Saturday.''

As she opened a can of cat food for Elmo and put a pot-pie in the toaster oven for herself, Nicki considered her conversation with Carol. It had been a long time since she had given any thought to the book that had been written about her. It had been billed as the inspiring story of a young athlete's fight to put together the pieces of a broken life. But she had never thought of it as being an inspiration to anyone. And she was particularly surprised to learn that Carol had read it.

Nicki had spent the first months after her injury engaged in wild denials and empty attempts to fight back. She had always been amazed and impressed by the apparent ease with which Carol had adjusted to her situation and had felt that the young woman's matter-of-fact acceptance of her handicap had been a much more courageous approach than her own.

She took a beer out of the refrigerator and almost fell over Elmo, who came running up behind her. "What's with you, cat? You can't still be hungry.''

Intending to erase the tape, Nicki wandered over to the answering machine, then relented and played Doug's message one more time. Elmo continued to rub against her legs. "So, Carol thinks I have courage, Doug thinks I'm his girl, and you think you're going to con me into feeding you again. Sorry, fuzz-face, but you're each operating under a horrible misconception.''

CHAPTER EIGHT

THE REST OF THE WEEK went by quickly. Besides working especially long hours so she could justify being away for two days, Nicki had gone to the gym each afternoon. So had Ian. He had stood in his usual corner and watched her work out, but he had never approached her. She had decided that, for a time, she would abide by his apparent wish to avoid her. The time was up. If he were there again today she would try to talk to him.

She pushed her chair back from the desk and reached for her briefcase. The sound of footsteps running down the hall drew her attention to the door just as Doug skidded to a halt in front of her office. "Tah dah." He spread his arms wide and grinned at her. "Back from the trenches and all in one piece. God, I'm glad I caught you."

She closed her eyes against the surge of pleasure that rushed through her at the sight of him. The white pleated trousers, pale blue, striped shirt open at the throat and navy silk blazer—all obviously cruise wear—told her that he must have come directly from the airport. The shining gray eyes and flashing smile, both of which brightened the deepest tan she'd ever seen, told her that he was genuinely happy to see her. And the sickening depression that settled over her at the realization she had plans for the weekend, told her she had made a terrible mistake.

"Well, hello. I didn't expect you until tomorrow." Did her voice sound as shaky to him as it did to her?

"I know. I was hoping to surprise you."

"You succeeded. How was your trip?"

"Brutal. There was nothing to do but miss you."

"And work on your tan."

"That was the worst. Lying in the warm sun—alone, swimming in a cool pool—alone, watching laughing couples smooth suntan lotion on each other while my own unprotected back was being burned to a crisp."

"Ah-ha, an ulterior motive. You just wanted me there to help regulate the tanning process."

"Wrong, curly-top. I just wanted you there—period. But now I'm here and so are you, so what shall we do this weekend?"

Nicki felt as though her stomach plunged to her toes and back again as she stood up. "I'm going out of town."

Doug laughed. "Sure you are. Is this how you get back at me for all those little lies I told?"

"I'm serious. A good friend called and asked me to teach her to cross-country ski. I said I would."

"Why?"

"Why not?"

"Darn it, you know I assumed we were going to see each other this weekend."

"And you know you had no right to make that assumption."

Doug turned abruptly and started to leave, then stopped and stepped into the office instead, closing the door behind him. "Nicki, didn't that kiss mean anything to you?"

She wanted to protect herself and tell him no, but the dull pain in his eyes wouldn't let her. "Of course it did. But I wasn't sure what it meant to you."

He looked toward the ceiling. "Please, someone tell me what I'm doing wrong."

"I told you last Saturday, I don't know how these things are done. I can't read the signals."

"That's an understatement if I ever heard one. Okay. Let's take it slowly. When are you leaving on your trip?"

"Tomorrow."

"Good. Then, since I am very much interested in spending time with you, I would be thrilled if you would consider joining me for dinner this evening."

"I'd love to but I can't. I have to check on a client right now, and I have a pile of work to finish when I get home."

"You work too hard."

"So you've said. I don't agree."

"Right. Try a different approach, Doug. Since I would gladly endure trial by fire for even a few moments of your company, and I realize you have a night at hard labor ahead of you, may I take you out for a drink after you finish what you need to do?"

She smiled. "Thanks, but I don't think I'd be very good company. I'll be too exhausted to go out."

"Don't make me grovel, Nicki. I bought a present for Elmo and I intend to give it to him. I'll be at your place at nine. Does that give you enough time?"

"I hate pushy men."

"Tough." He left the room, then peeked back in. "You will be there, won't you?"

"I'll be there."

"Terrific. See you later."

THE WEIGHT ROOM WAS EMPTY when Nicki first got there, but she noticed Ian come in before she had completed her warm-up.

She ignored him for a while, going through the first part of her routine and stopping for a rest before beginning the second segment. If he were ever going to approach her this would be the perfect time. Instead, he wandered over to the weight rack and began idly twirling one of the bars.

She walked up behind him. "Ian, would you like me to get you started on a lifting program to increase your strength?"

He glanced over his shoulder at her. "Are you kidding? I'm already stronger than you are."

"No doubt you are, but the principles are the same and I happen to know quite a lot about it."

"So good for you. I know all I need to know. I just don't do it anymore, that's all."

"Why don't you try?"

"No thanks," he mumbled, giving the bar another vigorous spin.

"Afraid?"

He turned to face her. "Hell no, I'm not afraid. Why should I be afraid?"

"That's what I'd like to find out. Don't you think it might help you to talk about what you're feeling? A lot of people have to learn to live with handicaps more severe than yours."

"Like you, for instance?"

"Yes, like me."

"Yeah sure. Well it's not the same. I mean who cares? A gimpy attorney can be just as good as the next one. Unfortunately, it's not that simple for me."

He turned to walk away but Nicki grabbed his arm. "Keep it up, Ian. If you work hard enough at it, you'll manage to alienate everyone who wants to help you. Then, when you're finally ready to crawl out of this hole you've dug for yourself, there won't be anyone left to throw you a line."

He shrugged away from her. "I don't need any help."

"Okay. But if you change your mind, call me."

Her hands were shaking when she turned back to the weights. There was no point in trying to lift now. She headed for the locker room. After all these years, she should be immune to rude references to her limp, especially coming from someone who was hurting every bit as much as she was. So why was it that she felt an almost uncontrollable urge to cry? She stepped under the shower and began to massage her aching thigh. What would Carol think about her courage right now?

NICKI WAS STILL FEELING a bit melancholy when she opened the door to Doug at exactly nine that evening. Despite her mood, she had to laugh at the sombrero plopped rakishly on his head.

He swept the hat off with a flourish and bowed at the waist. "Good evening, señorita." When he stood up he handed her a dusty bottle of tequila.

"You brought my cat tequila?"

"Of course not. Elmo only drinks beer."

"Elmo drinks beer?"

"Sure, but he prefers a nice German import to the Mexican brews, so I didn't get him any." Doug winked at her as he took off his jacket. "Close your mouth, curly-top. If you spent less time working and more time relaxing with your friends and family here you'd have learned that a long time ago." He bent down to greet the cat, who was rubbing against his legs. "She neglects us both, doesn't she, boy?"

Nicki shook her head in disbelief. "What am I going to do with you two?"

"I don't know about the miniature lion, but I have some great suggestions for handling me. First, point me to your salt shaker, then put some mariachi music on the tape deck and have a seat."

"Sorry, I'm a little short on Mexican music."

"You're hopeless. There are a couple of tapes in my jacket pocket." He took the tequila, picked up a large bag that he had propped against the door frame and headed for the kitchen. Nicki started to follow. "Stay there. I've got this under control."

A few minutes later she heard a loud whir. "Doug, what's that?"

"I'm blending the drinks."

"I don't own a blender."

"You do now. Have you eaten anything?"

"Not lately."

"How is it that I knew that?" He grinned at her as he came around the corner carrying a tray laden with tortilla chips, guacamole, bean dip and an enormous pitcher of margaritas.

"What's this?" She pointed to a bowl of frothy liquid.

"Beer, of course. I thought Elmo might want to toast my return." He set the bowl on the floor, and the cat ran to it and began to drink. Doug shrugged. "I guess he doesn't want to wait for a toast."

Nicki leaned forward. She kept expecting Elmo to realize what he was drinking and back away, but that clearly wasn't what he had in mind. "That's incredible." She glanced at Doug as he sat down next to her on the couch and began to arrange the tray of goodies on the coffee table. She couldn't remember when she had last felt so happy and content. "And so are you."

"I try." He handed her a glass rimmed with salt. "Here's to the end of stormy seas."

Doug leaned toward her for the toast. As Nicki clinked the rim of her glass against his and felt the gentle pressure of his fingers resting on her thigh, she couldn't help but think that the storm might just be beginning. She took a sip of her drink and reached for a tortilla chip. "So tell me about this gift you brought back for Elmo."

Doug blushed, sat back and cleared his throat nervously. "I'm afraid I had to tell another little lie."

"Oh? And why is that?"

"Because you were shutting me down, as usual. I thought if I made you curious enough you'd have to let me come over."

"Are you telling me there is no gift? That poor Elmo has spent the whole evening in a frenzy of anticipation for naught? You are a cruel man, Dr. MacNair."

Doug walked to the kitchen and returned with a package. "There's a gift all right, but it's not really for Elmo." He poured a splash more beer in the bowl. "Sorry, old man."

Nicki tore open the paper bundle and pulled out a Mexican blanket woven with an intricate geometric pattern in muted tones of blue and mauve. "Doug, this is absolutely gorgeous."

He nodded. "I'm glad you like it."

Standing up, Nicki spread the blanket across the sofa to get a better look at it, and as soon as she stepped back, Elmo crawled underneath it and curled up.

Doug laughed. "Now I never thought of that. I guess it's a gift for both of you, after all."

Nicki felt his arms slip around her waist and she leaned back against him. "If I decide to keep it on the bed, that is."

Doug chuckled. "Don't do anything rash. He seems perfectly happy out here."

He gave her a squeeze, and she fought the urge to pull his arms more tightly around her and absorb his warmth before he set her free.

He removed first the blanket, then Elmo from the couch and sat down. "So, what time do we leave on our ski trip tomorrow?"

"We?"

"Sure, why not?" He gestured toward the coffee table. "Eat some of this. If we're going away we don't want leftovers."

"Doug, there are a million reasons why not. I'm going with a woman friend. She doesn't even know how to ski. And you don't have a reservation." She waved a guacamole-covered chip for emphasis.

"I only counted three and those are easily disposed of. One, she'll love me. Two, I'm a great teacher. And three, I'll sleep in the car—if you insist."

"No!"

"Good, then I won't sleep in the car."

"No, you can't come."

"You can't stop me. If you won't take me with you I'll go to the same place myself. And you know it's dangerous to ski alone."

"You don't know where I'm going."

"Wild Turkey Inn in Indiana. There's a note on your kitchen counter to call Billy to check the reservation—two rooms."

"One for Carol and one for me."

"I'll share."

"You'll stay alone. Carol and I will share."

"So I can come?"

Nicki sighed. "Doug, do me a favor. Stick with medicine. I'd hate to have to face you in the courtroom."

"Hot dog, a verdict in my favor."

"So what else is new?" She leaned against the back of the couch and munched another chip. "I wonder what you'd do if you ever failed to get your way."

"I'd turn into a raving lunatic."

"Would I be able to notice the difference?"

He shrugged. "Probably not. Drink up. I assume we're leaving early."

Nicki couldn't believe what she'd just done. Even on her own, she wasn't sure she would be able to get through a whole weekend with Doug without losing either her mind or her heart. And given his past behavior, she had to worry about how he would react to Carol, once he knew her history.

She finished her margarita and ushered Doug to the door, assuring him she was quite capable of cleaning up the dishes. She handed him his jacket. "See you tomorrow—I guess. Make it around six, no seven, that's right, seven," she stammered while trying to think of some way to get out of the awkward situation.

"I'll be here." He hesitated and bent slightly toward her, but stopped when she backed away. "I've got a station wagon. Should I drive?"

"My, you do have a car for every contingency. Thanks, but that won't be necessary. Carol will be driving. She's coming down from Chicago."

"That's all the more reason for me to drive the rest of the way and give her a break."

"Doug, this really isn't such a good idea."

"Am I being too pushy?"

"Not for a bulldozer."

He nodded slowly. "I was afraid of that. If I promise to slow down a bit, can I still come along? It'll just be friends out to ski."

"That's part of the problem. I don't think you and my friend can be friends."

"Why not?"

"Do you follow malpractice cases closely enough to know who Carol Stuart is?"

"Sure. She was your last big victory before you came here to teach."

"She's also a good friend of mine and a spunky young woman who doesn't want to let her injury get in the way of the things she wants to do."

"Like learning to cross-country ski?"

"Exactly."

"Well good for her. I might even be able to help. I used to coach handicapped kids when I was an intern."

"I didn't know that."

"Why should you have? Listen, Nicki, if your big concern is that you think I'm going to give Carol a hard time because she won a malpractice verdict, then you can relax. I'm a little more fair-minded than that."

"You certainly weren't with me at the start."

"No, but you've given me a new outlook. Let me come along and have a chance to show you that I've changed."

"Okay. But I won't have Carol hurt or subjected to your temper tantrums. She doesn't deserve that."

He raised a hand solemnly. "Scout's honor. You'll be proud of me. And just to prove that I'm on good behavior I'll make this a hands-off good-night."

Nicki started to protest but caught herself. If she were going to make it through this weekend without letting Doug overwhelm her, she probably would do better not to begin it with one of his dizzying kisses. "Good night, Doug. See you in the morning."

As she carried the tray and pitcher to the kitchen, she noticed the blender that Doug had acquired for the evening. He certainly was amazing—uncommonly considerate and completely crazy at the same time. Just the thought of how he'd swept into her life left her breathless, but she should not allow herself to forget that he might be gone just as quickly. She glanced at the clock. Why did 7:00 a.m. seem to be such a long time away?

DOUG ARRIVED RIGHT ON TIME, appropriately outfitted in a bright red turtleneck, gray down vest, black jeans and knee-high canvas gaiters.

Nicki caught his surprised look as he scanned her own skintight racing garb. She smiled as she handed him her small overnight bag and easily shouldered her own skis and poles. "Carol just called from the gas station on Seventh. She'll be here in a minute so we might as well go down."

"Did you warn her about me?"

"There is no way to effectively warn anyone about you. I did, however, explain that you had invited yourself along."

"What did she say?"

"She wanted to know if you were cute."

"Oh? And what did you tell her?" he asked as he loaded her gear into his station wagon.

Nicki pretended to size him up before answering. "I told her I wasn't sure, but that you dress well. Do you always have the perfect attire for every activity?"

"No. I don't have a smoking jacket for sipping sherry in my study, a long fur coat for going to art exhibits and theater openings, or my own bowling shoes."

"Do you do those things?"

"What do you think?" He tossed her skis on the roof rack and began to tie them down.

She watched him as he moved swiftly and efficiently around the car, pulling ropes tight and checking clamps. His thick hair had been mussed by the wind and his deep tan appeared even darker in the pale light of a winter sunrise. Periodically, he paused to rub his ungloved hands together or stomp his feet against the cold. She tried to conjure up a picture of Doug in his leisure time.

"I think you do sip sherry, but in a sweatshirt, go to the theater but not art exhibits, and probably only bowl if you're with a crowd that doesn't take it seriously."

"Right on all counts. You are insightful this morning—as well as beautiful. Those ski clothes look perfect on you. I get the feeling you just might be a pro."

Before she could comment, Carol pulled up to the curb and Nicki breathed a sigh of relief. She hadn't really intended to keep her past a secret, but she also didn't want to talk about it if she didn't have to. "Hi Carol." She raised her hand in greeting as she walked over to her friend.

"Hi yourself. And what do you mean 'he's okay'?" Carol jerked her thumb toward Doug. "If that's the man in question, he's fantastic. It's about time."

"He's a friend and nothing more."

"Too bad. Speaking of friends, your 'friend' Ron sent a box of files for you."

"Damn him. Can't he do anything himself?"

"I doubt it. I really don't know how you got tied up with him, Nicki. You know all he's interested in is politics. This practice is just a way for him to amuse himself until he's ready to launch a campaign."

"I wouldn't have believed that a month ago, but it sure seems to be the case. How is it that you're playing messenger?"

Carol began to fiddle with her keys until she found the one for the trunk. "I just went by to ask him something and he dumped this on me."

"Oh please, don't tell me you're getting free legal advice from him now."

"It wasn't about me...." She spun around to greet Doug, who had come up beside them. "Hi there. I'm Carol Stuart and you must be . . . I haven't a guess."

"Doug, Doug MacNair. Nice to meet you."

Nicki watched as Doug offered his right hand then, apparently picking up Carol's hesitation, smoothly switched to his left. It was a small gesture but it immediately put Nicki at ease. Leaving them to get acquainted, she took the files to her apartment. By the time she returned, they were already laughing together.

"Hey, Nicki, haven't you gotten around to telling this guy that short-people jokes are in poor taste?"

Doug put up his hands in defense. "I didn't say short. I said petite. I simply asked her if all gymnasts were so petite."

"Sure he did. Right after he pointed out that even if I sat on your shoulders we wouldn't make a whole person. I was just about to tell him that you weren't a gymnast but a—"

"That's right, I wasn't. Should we get going before you two come to blows?" Nicki picked up Carol's skis and headed for the station wagon.

WHEN THEY CROSSED into Indiana, Doug glanced over at Nicki napping peacefully beside him, then nudged her gently. "Wake up, sleepyhead. You and Carol here have been slumbering sweetly ever since we pulled away from the curb. Now I need help. You said you wanted to go to the lodge first, and I don't know where that is."

Nicki groaned, peeked up at him from under a mass of curls and shifted her position to sit upright and look out the windshield. "At the moment, neither do I. Where are we?"

He gave their location, and after thinking a minute, she told him where to turn off the interstate, then directed him to a large log building surrounded by a number of smaller cabins. Leaving Carol in the car to adjust to the cruel reality of being awakened, Doug and Nicki went into the lobby to check in. "Neat, clean, but hardly romantic," he teased.

Nicki glared at him. "Carol and I hadn't planned a romantic weekend." She turned to the athletic looking man behind the desk. "Hi, Billy, how's it going?"

"Nicki. Long time no see." The man came around the counter to give her a bear hug. "It's going pretty good. We've sure had enough snow this year. How has your leg been treating you?"

Nicki smiled. "Can't complain. I'm here aren't I? As long as I take it easy, it's all right. Billy Waite, this is Doug MacNair, old friend meet a new one."

Doug shook hands and Billy gave him a knowing wink as he turned back to Nicki. "The reservation was for two rooms, right?"

Nicki mimicked the wink. "Yep—one for Carol, one for me. Doug, here, didn't decide to come until the last minute, so we'll need another room for him if you've got one."

Billy sighed heavily and shook his head. "If you want an extra room I'll get you an extra room."

Carol wandered in just as they got their keys. After dropping off their bags, they headed back outside to begin Carol's initiation into cross-country skiing, starting with some practice in front of the lodge before they headed over to the official state park trails.

It didn't take Doug long to realize what a talented athlete Carol must have been. She needed to adjust the way she used her poles to compensate for her weak right hand, but her excellent sense of balance and rhythm made it easier than Doug would have expected for her to overcome the problems her handicap caused.

Doug considered himself a strong cross-country skier and had planned on helping with Carol's instruction, but a few minutes' observation of the two women together convinced him that his expertise was not needed. He leaned back against a tree and crossed his arms. There was something about the way that Nicki took charge and the way that Carol let her that he found fascinating.

The young woman who had been too self-conscious to greet him with her right hand didn't flinch when Nicki took it and began to teach her how to hold the poles by wrapping her own fingers over Carol's. Doug thought the spunky gymnast would have considered herself an expert on the rhythm and grace of athletic movements, but she responded obediently to all of Nicki's barked commands to set her shoulders, bend her knees, stop moving like a robot and take the glide.

Nicki, to all appearances, performed her job as instructor like a drill sergeant, totally lacking in compassion. It was only when Doug saw the pride and relief in her eyes as she hugged Carol and proclaimed her ready to try the trails, that he understood the pressure she had been under. He was disappointed in himself for not realizing sooner how devastating it would have been for Carol to fail. Having never had to overcome a physical handicap himself, he hadn't considered the possibility of failure. Nicki obviously had.

He thought about her limp for a moment, wondering what had caused it and how much it had cost her. Seeing her work with Carol convinced him that she had definitely been athletic at one time in her life. Even now, she moved with a confidence and control that signaled someone very much in tune with her own body. He liked that about her. He enjoyed watching her. But he knew that her special brand of self-awareness was also the sign of a person who was used to standing alone. Maybe she wouldn't be able to let someone else become a part of her life. He pushed the thought away as he began to load their gear into the station wagon for the drive to the trails. Maybe no one had ever tried.

As they started down the beginner trail, Nicki took the lead and set a slow, easy pace—both for Carol's benefit and her own. She did not want to strain her leg the first time out.

She settled into the smooth rhythm of the kick and glide. Cross-country lacked the excitement of a downhill race, but it gave her a sense of peace and well-being. Taking a deep breath of the cold, clean air, she allowed herself to be lulled by the soft whisper of her skis on the trail as she scanned the glistening landscape that lay before her.

The pines, their boughs laden with snow, looked like a distant corp of ballerinas all decked out in layers of tulle and lace. As she skimmed along the path that wound between and beneath them, the spicy fragrance tickled her nose, and a gust of winter wind covered her with a dusting of fragile flakes. No two alike, she reminded herself as she blinked through the water droplets on her goggles.

She dug the edges of her skis into the snow to begin an arduous uphill stretch. Glancing over her shoulder to be sure Carol could make the climb, she was pleased to see Doug ski up beside the young woman and begin to coach her on the necessary technique. Nicki turned her concentration back to the trail. This particular motion was one that put a good deal of stress on her hip and leg.

As soon as she reached the crest of the hill, she angled her skis, bent her knees and pushed off. The descent was, after all, the payback for the climb, and she wanted to get the most out of it. She sped down the hill, expertly negotiating two curves, then plowed to an abrupt halt as a skier took a fall right in front of her. *Damn*. Now she'd lost her momentum.

She waited impatiently for him to get up and out of the way, and when he didn't, a wave of fear washed over her. Looking behind her, Nicki saw that Doug and Carol had stopped to catch their breath at the top of the hill. She

waved her poles frantically to signal Doug then inched her
way down the remainder of the steep slope until she reached
the skier. Middle-aged and slightly overweight, he lay on his
side in the path, knees pulled up as close to a fetal position
as his skis would allow. He was gasping for air and his
hands, still encumbered by the ski poles, were clutching at
his chest.

Before Nicki could even think what to do, Doug skidded
to a halt beside her, kicked off his skis and leaned over the
stricken man. "It's his heart. I'll do what I can, but he'll
need help fast. Do you know CPR?"

"Yes, but so does Carol." Carol had stayed at the top of
the hill. Nicki motioned for her to take off her skis and walk
down, then she turned back to Doug. "I'll go for the ranger
and have him get an ambulance sled in here."

She went into a crouch and, placing one ski on a diago-
nal to the other, pushed off. Since speed was an issue, she
would have to abandon recreational cross-country techniques and use the racer's skating style. That was going to
cost her.

She left the trail to take a shortcut across the open fields.
The icy wind, no longer tamed by groves of trees, slashed at
her face and hands, numbing them. In spite of the cold,
Nicki was sweating profusely. She pulled off her steamy
goggles and tossed them aside. They were more hinderance
than help now.

Each time she kicked with her right leg a bolt of fire shot
from her ankle to her hip. Nicki bit her lower lip against the
pain. She could take this. She could control this. If only her
leg didn't give out on her completely. She'd never put all of
those pins and pieces of plastic to a test like this before.

It took her only ten minutes to reach the start of the run,
but it felt like hours. The intense, burning throb in her right
leg was a constant torment. Luckily, the ranger's car was in

the lot and she had him radio instructions for an ambulance to proceed to mile marker two on the beginner trail. The ranger drove out to the main road to direct the ambulance in and Nicki grimaced as she hobbled to Doug's station wagon only to find that it was locked. Now, without the exertion of skiing, she was becoming cold and the unrelenting pain made her feel weak and ill.

She leaned against the car to take the weight off of her leg and tried to think. Doug would most likely accompany the heart attack victim to the hospital. That was the correct thing for him to do, but right now she really wanted him to be with her. She would welcome the warmth of his arms around her.

As a last resort, she tried the button on the liftgate and breathed a sigh of relief as it popped open. Crawling painfully into the back of the wagon, she pulled an oil-spattered tarp around her shoulders and settled in to wait.

CHAPTER NINE

As NICKI HAD EXPECTED, Doug did go along to the hospital, so it was Carol who returned to the car with his keys, drove back to the lodge and helped Nicki to her room. As soon as Carol was gone, Nicki slumped onto the bed without even attempting to remove her boots. She tried to get into a comfortable position. For the first time in years she felt trapped inside her body.

She clenched her fists, closed her eyes and let her thoughts wander. The first image that came to mind was that of Doug kicking off his skis and falling to his knees next to the man on the trail. This afternoon had been the only time she'd seen him function as a professional, and she had been impressed. The Doug she knew seemed so wrapped up in having a good time that it was hard to picture him as anything other than a fun-loving playboy. But the Doug she saw on the trail, helping Carol and aiding the stricken skier, was someone new to her—someone she could respect very much. She found herself intrigued by Doug's ability to blend both aspects of his personality. Just what she needed—something else intriguing about Doug MacNair.

Nicki struggled to her feet and limped to the bathroom, hoping a soak in a hot tub might give her aching body some relief.

By the time she was pulling on a clean ski sweater an hour later, she did feel a little better. But the bath probably had not helped as much as the shot of brandy from the bottle that Billy had had Carol bring her. She was just debating whether to have another when she heard a knock at the door.

"Coming." She hobbled over to open it and Doug breezed into the room, black bag in hand. "How is he?" she asked before even closing the door.

"He's doing fine, but you look terrible, curly-top."

"Is that a professional diagnosis or a social commentary?"

"Purely professional. You are a beautiful woman but, right now, I have to agree with the diagnosis Carol just rendered while insisting that I come see you immediately. You're hurting. Come over here and let me check you out."

"Over my dead body, which is closer to the truth than I'd like to admit, I might add. I know a line when I hear one."

"Nicki. I am a doctor."

"I'm aware of that. You already treated me once, remember?"

Doug walked over and rested one hand on her shoulder while lifting her chin with the other. "I want you to listen to me. You could have done some serious damage to yourself out there, and as a physician, it's up to me to do what I can to help."

She raised her eyebrows at the stern sound of his voice. "I appreciate your position, but I've lived with this for years. I know when there's cause for concern and when I just need a good rest."

He walked to the bed, turned down the bedspread, stacked and fluffed the pillows then glared at her. "So why aren't you resting?"

"Because I'm not ready to rest. I'm too keyed up to settle down."

With one long stride he closed the space between them, picked her up and put her on the bed. She started to get up, but he stood in her way.

"No, Nicki. I want you to stay right there. If you don't want to sleep, I'll sit and talk to you, but you are not to move. Is that clear?"

"I don't take orders well, Doctor."

"I'm sorry. I was being heavy-handed, but please do yourself a favor and sit still for a while."

Nicki fell back obligingly against the pillows.

Doug grinned. "Thank you. May I stay?"

"I'd like that." She did feel better having him there. The last thing she needed was to be alone with her memories right now.

"I ate at the hospital. Do you want me to order you something?"

"No thanks. Billy sent a sandwich and brandy. Have a drink."

He picked up the bottle and walked into the bathroom for a glass. "Have you had much of this?"

"One or two swallows. Why?"

"I wanted to leave you something for the pain, but it's probably not a good idea to combine it with alcohol."

She shrugged. "It wouldn't have mattered. I don't use drugs. I spent too many years in a painkiller fog to go that route again."

"Would you like to tell me about it?"

"About what?"

"Everything. Your life. What makes you the way you are."

"I'm not sure I even know the answer to that last one."

"Start with the basics then." He took a sip of his brandy. "When did you learn to ski like that?"

"Okay, let's see. Like that, when I was twelve, but I started downhill skiing when I was toddler."

"And I take it that it was more than a hobby."

Nicki smiled sadly. "For ten years it was a way of life."

"And then?"

"And then I fell off a mountain and off my pedestal all at once. America lost their sure bet for the gold, my family lost the chance to see the name Bernard in the record books, and I lost my identity."

"Is that when you stopped using your stepfather's name?"

Nicki hesitated as she tried to think of a way to avoid the direct question. "Nicki Bernard was a world-class skier. That's all she'd ever been to anyone, including herself."

The slight narrowing of Doug's eyes told her that she probably hadn't gotten away with it. "Well, you certainly managed to bounce right back."

"Is that what you think?"

"Sure. Don't you?"

"Sometimes—on a good day. Today has not been a good day."

"Of course it has. You were terrific. If it weren't for you, that man would have never gotten help in time. As it is, he has a solid chance at being as good as new."

"Oh, Doug, I'm really glad to hear that." She tried to sit up higher in the bed and groaned. "I wish I could say the same for me."

"Tell me where it hurts."

She rolled her eyes. "When are you going to give up?"

"When are you going to give me some credit?" He knelt by the bed. "Now don't panic. I'm just going to touch your leg for a minute."

She didn't panic, but she did flinch when she felt him slip his hands around the tender area above her knee. She closed her eyes, waiting for the pain, but it never came. He gently manipulated the tight muscles to relieve some of the pressure. She'd been through enough sessions like this in the hospital to realize that he knew exactly what he was doing. "Physical therapy too? Is there any type of medicine you don't practice?"

"I told you, I used to work with sports teams for the handicapped. Sometimes the simplest treatments work best."

"Hardly a long-term cure, I'm sure, but it certainly feels wonderful right now."

"Good." He continued to work over her. "Tell me about your own long-term cure. Who screwed up what to make you bitter against doctors?"

"I'm not bitter against doctors." Nicki struggled to get up but he held her firmly in place.

"Then why the malpractice specialty?"

"Because I know how good 'good' medicine can be. Do you remember when you first met Elmo and asked about his name?"

"Sure. You named him after Elmo Vandercamp. Now there's a good doctor."

"You are looking at a woman who has been credited with one of the most spectacular falls in skiing history. I probably shouldn't have lived to tell about it, I certainly shouldn't have walked again, but fortunately for me, Dr. Vandercamp is a ski buff. He was watching the race, saw it happen and was at the hospital by the time they brought me in. The man isn't just a good doctor. He's a miracle worker."

"So I don't get it. Why punish the system that gave you a miracle?"

This time she did succeed in sitting up. "Don't you see? I don't want to punish it. I want to preserve it. Medicine should belong to the Elmo Vandercamps and the Doug MacNairs, not to a bunch of incompetent, unfeeling young hotshots who think they're gods yet don't have the brains to test for compartment syndrome. I broke every bone in the lower half of my body, some of them in several places, and I came away with a bunch of scars, a limp that acts up now and then and some shattered dreams. Carol Stuart had a simple broken arm and she lost just as much as I did. That's not the way it's supposed to be."

She raked her hand through her hair and ducked around Doug to stand up and pace. "Sometimes there are legitimate mistakes, accidents that happen no matter how careful everyone tries to be, bad results that can't be helped or avoided. I know that. But sometimes there are just bad and careless doctors. I can't change that, but at least I can see their victims get compensation."

"And that's your expertise."

"Exactly. I know what it's like to wake up in a hospital bed and have to face the fact that you will never be perfect again—to have everything you've worked for put forever beyond your reach. There's an awful lot of pain and suffering and heartache that goes into what you call 'bouncing right back.' I'm an expert at convincing a jury to pay my clients for that."

"But no one paid you."

"I didn't deserve it. I did this to myself, so I'm the one who has to pay."

"That's not how Sarah feels. She said you weren't the only one hurt."

"Of course I wasn't. There were a lot of people counting on me. I did something stupid and let them all down. They were all hurt. But in the long run, even for that, I'm the one who has to pay."

"Because that's what they expect of you?"

"Because that's what I expect of me. It makes a big difference."

"It sure does. That's a much heavier burden."

"Back to psychology again, doctor?"

"It's your fault. I was perfectly happy with the physical therapist role, but you had to get up and start hopping around. How do you think Dr. Vandercamp would feel about your attempts to destroy all his good work—first racing across rough terrain and now this?"

Nicki sat on the bed next to him and shook her head. "It's not like that. Everything is stable. It's just a matter of how much pain I'm willing to take, and when someone's life may be at stake, there's not really much choice."

"A lot of people would have made a different choice."

"Sure. And there are also doctors who would have refused to help. It's not even your specialty, and if something goes wrong, you could be sued."

"That's the breaks. At least I know where I can find a good lawyer." He reached over to massage her neck. "And you've found a good physician, so lie down and let me give you a back rub."

The gentle pressure of his hand against her tight muscles encouraged her to comply. She rolled over on her stomach and rested her chin on her folded hands. It was comforting to think that he wanted to care for her, to ease her pain. She needed that from him tonight. She felt the bed give as Doug sat beside her, and her stomach lurched as she was hit with the full impact of what she had agreed to. She was used to being touched by trainers and team physicians before her accident and doctors and physical therapists afterward, but it had always been a completely impersonal experience. With Doug it would be different. His touch—the way that he touched her—would matter a great deal more than she wanted to admit. He had the power to bruise her much more than her skiing effort had, and she wasn't sure that he understood that.

Doug pulled off his heavy sweater, tossed it on a nearby chair and pushed up the sleeves of his turtleneck. "Would you care to do the same?"

"No thanks."

"I can't do this right if you won't cooperate."

"I am cooperating. I'm positively docile."

"You are also fully clothed. Not good for a massage."

"Nice try, MacNair. Like I said, I know a line when I hear one."

"Just take off the sweater and leave on whatever you have underneath it."

She toyed with the idea of complying with his request—to ignite in him the same desire that the thought of his hands on her naked skin had sparked in her. But her reluctance to reveal what she was feeling stopped her. "There is nothing underneath it," she whispered, and felt her cheeks grow warm as she heard the sharp intake of his breath.

"Ah, Nicole, I really wish you hadn't told me that. You're a cruel woman."

"It serves you right for being so pushy." She hoped her voice didn't reveal the smug satisfaction she felt at his reaction.

"I should have learned by now that I can never get the best of you." He chuckled as he began to knead the bunched and knotted muscles of her lower back.

He was exactly as she'd hoped; gentle, considerate, caring. She knew it was impossible for him to be firm enough to accomplish his purpose without causing her some discomfort, but he made up for that by being so endearingly apologetic every time she winced. None of her trainers had ever worried about whether they'd hurt her, but she hadn't expected or wanted them to.

As Doug's hands moved expertly over her aching back, hips and thighs, her pain began to melt away. Feeling limp and exhausted, Nicki settled in more comfortably, turning her face to one side and snuggling up to a pillow. Again a sense of contentment washed over her, just like it had last night over the margaritas. When she was with Doug, all the tensions inside her—all the demons that kept her operating in high gear—subsided, and she could be truly relaxed.

He began to hum and Nicki smiled to herself. "My, you even provide the background music. You do have a real talent for this."

"No talent necessary. It's all pretty scientific." He slid his hands to her shoulder blades. "But I'm afraid this is hardly my best effort. I'm operating at a severe disadvantage."

"Such as?"

He stood up. "The bed is too low to give me the proper leverage, and if I keep bending over you at this angle, I'm going to break my own back." Slipping off his shoes, he got on the bed and straddled her in a kneeling position. "Hardly discreet, but this should work."

"Doug, why don't you just stop now?" Even as she said it, Nicki knew she didn't want him to stop.

And he must have known it, too. "Oh no you don't. You've had to endure the rough stuff, now we start the good part."

The huskiness of his voice and the breathtaking sense of his body poised over hers, filled her with anticipation. As he settled back on his heels, she could feel the muscles of his legs pressed against her outer thighs, and a steady yearning began to grow inside her. She tightened her jaw against it, feeling foolish for getting carried away by a simple back rub, yet wondering if what was happening between them was all that simple anymore.

She was completely sensitized to his every motion. He rocked forward to move his hands to her shoulders and his thigh muscles tightened. So did hers. He rocked back to massage her buttocks and his muscles relaxed. Hers did not. He cupped his hands over her sides as he applied pressure along her spine with his thumbs, but the pressure she felt was in her breasts, which tingled at the nearness of his fingers. Finally, he abandoned the therapeutic kneading and began to trail his hands up and down in long, caressing strokes. Nicki could not suppress a murmured sigh, a sigh that Doug must have noticed. She could sense a new urgency in his movements. He had eased her pain. Now he wanted to give her pleasure with his touch and, mesmerized, she surrendered to him.

Doug hesitated for a moment. He could no longer pretend that he was administering treatment and nothing more. From this position he could see the slight rise and fall of Nicki's shoulders every time she took a breath. He could feel the involuntary tightening of her muscles every time his hands brushed her sides near her breasts. Her rumpled, uncontrolled curls wisped against her collar as she moved, alternately hiding and revealing the soft skin at the base of her neck. She looked so fragile, so vulnerable, stretched out beneath him.

He shifted his weight, hugging her hips with his knees as he reached up to bury his fingers in her hair. She tensed slightly, signaling that she too was aware that the mood had changed.

"My head is the only part of me that doesn't hurt." Her voice sounded as though she had just awakened from a dream.

"Sorry, but this is part of the complete MacNair package. Does it feel good?" With his thumbs, he traced a pattern from the back of her ears to her temples.

She nodded, shoulders and curls moving in tandem. "I'm in heaven."

"I'm glad one of us is, because I'm about to be damned."

"For what?"

"I want to touch you, Nicki."

She paused before responding and he waited, hoping her desire would overcome what he imagined would be her instinctive need to pull away.

"You have been touching me—for almost an hour."

"And now I want to really touch you. You know the difference. Are you avoiding the decision simply to torment me or because you aren't sure?"

She levered herself up a bit and turned her head so her eyes met his. "I guess I'm a little afraid. This is all so new to me. I know what I'm feeling, but I don't know if it's what it should be."

Her candid admission took him completely off guard. He had to fight the urge to gather her up in his arms and warn her about the dangers of revealing so much. He knew, in that instant, that he loved her—loved her unique brand of honesty and needed to protect her from those who would be only too willing to use it to hurt her.

He touched her shoulder to encourage her to lie down again and kissed her cheek. "There are no guidelines on that, curly-top. You feel the way I make you feel or, rather, the way you let yourself feel when you're with me. If that's intense enough, you'll ache for me the same way I ache for you."

Nicki smiled hesitantly. "Well, if aching is the goal, I reached it a long time ago."

"But I promised to take your pain away. Let me try again." Doug reminded himself to be gentle as he lifted the bottom of her sweater and slipped his hands underneath, expecting to skim warm, silky skin. Instead, he encountered a crosshatch of irregularities that he recognized immediately as scars. His chest tightened at the realization of what she must have gone through. Afraid that she might be embarrassed, he made no comment, but guided his fingers lightly along her sides to her breasts. She arched slightly, giving him easier access to the tender buds that hardened against his palms.

He felt as though a dam had burst within him. Leaning forward, he wrapped his arms around her and pressed his lips to the back of her neck. "If you're going to stop me, do it now."

She knew she should. She had promised herself that she wouldn't allow this to happen, that she wouldn't allow Doug to charm her into a relationship she was bound to regret. But right now she was afraid she would have bigger regrets if she turned him away. She'd never known this burning need to be loved by a man before—never thought it was possible for her. She couldn't let it go. "I won't stop you."

He smiled and moved aside. "Turn over. I need to look at you."

Nicki knew she was blushing, but she complied.

Pushing her sweater up, he studied her silently for a moment, then closed his eyes as he cupped his hands over her breasts and kept them there, as though touching her that way gave him some special strength. The heat from his palms surged through her. "You are incredibly beautiful," he whispered.

"You don't have to flatter me." She fought the urge to pull her sweater down. "I know I'm incredibly tiny."

"Well, let's see." He studied her with mock seriousness. "It looks like everything is in perfect, petite proportion to me."

"Doug, please don't laugh at me. I've told you, I'm pretty insecure about these sorts of things. I haven't had a lot of experience."

He reached out to stroke her cheek. "I'm not laughing at you, Nicki. I'm delighting in you. And I'll have you know that everyone is insecure about these sorts of things. Experience has nothing to do with it." Nicki gasped as he bent down to plant a kiss on the tip of one breast then the other and finally moved to lie beside her. "Sorry. You are so tempting that I'm getting a little ahead of myself."

Before she could ask what he meant, he leaned over her and brought his lips to hers in an urgent kiss that left her no choice but to respond. Instinctively she locked her fingers behind his neck and held him captive. The tip of his tongue brushed her lips, begging access, which she granted. She allowed him to explore her, to tease the roof of her mouth, to taste of her, then demanded the same rights for herself. She pulled him closer still. His chest pressed against hers, and she could feel his heart thumping wildly.

When she released him, he got to his knees and straddled her again. "That wasn't the kiss of someone lacking in experience, love. You've been driving me crazy. Now it's my turn." He grasped her arms, pinning them to her sides, and looked down at her, his eyes shining with such intensity that she knew a flash of fear. She strained against his grip and he pulled back, opening his hands to set her free. "Please, don't think you have to fight me, Nicki. You must know I would never force you to do anything against your will."

"I'm sorry. You just looked so fierce."

"Then I'm the one who should be sorry. I want you so much I keep losing control." He paused and shook his head. "My need for you is fierce, but it has to be matched by an equally fierce need in you."

"I've never had anyone want me that way before. I don't know what to expect."

"Expect to be loved."

He began to massage her chest and stomach the same way he'd massaged her back before, caressing her with long, soothing strokes, running his palms over her breasts until she wanted to grab his hands and clasp them tightly against her. But he evaded her grasp, and rather than taking her sign to increase his pressure, he pulled his hands away. She moaned in disappointment.

"Patience, Nicki, patience." He leaned forward and touched the tip of his tongue lightly to each nipple. As she writhed beneath him, Doug repeated his tease again and again, each time applying a little more pressure, each time licking a slightly larger arc in the circle. Finally he cupped her breasts in his hands and suckled each in turn until she could stand it no more and reached up to force his head away. He fought her for a moment, then gave in and settled for laying a trail of kisses across her stomach to her waistband and back up her breastbone to the base of her throat.

He moved to kneel beside her. "Not too much longer now." Again he slid his fingers down her torso, but this time he continued the journey down her outer thighs and up her inner thighs, pausing a tantalizing moment before she felt him unsnap her jeans. As he lowered the zipper, she put her hand out to stop him, then pulled it back. There was no point in denying that she wanted this. He kissed her stomach where the material parted and rested his hands on her waist. "I need your help now, love."

She arched her back to make it easy for him to draw the tight denim down over her hips. The sharp pain that knifed all the way up her right side and down again left her too stunned to even call out. The room reeled for a moment and she couldn't bring it back into focus. Stinging tears blurred her vision. She shook her head to clear it, but it did no good. Hoping that Doug hadn't realized what had happened, she slid her arm under her back as a lever and tried to lift herself again.

She felt his powerful hands closing over her hips to restrain her. "Are you crazy? Don't try to move." Doug's familiar voice cut through her dizziness and she blinked until his features became clear. He was kneeling beside her, breathing heavily as though still caught up in his passion, but his eyes were frightened and fixed on hers and his complexion was ashen. "Just lie there until we can figure out what happened and be sure you aren't doing any more damage."

"I know what happened. The same thing that always happens when I move like that without supporting my back. Believe me, I'm used to it." She made a futile attempt at a smile. "I'm fine, Doug. Really."

He rested on his heels. "Damn it all."

She winced at his invective, hating the idea that she'd been careless and disappointed him. "Please don't be upset."

"Upset? You bet I'm upset. How could I have been such a total idiot? Talk about stupid. What a selfish, unthinking..."

"Ah, Doug, I hate to interrupt you when you're on a roll, but I hardly think self-flagellation is necessary. It was my fault, not yours. I'm the one who should have known better. I'm sorry."

"Sure, everything is always your fault. No matter that I'm a doctor who knew about your injury and also knew that you'd already given your body a beating today. You had no right to expect me to have the common sense to leave you alone instead of tricking you into being physical with me."

Nicki felt as though she'd been slapped. "Well, that puts a different light on things. I wasn't aware that you had tricked me." She reached up to pull her sweater back into place.

Doug blinked at her as though he couldn't quite understand what she was saying. "Well, I certainly didn't plan it that way. But if only I'd been thinking, I would have realized that things could get out of control."

" 'If only I'd been thinking.' Those seem to be my famous last words. Don't worry about it, Doug. It really wasn't your fault. Now, I probably should try to get some sleep."

His face still tense with concern, he eased off the bed and picked up his sweater and bag. "Is there anything I can do to make you more comfortable?"

"We just tried that, remember?"

"Right. How about those painkillers?"

"No thanks. As you can see, I make enough mistakes when I'm in full control of my faculties. Imagine what I'd do if I were doped up."

"This wasn't a mistake, Nicki. Poor timing, maybe, clumsy execution, perhaps, but not a mistake." He bent down to kiss her on the forehead. "I'll be by first thing in the morning to see how you're doing." Doug flicked off the lights before he left the room.

CHAPTER TEN

As soon as the door closed, Nicki reached over to turn on the lamp beside the bed. The familiar throbbing in her thigh warned her that she would be awake for a long time, and she had no intention of sitting in the dark.

Ever since her accident, she'd been unable to cope with being alone and in pain in darkness. She had spent too many nights lying in a darkened hospital room with only machines and monitors to keep her company, staring at the ceiling and grappling with the uncertainty that had become her life.

She closed her eyes against an aching tremor, caused not by her leg, but by the whirlpool of memories that spun within her.

Nicki could not remember a time when her life hadn't revolved around skiing. Her father had been a coach for the Aspen Ski Club, and by the time she was eight, he had her participating fully in the program.

At age ten, she had already swept her division in all major competitions, been a medalist in the Junior Olympics and caught the eye of not only the U.S. Ski Team's coaches but of Max Bernard, a dynamic independent coach who had competed in the Olympics himself. Although neither he nor any of his protégés had ever won a medal, he still had an outstanding reputation among insiders on the ski circuit.

Max convinced Nicki's family that he could prepare her for a win in the Nationals, which would put her on track for a shot at Olympic gold. So John Devlin had stepped aside and allowed Max Bernard to take over Nicki's training—and her life.

Two years later her father was killed in a plane crash and, to everyone's surprise, Max began to court Nicki's mother. They were married after less than a year, and Max had insisted on adopting Nicki and Sarah and having them take his name.

Life became one race after another—one win after another. Nicki had lived up to Max's expectations that she would be one of the very rare skiers who could compete effectively in all three of the Alpine events: slalom, giant slalom and the dangerous and demanding downhill race. By age sixteen, she was almost assured of a trip to the next Olympics.

The price for that success was a life that excluded everything but skiing. She did whatever Max told her to do, whenever he wanted her to do it. She knew she carried the dream not only for herself but for her whole family. There was no time for friends, dating or even regular school—no time for anything but winning.

When Nicki began to work full-time with the U.S. Ski Team, Max had to let the team coaches take over her training, but he accompanied her to every camp and every race. The rigorous schedule was not new to Nicki, but her years with Max had been isolated ones, and she felt ill-prepared to enjoy the interaction with other team members. Although they were all Olympic hopefuls who shared her background and understood the dedication needed to excel, most of them had been training together for years. Nicki was a newcomer, an outsider. There was, however, one young man who seemed to make an effort to get to know her. Christopher Williams was four years older than she was. He was also handsome, charming and sexy. Nicki was first flustered, then flattered by his attention.

Olympic hype was in full swing and the public always liked stories of romance between two athletes. It wasn't long before Nicki began to see articles linking her name to Chris's, which made her extremely uncomfortable, but Max couldn't see the harm in it. He had been anxious to capitalize on the new methods available for athletes to earn endorsement money without sacrificing their amateur status, and Chris was an expert on how the system worked.

The attractive young couple made numerous appearances for ski equipment and clothing companies, and both Chris and Max were thrilled by the rapidly growing trust accounts. But Nicki was miserable. She felt that it was basically dishonest to represent themselves as a couple just to gain more endorsement opportunities. And to make matters worse, she was so attracted to Chris that having to work with him under those circumstances was awkward. She wanted and needed him to be more than just a business associate.

She tried to talk to her stepfather about her feelings, but he dismissed her concerns, pointing out that her finances were his business. All she had to do was ski and he would take care of everything else. He reminded her that Chris had been having a run of bad breaks and had had a poor season. He needed Nicki to stand by him and help him get the publicity and funds necessary for him to continue his training. As usual, she agreed to comply with Max's wishes for a while longer, at least until Chris got back in form.

As Nicki's training intensified, Chris became more attentive. Wherever she went, Chris was there waiting to walk with her. He joined her for meals, called her during their meager free time—just to talk—and eventually started to ask her out. She began to believe that, in spite of her youth and inexperience, Chris was genuinely interested in her.

The more time they spent together, the more real their romance seemed. The first time he kissed her she saw stars, just like in the love stories she had read but never hoped to experience. The first time he fondled her breasts, she felt a dizzying surge of self-confidence at the thought that someone could actually get pleasure from touching her that way. The skiing was still important, still the driving force in her life, but at last she had something else. She had Chris.

The press had begun to refer to Nicki as Chris's fiancée, and this time she hadn't objected. Nicki had already made her commitment to him and, although they had not yet made love, in her mind they were lovers.

The press also began to make Nicki a star. No woman had ever taken gold medals in all three Olympic events, and that was what Nicki knew was expected of her. As a result, her race schedule was much more strenuous than Chris's, who only did slalom and continued to have an off-season. Often he would be finished and ready to relax when she would be skiing back-to-back events and trying to maintain the mental competitive edge that she needed to win. Such was the case during her last competition at home in Aspen.

The event should have provided a festive foretaste of the Olympics, but weather conditions had deteriorated and races had been repeatedly canceled and rescheduled. Chris completed his event in the afternoon of the second day and he won, defeating two skiers who had beaten him several times in the past. He was euphoric.

Nicki was not scheduled to race in the giant slalom until the next morning. They had dinner together and returned to their respective quarters. Shortly thereafter, Chris came to her room with a bottle of champagne.

She tried to send him away, reminding him that she was still facing a major race, but he was obviously in a mood to celebrate. He got angry and accused her of not caring enough for him to toast his success. Finally, she let him in. She had only one glass of champagne, but Chris emptied the bottle, and it became clear that he had no intention of leaving.

For the past month they had teased and argued about whether or not they were going to sleep together. But that night Chris had been much more insistent than before. He felt the race had been a turning point for him and should be a turning point for them as well. He said all the right things about how important she was to him, how he needed to share the happiness he was feeling with her and how making love with him would prove that she shared his hopes for their future. He was charming and affectionate in a way that made an insecure seventeen-year-old feel womanly, and in the end, she gave in. Knowing it was her first time, he was reasonably gentle, and she felt as though she'd shared something special with someone she loved. She had curled up in his arms and they had fallen asleep.

The next thing she knew it was morning. She had overslept, and her stepfather was banging on her door, announcing that her coach was looking for her. There was no way for Chris to get out of the room, and nowhere for him to hide, so they both pulled on jeans and shirts and Nicki opened the door, hoping to step into the hall to talk to Max. But he pushed his way past her. As soon as he saw Chris, he drew to a halt, then looked at the unmade bed and back at Nicki. She would never forget the disgust in his eyes as he slapped her and told her that he had not wasted the last six years just so she could sleep around with every ski bum on the circuit.

She turned to Chris, expecting him to say something to defend her, but he simply stared at the floor. As Max stormed out of the room, he yelled back to Chris that any deal they had was off. She ran after Max, grabbed his arm and tried to explain that Chris hadn't hurt her or forced her into anything. They were in love. It had been her decision.

He brushed her aside, telling her that he was the one who made her decisions for her. Then he ordered her to report to her coach for the start of the race and walked away.

She went back to her room, hoping for a reassuring hug from Chris, but he had left. As she dressed, she knew that she was in no state to race. She was emotionally exhausted, couldn't stop crying and certainly wouldn't be able to concentrate on skiing. She wanted to tell her coach that she needed to scratch, but Max was waiting for her outside the dorm. He told her, with icy detachment, not to even think about canceling. She would ski and that was that.

It never occurred to her to fight him on the issue. Max had been right when he'd said he made her decisions. He had always taken care of everything for her, always controlled her professional life. Rather than being angry with him for making her ski, she was actually relieved that he was still interested in her career and wanted her to race. She didn't want to disappoint him.

By the time she got into starting position and adjusted her goggles, tears had frozen on her eyelashes and her stomach was in knots. She moved up against the starting wand in a daze and her reflexes shot her forward at the starting signal. She had memorized the blind turns and potential rough spots on the course, but her mind was empty except for an instinctive inner conviction that she owed Max, owed everyone, this race. She made the first gate but was a fraction too slow in her turn for the next one. As she gathered speed, she knew she should miss the gate, but that would disqualify her for the run and she couldn't make herself do it. She pulled hard to compensate, always a mistake but a critical, almost fatal one, in the snow conditions. She spun into a slide she couldn't correct, and as she plunged off the course and through the snow fence, the world turned upside down.

After all of the spills she'd taken in the past, she knew that this one was going to be different, not because of the pain but because of the absence of it. She had always felt in control when there had been pain. She'd known instinctively how to protect the part of her body that was hurting. But now there was no pain, no way to regain control—nothing. She was headed for nothing. She heard the crowd roar a collective "Oh my God," and then she had passed into darkness.

Nicki forced herself back to the present and groaned as she sat upright. She pushed herself off the bed and paced around the room as if to assure herself that she really could walk, then changed to her nightgown, poured herself another brandy and crawled back into bed. After cupping the glass in her hands for a minute to warm it, she took a sip of the tawny liquid, savoring it. It felt so good, so soothing going down, but she would not drink enough to dull her senses.

She didn't want to do anything to dull her recollection of the shame and anger she'd felt the night she realized exactly how she'd been betrayed.

Chris and Max, in their roles as her devoted lover and concerned stepfather, had made only one trip to the hospital. They had both wanted to be there to garner sympathy and mouth the proper platitudes at the press conference. In her room, under the guise of visiting her, they had had a heated, whispered argument while Nicki had pretended to be asleep.

She had been too blind to see that her talent had been their only hope for success. Now that hope had vanished—each blamed the other.

Max had accepted Chris so readily because the young man's physical appeal and ruthless approach to the development of a desirable public persona would enhance Nicki's image and earning power. Her stepfather had been confident that Nicki could bring him the medal he had coveted for so long, but he hadn't been at all certain that a little girl, totally absorbed in her skiing, could earn as much money as a more gregarious and fame-conscious athlete could. He had been counting on her to finance the skiing school that he intended to build after the Olympics, so he'd wanted an angle to make her as attractive as possible to the press. He'd found that in Chris Williams.

Max had offered to take Chris on as a hidden partner in return for Chris's agreeing to be known to the public as Nicki's love interest. When Nicki had become uncomfortable with the sham, Max had given Chris directions to make her believe that their romance was for real. But Chris's ego had led him to want to add Nicki to his list of conquests, and Max had not approved. He did not want her to break training, risk pregnancy, or marry before she had "earned out" for him, as he'd called it.

Chris had rallied brilliantly to his own defense, assuring Max that he had no intention of marrying Nicki. He had simply been trying to obey Max's request to keep her happy. She had wanted a lover. He had complied. Chris had been quick to point out that it was Max who had gotten angry over something that really had been no big deal. It had been Max who had overreacted and Max who had forced Nicki to ski, even though anybody who cared about her would have known she had been too upset to do well. Pulling out of the race would not have affected her team standing, but

Max had been more concerned about a potential sponsor in the crowd than in his stepdaughter's well-being.

Nicki took a last swallow of brandy and set the glass aside. Even now, over ten years later, she still blushed with embarrassment at the extent of her own gullibility.

Chris had disappeared from her life without so much as a goodbye. Her stepfather had stayed only long enough to get a divorce from her mother, making it clear that his interest in the family had ended along with Nicki's ability to win championships in his name. Her mother had had a breakdown, and Nicki had been left to pick up the pieces, not only of her life, but of Sarah's and their mother's as well.

So far, she had done a pretty good job of it, but she had almost allowed Doug to lead her on a detour from the path she had so carefully planned for herself. Fortunately, the painful reminder of her accident had enabled her to regain her perspective.

Nicki leaned forward to prop a pillow under her aching knee. She had learned her lesson once. Now she had remembered it. And if she could just keep herself from being swept up in Doug's charming grin, she might not forget it again.

CHAPTER ELEVEN

AS SOON AS DOUG saw Nicki the next morning, he knew he had trouble. She had greeted his cheery, "Morning, curly-top," with a grimace, managed to elude his attempt to claim a kiss and cursed audibly as she hobbled back to sit on the bed after opening the door for him. When informed that Dr. Doug MacNair only made house calls to very special patients, she had asked how she could get her name removed from the list. All in all, he'd decided, she was in a pretty vile mood.

He walked over to the bed and crouched on his heels in front of her. "Am I right in assuming that you aren't going to jump at the chance to share a romantic room-service breakfast with your favorite physician?"

She scowled at him. "I'm not even up to crawling, let alone 'jumping,' and if you'd ever sampled the cooking here, you'd reconsider as well. There's a fast-food joint down the road."

"Well, that could be fun too. What should I bring you?"

"Arsenic. I'm feeling suicidal."

"How about some painkillers instead?"

"No thanks. I told you, I thrive on pain."

Doug sighed deeply and stood up. "Actually, right now, you *are* being a bit of a pain. I'm just trying to be helpful."

"If you really want to help, you'll leave me here to sulk in peace and take Carol skiing. She can't go out alone, and I hate to have her weekend ruined because of me."

"I'd be happy to, but we can't ski all day. And I haven't had breakfast yet."

"Take Carol to breakfast. She'll love it. She thinks you're gorgeous."

"The kid's got taste, but I don't want to take Carol to breakfast. I want to spend some time with you."

"I never have much of an appetite when I'm dying."

"I'll order. You can watch me eat and see if you change your mind."

"Doug, read my lips. First you'll see an *N* then an *O* as in *no*. No. I don't want breakfast. No. I don't want to watch you eat. No. I don't even want you to keep me company. I want to lie here on the bed, whimper softly and be miserable. Go away."

"You're serious?"

Nicki flopped back on the bed and covered her eyes with her arm. "I'm ignoring you, Doug. You are no longer here."

He put his hands up as he backed to the door. "You're adorable when you're grumpy, you know that?"

He was laughing as he stepped into the hallway and bumped right into Carol.

"Good morning." She pointed to the door he was closing. "I was just going to check on Nicki."

"Bad idea. I don't think she wants any visitors. She's not too happy about having to slow down for a few days."

Carol sighed and shook her head. "Man, I know the feeling."

Doug hesitated for a moment. "I guess you do. I'm trying to understand what it must have been like for her, and for you, but it doesn't really touch me in a way I can relate to. I look at both of you and I see two attractive, intelligent, dynamic women. I guess you both feel like you lost the most important part of who you were, but you seem so complete to me. I just can't imagine her being anything better, anything more special than she is now."

"It's not necessarily a matter of better, Doug—just different. It's kind of like hearing yourself on a tape recorder, or seeing yourself on a video. No matter how good the voice sounds, or how terrific the face on the screen looks, it's never quite what you expected. There is always that disorienting first moment when you don't recognize yourself. Well, that's how I feel every morning when I wake up and realize I'm not quite what I expected to be." She winked. "Still terrific, mind you, but different. It can be pretty confusing."

"And you think Nicki feels the same way?"

Carol nodded. "I stole the idea from her." She rested her hand on Doug's arm. "If you're really serious about wanting to understand what Nicki's been through, I have a book you ought to read."

"A book? Great." He paused. "But I never discuss literature on an empty stomach. Could I interest you in breakfast?"

"Breakfast, lunch, dinner, mention food—I'm interested."

After a quick meal, Doug and Carol spent the morning and early afternoon skiing and talking. Carol's stories about Nicki and the way she handled her cases confirmed Doug's suspicions. In spite of Nicki's efforts to play the part of the detached businesswoman, she genuinely cared about all of her clients and had provided not only legal counsel but moral support. No doubt Nicki got a lot of satisfaction from helping others who were going through what she had gone through, but Doug was more determined than ever to convince her that she also had to save some time for herself.

When they returned to the lodge to pick Nicki up for the drive home, she was standing in the ski shop with Billy. She smiled and waved to them. Doug thought that she must be feeling a little better, but when she walked to the car, he could see that her limp was much more pronounced than usual.

He got out to secure her skis to the roof rack, and Carol started to move to the back, but Nicki stopped her. "I need to be able to stretch out, if that's okay." She slid onto the back seat, put her feet up and pulled her ski jacket over her head.

For most of the drive, Nicki dozed and Carol chattered on about her upcoming wedding and what a difference falling in love had made in her life. Only when she concluded her monologue by telling Doug, in a louder than necessary stage whisper, that Nicki ought to try finding a love interest too, did the lump in the back seat stir.

"Matchmaking is such a nasty habit." Nicki stretched and yawned. "Especially when one is so obvious about it."

Carol shrugged. "You can't blame me for trying."

"Sure I can. Just because romance is high on your list of life's little necessities doesn't mean everybody has the same priorities."

"I suppose, but Eric sure means more to me than a gold medal would have. The accident changed a lot of things, some for the worse, but some for the better, too. Going to a regular college and meeting Eric was a good thing. So is my relationship with my parents. I never really felt like a part of the family while I was training. I hardly ever saw them. But now we've gotten close again and it's fun." Carol twisted around in her seat to face Nicki. "Maybe that's why I adjusted a little faster to what happened than you did. My whole family rallied around me. You had to deal with your stepfather running out and your mother being unable to cope. That was tough."

Doug sensed Nicki stiffen, just as she always did when her stepfather was mentioned. He glanced in the rearview mirror just in time to see her put her finger to her lips and shake her head at Carol. So there were still some things she didn't want him to know. He had been hoping they'd moved beyond that. He sighed to himself. Well, as he'd told her once, he was a patient man.

WHEN THEY ARRIVED back at Nicki's apartment building, Carol announced that she was leaving immediately so she could pick Eric up at the airport. Doug loaded her equipment in her car while Nicki and Carol said goodbye.

"You will come for the wedding, won't you?"

"I'll be there. I promise."

"Bring Doug."

"That I won't promise."

"You're making a mistake, Nicki. He's a nice guy, to say nothing of his being a hunk, and I think he really cares about you. You ought to give him a chance." She took Nicki's hand and squeezed it. "I was afraid to trust Eric at first, too, and look how well that turned out. Life is a lot easier when you've got someone else to lean on now and then."

"For some people that's probably true, but you forget, I spent two years fighting to get off crutches. I like walking on my own."

"Whatever you say, but he sure looks like a keeper to me."

"Well, well, talking fishing again, Nicki?" Doug came up beside them wearing a big grin.

Nicki felt herself blush. "How long have you been eavesdropping?"

"I just got here in time for Carol's closing argument." He turned to Carol. "Thanks for the vote of confidence."

Nicki gave her friend a goodbye hug. "You better get going or Eric will think you forgot him."

Doug and Nicki waved as Carol pulled away. Then Nicki bent down to pick up her bag. Doug beat her to it. "Believe me, it won't represent a return to your crutches if you let me carry your luggage."

"I thought you didn't hear anything I said."

"I lied."

Inside the lobby, Nicki jabbed angrily at the elevator button, then turned on him. "You know, I'm getting pretty damn tired of hearing that."

He looked stunned. "Hearing what?"

"You know 'what.' You lie whenever it suits your purposes and then you seem to think that admitting it makes it okay. Well it doesn't. And don't you dare tell me they're just little lies because, as far as I'm concerned, there are no such things."

The elevator came and they rode up in silence. She opened her door and Doug followed her into the apartment and took her things to the bedroom while she checked the answering machine. The first three messages were from Ron wanting reports on work she was doing. The next one started with a stammered, "Ah, hi, ah, Ms Devlin..."

Doug reached around her and turned off the machine. "I'm sorry."

"What are you doing?" She reached for the button again and he grabbed her hand.

"I'm apologizing, Nicki. I said 'I'm sorry.'"

"So?"

"So you're supposed to forgive me."

"Really? Just like that? I don't think I'll play your game just now, thanks." She turned on the machine again.

"This is Ian, Ian Dorchester. I'd kind of like to talk to you, if you have time. I'll be at the gym Sunday afternoon until around five."

It was already after four. Nicki limped across the room to get her briefcase.

"Where do think you're going?"

"Come on, Doug. Don't pretend you didn't hear that. You were standing two feet from the machine."

"I heard. And I say you're staying right here. You can barely walk."

"Don't give me orders, Doctor. What am I supposed to do about Ian?"

"The kid will call again. It didn't sound like an emergency. He just wants to talk."

"For him, that's a major breakthrough. I'm not going to stand him up." She tried to brush past Doug and stumbled against a chair.

"If you aren't careful, you aren't going to stand up period. Be reasonable, Nicki. You're hurting. Is this ridiculous case more important to you than your own body?"

"This 'ridiculous case,' as you call it, is as important to me as your patients are to you. It involves real people who need my help." She went to the hall closet and pulled out the cane that she'd saved for emergencies like this.

Doug took it out of her hand. "I can't let you leave when you're like this."

She snatched the cane back. "I'm afraid it's not up to you. It took me a while, but I've developed the habit of making my own decisions."

"Well, if this is the kind of decision you make, you sure aren't very good at it. Why can't you let someone with a little more common sense take control until you learn how?"

Nicki felt such a hot flash of anger that she couldn't even speak for a minute. She walked over to the door and yanked it open. "Get out of here, Doug. Get out before I do or say something that I'll regret later."

"If you keep putting your business and your clients before yourself, you'll look back on your life someday and realize that you have plenty to regret. I just hope you wake up before it's too late."

He took the stairs rather than the elevator, and as Nicki heard his footsteps receding, she felt more empty and confused than angry. She had decided last night to terminate their relationship. So why was she upset that an argument had accomplished what she'd planned to do anyway? Maybe it was because she felt a little guilty for having steered him into a quarrel. Doug had no idea what memories had visited her during the night. He had no reason to believe that anything had changed between them, yet she had been trying to distance herself from him all day, and she knew she had jumped at the chance to challenge him for lying.

As Nicki slipped on her jacket and started for her car, her anger began to build anew. Why should she feel guilty? Blaming herself was proof that she was falling back into old patterns. Doug had tried to step in and control her actions in a way she could never allow anyone to do again.

When Nicki arrived at the gym, Ian was already there. He watched her as she made her way across the weight room, leaning heavily on her cane.

"Leg acting up?" he asked as she lowered herself onto the bench beside him.

"Yeah. It's no big deal—all a part of being 'gimpy.'"

He looked at the floor. "I'm sorry about that. That was a rotten thing to say."

"True. But I'll forgive you this time. What did you want to talk about?"

"Nothing much. I thought you might help me with that weight program, but it doesn't look like you're up to it today."

"We can work on it. I don't have to be able to lift to help you."

"That would be great." He handed her a dog-eared index card. "That's what I used to do before the attack."

Nicki studied the workout notes carefully. They indicated someone who was very serious about lifting. "You were doing an awful lot of weight for someone your age. Did your coach know about this?"

"He knew. It didn't cut in on the swimming."

Nicki looked at the card again. "Okay, I've got a few ideas about where to begin. But first I want to know what changed your mind about wanting me to help you."

"That book you sent me."

"I didn't send you anything, Ian."

"But I'm sure it came from your office." He began to rummage in his gym bag and finally pulled out a copy of *To Dance No More*. "This one. I got it Friday, special delivery."

Nicki took the book from him and began to flip through it. This must have been what Carol had stopped at the office for, to have Ron forward a copy of the book to Ian.

"I haven't finished it yet, but there are a lot of places where I felt like you were inside of me writing down exactly what I was feeling—like all the guilt stuff. I know it will make my folks happy if you find some way to blame the hospital for what happened, but you and I both know, I'm the one to blame. I forgot the insulin. I decided to swim anyway. It's my fault and no one else's."

"Ian, I know it's hard not to blame yourself. That's part of an athlete's training—when we lose it's our fault and no one else's—but your situation is different from mine. I made all my mistakes myself and those mistakes are what caused my injury. In your case, something went wrong at the hospital, and we have to determine what and why. Maybe someone was at fault, maybe you were just unlucky.''

"But your stepfather made you ski, so wasn't it his fault?"

"I could have told him no. He didn't have the power to make me ski. I just didn't have the courage to disappoint him."

"And you ended up letting everyone down, just like I did. My diving was always the most important thing to the whole family, and I promised them I wouldn't let anything interfere with that. Then I had to go and forget my insulin before the first really big meet. My folks were against that camping trip in the first place. I couldn't disappoint them by not swimming."

He leaned forward to rest his elbows on his knees and bounced his gym bag on the floor in front of him. "So now I've ruined everything they had planned for me."

"What about what you had planned for you?"

"I didn't have plans. I just wanted to keep winning. I'll never be able to do anything else that will make people as proud of me as the diving did. It's like you said in the book. Winning wasn't just something I did for me, it was the way I paid everyone back. As long as I was winning, they couldn't expect anything else from me. Now I've got nothing to offer."

"That's not true, Ian. There are a lot of things you can do to make people proud of you and, more importantly, to make you proud of yourself."

Their conversation was interrupted by the boisterous laughter of four young men carrying racquetball racquets, who passed by on their way to the locker room. Ian's eyes followed their progress.

"Ms Devlin, when you were skiing, did you have a lot of friends?"

"I knew most of the skiers who were competing the same years I was."

"I mean real friends. Not people you had to go out and race against the next day, but people you could talk to about what you were feeling, or just hang around with."

"No, I didn't really have any friends like that." She felt a twinge of sadness both for herself and for him.

"Do you now?"

"No, not now, either. I'm still sort of a loner."

"Me too, but I don't really like it that way."

"Then why don't you change it?"

"I don't know how. What do I do, walk up to a group of guys that have been buddies for years and say I want to make friends?"

"If you want it badly enough it's worth a try."

"Yeah, I guess so, but it's kind of scary." He began to bounce his gym bag again. "Didn't you ever feel like you just wanted it all to go away, like you wanted to go to sleep and never wake up?"

"I did at first, but that faded pretty fast. Do you still think that way now?" She hoped her voice didn't reveal her concern.

"Not so often anymore. But I get tired of people always feeling sorry for me."

"Ian, that's not going to stop until you get to the point where you stop feeling sorry for yourself."

"I'm working on that, but it doesn't seem like it's ever gonna happen." He stood up. "Do you still want to work with me on the weights?"

"I'd love to, but do you really need me or did you just want someone to talk to?"

"Both." He grinned and offered her a hand to help her up. "Do you mind?"

"Of course not, I'm just glad you're talking to someone."

"Once I started reading about you, I thought maybe you would understand. But it was a long time ago for you. I wasn't sure you'd remember how it felt."

"I wish I could tell you that it goes away, Ian, but I still remember like it was yesterday. You just have to learn how to live around it." She picked up his weight card and walked toward the lifting benches. It was easy for her to talk to him as if everything would be okay, but he seemed to be balanced on such a fragile thread. She worried how he was going to react to the day-to-day realizations of how his life had changed—to the little things like having to reduce the amount of weight he could lift. She would just have to try to be there when he needed her.

Ian stood next to her, watching, as she made notations in the margin of his card. "I hope I can get to where you are someday," he said while kneeling down to begin slipping weights on the bar. "And I'm not talking about with weights."

She rested her hand on his shoulder. "Ian, I hope you can get a lot further than that, and I'm not talking about weights, either."

BY FRIDAY, Nicki's leg was feeling much better, but the rest of her was exhausted. It had been difficult getting around all week and tiring to be in constant pain. She had worked long hours on the projects for Ron, set up some meetings with possible expert witnesses for the investigation of Ian's case and tried to keep up with lesson preparations and lecture notes.

In addition, she had seen Ian several afternoons during the week, and each time she was with him, she found herself becoming more and more concerned by his volatile mood swings. He could flash from being funny, to sullen, to nasty with no warning or apparent motivation.

To make matters worse, her concentration had been off all week. Although she hadn't had time to dwell on her argument with Doug, she could never get him completely out of her mind. She had to admit that she was nervous about seeing him in her Friday class, and yet she was looking forward to it. She knew she secretly hoped that he would make some attempt to talk to her.

She waited in the hall outside the classroom, but it was Stephanie, not Doug, who approached her.

"Hi, Nicki. Drs. MacNair and Carlson are tied up in a very important meeting, so they sent me over to sit in on the class for them."

Nicki swallowed a wave of disappointment and wondered if Doug was just using this as an excuse to avoid her. "Sure, that's fine."

"Okay if I tape?"

"If you do me a favor in return. I need some expert advice on a client of mine."

"How about going for coffee and consultation after class?"

"Deal."

The classroom discussion had been a lively one, and Nicki felt as though she had gotten some very important points across. When she and Stephanie had left the law building to walk to the coffee shop, her favorite type of snow had been falling—big fluffy flakes that quickly made a soft blanket on the ground and pillows of every bush. Snow like that was something she'd missed since moving to Chicago, where everything became dirty slush so quickly. She sighed contentedly as she took a taste of her Viennese coffee.

"Unwinding at the end of the day?" Stephanie asked.

"A little. I still have a lot of work ahead of me tonight, but right now I'm feeling pretty lazy."

"You should be feeling pretty proud. You are a terrific teacher."

Nicki smiled. "Thanks. I really enjoy it. I always thought I'd never be happy doing anything other than trial work, but this has been a great experience. I'll hate for it to end."

"Can't you do some teaching in Chicago?"

"Oh sure, but it's hard to fit it in with a full-time practice going."

"If you enjoy it so much, make room for it."

"Of course, no problem. Why didn't I think of that?" She waved her hand and grinned. "I almost forgot you were one of Doug's disciples." She took another sip of coffee. "Listen, I didn't intend to talk about me. I want your advice about a young client of mine who is having some trouble rebounding emotionally from an injury—off the record—nothing to do with damages, pain and suffering or any of the legal goodies, I'm just really worried about him."

Nicki proceeded to tell Stephanie about Ian's background, what she knew about his relationship with his family and his behavior since his accident. "He swings from high to low before you can blink, and his depressions are so black they are frightening."

Stephanie shook her head. "Well, there's not much I can tell you. He obviously needs help. I wish you could talk him into coming in for counseling, preferably with his parents."

"I've tried. He says his parents are against it, and he's begged me not to talk to them about it. I can't go behind his back."

"No. At least not yet. It sounds like you're the only one he trusts enough to talk to right now. You have to stay on his side. He's lucky he has someone who can understand his situation so well."

Nicki folded her hands under her chin. "What makes you think I would have any special insight?"

"From things Doug has said, I assume that you must have experienced a lot of the same problems that Ian is having."

"Since when has Doug been talking to people about me?"

"When isn't Doug talking about you? He's been bending my ear since Sunday."

Nicki's heart began to beat a little faster. "Oh? And just what did he tell you about Sunday?"

"That he was a jerk. You called him on it. He apologized. You wouldn't forgive him. He got upset and was an even bigger jerk than he'd been in the first place. You kicked him out. He deserved it. But, 'Damn it, she works too hard.' And he hopes he didn't blow it, but he thinks maybe he did, and how long do I think he should wait before he calls you?"

Nicki smiled and shook her head. "Sounds like a full report. How long is he going to wait?"

"Let's see. I think he's actually going to talk to you this weekend, but in the meantime, he calls your machine two or three times a day just to hear your voice, then hangs up."

"I've been wondering about all those calls." She sat back for a moment to revel in the knowledge that he'd wanted to hear her voice. "Don't you feel guilty for telling me about your confidential conversations?"

"Heck no. He's not paying for my time. But please say that you do intend to make it up with him soon so I can get back to my own life. He's becoming a pest and you know how jealous Paul is."

"How's it going with Paul?"

"All the signs are hopeful. I can't believe the difference in him. He even took Monday off so we could spend the day together. I was sure he'd be calling the office every five minutes, but he never mentioned work once—amazing. I owe you for that one."

"I really didn't do anything, but if you want to feel indebted that's okay with me. I'm probably going to need continuing counsel on Ian."

"That I'll give, gladly, but please do something to get Doug off my doorstep, will you?"

"I can't believe he doesn't have a whole harem of beautiful women to keep him busy. Why me?"

"Probably because he thinks you're terrific. And don't kid yourself about Doug's harem. He's always been a pretty reserved guy—too busy for a social life and all that. Doug the debonair is as new to him as it is to you."

"So everyone keeps telling me." She shrugged. "I'm afraid I can't make any promises about taking him off your hands though. Every time we're together we argue."

"You'll get used to it. That's just the way Doug is."

"Charming." Nicki glanced at her watch. "I've got to get going. Ian will be expecting me at the gym." She put some money on the table to pay the bill. "This one's on me. Thanks for the advice."

"I didn't say much." Stephanie reached out to stop her from leaving. "Listen, Nicki, I said you're important to Ian right now, and I meant it, but you can't run yourself ragged trying to help him or you won't be able to help anyone."

"I know my limitations, Steph, and by the way, you can pass that on to Doug. Take care and keep your eye on Paul."

"Both eyes, and you take care, too."

"Believe me, I'm trying to do just that."

CHAPTER TWELVE

DOUG HAD JUST FINISHED with his last patient and was putting on his sport coat when Paul burst into his office and clapped him on the back.

"I see you're off to spend the weekend celebrating. Congratulations, buddy."

"I'm off to brood about whether to call Nicki tonight or tomorrow and what are you talking about?"

"Come on, Doug, why do you think they didn't adjourn the risk management meeting when you said you had to leave?"

"So you guys could talk about me behind my back?"

"Exactly. Bailey took advantage of the opportunity to drop some subtle hints as to who he thought would do the best job as Director of Risk Management. He made it quite clear that, as far as he's concerned, you are the only choice."

"Great. That's really great." Doug knew he should be elated, but after spending all afternoon contemplating the best way to get back into Nicki's good graces, he couldn't help but focus on the problems this development would cause.

"Doug, what is the matter with you? You've been working toward getting this position for two years. Now it's almost in the bag and you're miserable."

"It's nothing. I was just thinking about Nicki, that's all."

"Makes you feel that good, does she? She might not be as perfect for you as you think." Paul sat down on the chair facing Doug and slouched casually against the arm.

"She's perfect all right. It's just that she might not see it that way."

"Hmm. I don't know. She's a pretty feisty little thing, she'll probably want some say in the matter."

"Exactly. And as soon as she hears about this, what she's going to say is that dating me is impossible."

"If I go out and come in again, is there a chance this conversation is going to start making sense to me?"

"Given how slow you are, I doubt it, but I'll try to explain it to you. Nicki is a malpractice attorney and I am a physician."

"Should I be taking notes?"

Doug glared at him. "Our respective professions, in and of themselves, present enough opportunities for disagreements. Add the complication that Nicki is currently investigating a case that may result in her having to file a lawsuit..."

"...against the hospital where you will be serving as Director of Risk Management."

"And taking an active role in all decisions involving how the hospital will defend itself against such lawsuits."

"Sounds like a conflict of interest to me."

"Give the man a cigar." Doug put his head in his hands. "So what am I going to do? She's always looking for a reason to shut me down and this sure sounds like a good one. Even I have to admit that we could have a problem."

"So? She doesn't have to find out yet, does she?"

"Oh no you don't. Remember how I got in trouble with her in the first place. I'm not going to lie again."

"You're not lying. There's no guarantee you'll get the position. It's not official until the announcement is made, which won't be for a couple of weeks. In the meantime, she may decide she has no case."

"Keep talking. You're starting to convince me."

"There's no point in dooming the relationship before it even has a chance, over something that might never happen."

"Right. And as long as I'm willing to take the consequences, I won't really be doing anything wrong."

"Consequences?"

"If Nicki does decide to file a suit, I'll have to turn down the directorship or we *will* have a conflict."

"Couldn't you just say you wouldn't be involved in that case?"

"I don't know. Maybe. I'd have to do whatever Nicki felt was necessary."

"Doug, you hardly know each other. Are you saying that you would really throw away your whole future over this?"

"The future is full of possibilities, Paul, and right now I would do almost anything to be certain that Nicki Devlin could be one of those possibilities."

"I haven't seen you like this since Clarissa."

"A painful reminder that I could be making a big mistake, but I don't think so. Clarissa was selfish and uncaring. Nicki's problem is that she cares too much." He smiled. "She's much too dedicated."

"Which should be something you can understand."

"I can understand it all right. I just hope I can do something about it."

"If I were you, Doug, I'd back down on that one for a while. Nicki loves what she does and she's good at it, but all you do is give her constant grief about it."

"I'm just concerned for her. I don't want her pushing herself so hard."

"And how hard did you push at her age? Give it up, Doug. You've made your opinion clear. She's rejected it. She'll decide for herself when a change is in order. You just have to decide if you'll be able to settle for what she's willing to give you."

"Which is exactly why I have to take a chance with the directorship. I want to find out just how much she is willing to give. I have a feeling it's going to be worth it."

"Frankly, I think it is, too, but I hope you get to have both." Paul stood up and straightened his tie. "Good luck with your lady. I'm on the way to spend a blissful weekend with mine."

Doug watched his friend leave and debated whether to call Nicki that evening or to wait until Saturday. Actually, he didn't want to wait to call her period. He'd make a stop at his house to set the mood, then he'd just show up on her doorstep.

When he rang Nicki's bell a few hours later, it was Sarah, not Nicki, who answered the door, and it was obvious that she had been crying.

"Sarah, hi. What's the matter?" Doug put a protective arm around her shoulder and stepped into the apartment.

"Nothing. I was watching a sad movie. I just came up from my place to check something in Blake's files." She took some letters and photos from the coffee table, hurriedly threw them in an empty box and carried it down the hall to what Doug assumed was Blake's study.

When she returned, she seemed somewhat more composed. "I suppose you came by hoping to find Nicki and not me."

He smiled. "I admit that was my plan. And since you're already taken, I might as well stick by it."

"Chauvinist. For your information, I haven't been 'taken' by anybody. Right or wrong, I make my own choices."

"Hey, I'm sorry. I didn't mean it to sound that way. My mouth has been getting me into a lot of trouble lately, especially with the Bernard sisters."

Sarah sighed. "No, I'm the one who is sorry. I'm a little, no a lot, on edge today. Forgive me."

He nodded and Sarah sat down and signaled for him to do the same. "Doug, my last name is Bernard, but don't ever let Nicki hear you refer to her that way. She might let it pass but, trust me, it'll hurt her a lot."

Again he nodded. "I know that. I wouldn't have said it in front of her. And I'm embarrassed to admit, I probably only said it now because my curiosity is getting the best of me. Am I going to get the answer to what happened between Nicki and your stepfather by reading *To Dance No More*?"

"She gave you the book? I can't believe it. She hates it."

"She didn't give it to me. Carol Stuart did."

"Good for her. I've always liked Carol."

"You know her?"

"Sure. Nicki makes her special clients into family. It's part of the Nicki Devlin moral support structure, which, by the way, she will deny exists."

"What about Max Bernard?"

"Ah, dear Daddy. Yes, the book will give you the basic facts. Max married mother so that he could be more than Nicki's coach. He liked the idea of having a future Olympian take his name. When Nicki had her accident and could no longer compete, he dumped the whole family and moved on to another protégé. What the book won't tell you is how much that hurt Nicki, and I'm afraid I can't tell you, either, because she won't even talk to me about it. He was a user, and Nicki trusted him completely. I don't think she's ever forgiven herself for not seeing through him."

"She was just a kid."

"No excuse. Nicki doesn't believe in excuses—at least not for her own behavior."

"She's too hard on herself."

"Maybe, but I think it's a matter of her wanting to be able to say, 'You can't take any satisfaction from this because you didn't hurt me. I hurt myself.' Nicki thinks it is important to take full responsibility for your own mistakes. Then you have the power to be sure that the same mistakes don't get made again. It may seem easier to keep blaming everything that goes wrong on someone else, but then you also have to be willing to admit that it's that someone else, and not you, who is in control."

"And what about those situations that are truly beyond your control?"

"That's easy for Nicki. She doesn't acknowledge that there are any."

"That's ridiculous."

"Tell her, not me. I'm perfectly willing to blame my problems on anyone who comes along."

"Like me this afternoon?"

"Like you this afternoon. But I already apologized for that, so let's get to the point of your visit. Nicki is not here. I assume she is out somewhere with Ian, who is her latest responsibility. She'll be back sometime after he goes home for dinner, and she'll probably want to work. Ron the remora has just sent her another package." Sarah pointed to a thick express mail envelope.

"You sound bitter."

"To put it mildly. She doles herself out in pieces to whomever wants something from her, until there's not enough left."

"Not enough left for you? She wasn't here when you needed a shoulder to cry on, is that it?"

"I ought to slug you for that one, but I'll let you get away with it this time. The last time you saw Nicki and me together we had a fight, the first one in years, and it was my fault. Don't let it give you a distorted picture of the way things are. Nicki is the most important and most stable influence in my life. She's always been there for me, no matter what it's cost her personally or financially. When I cry to anyone it's to Nicki, and if Nicki ever cried to anyone, it would be to me."

"But, of course, she doesn't."

"Not for herself. She keeps all that bottled up inside her, but I've seen her cry for others many times. Nicki's problem is she doesn't think she deserves to cry. She blames herself for having had that accident and disappointing everyone who was counting on her to be a champion. She's spent the rest of her life trying to make up for that, one way or another. She completely supported mother and me until Mom remarried three years ago. She still pays all my school expenses and meets her imagined debt to Mom by continuing her ridiculous, one-sided partnership with Ron Foley, who is the son of Mom's husband's sister. And then, of course, she picks up strays along the way."

"Strays?"

"Like Ian Dorchester. The kid needs help. Nicki sees it as her mission to provide it. And the fact is, she's good at it. She shores you up so invisibly that you actually believe you're doing it all on your own. And eventually you gain enough self-confidence to do just that."

"That's a real gift."

"Nicki has always been gifted. Unfortunately, she has let her gifts become a burden to her."

"So why doesn't she change that?"

Sarah shrugged. "Either she doesn't want to or she doesn't know how to."

"I sure wish I knew which it was, because I'd like to help her."

"For her benefit or yours?"

"Meaning what?"

"Meaning, if you want Nicki to change her life because she's wearing herself to a frazzle, I'm with you all the way, but if you just want her to shove aside things that are important to her so she'll have more room for you, forget it. Then you're just using her like the rest of us."

"I wish I could honestly say it's all of the first and none of the second, but you know better than that. I think it would be good for her to start demanding her right to have a personal life. I also hope she'll want me in that personal life once she gets it."

"And she said you weren't an honest man."

"I wasn't, but she's cured me."

"Then let me ask another question and see if you'll be as candid this time. Why are you so interested in Nicki? Your careers are incompatible. You don't really understand where she's been or where she hopes to go. In fact, you haven't even known her long enough to know where she is right now. Yet, you are insistent on pursuing her. Why?"

He grinned. "That's easy—chemistry."

"Baloney. Blake's used that one on me. I don't buy it."

"No? That's too bad, because I don't know any better way to explain it. She's attractive, intelligent, witty and has more integrity than anyone I've ever met. But the reason I'm 'pursuing' her, as you call it, is because being around her makes me feel..." He stopped.

"Feel good?" Sarah volunteered.

"No, just *feel*—good, happy, content, tender—but also sad, melancholy and angry. It doesn't really matter which, it's the intensity of the emotion that overwhelms me. That and the fact that I can't seem to control it.''

"I didn't think you self-proclaimed handsome playboy types ever admitted to any emotions."

"We don't. You have to know how to read it all in our eyes."

"Your eyes?"

"Sure. That's how I know what Nicki's feeling. She thinks she never lets anything show, but her eyes are a give-away. So are yours."

"Really? Then that's my cue to leave before you observe too much. Besides, having presented Nicki's view of life and responsibility to you reminds me that I have some things to see to on my own. Are you going to wait here for Nicki?"

"Do you think that's all right?"

"Depends. Are you planning on stealing her valuables?"

"No, just her heart, and I promise I won't do that when she's not looking."

"Bad promise, Doug. That might be the only way you'll get it."

"I hope not. I'm really not a playboy, you know."

"I never believed that you were, but then I've been fooled before."

Doug jumped as Elmo leaped into his lap. "See? I have a character witness."

Sarah looked at the cat with distaste. "That beast has no character of his own so he can't possibly vouch for yours. But that's okay. I'm rooting for you anyway." She blew him a kiss on her way out.

Doug noticed that when Sarah left, she picked up a suit-case and trench coat. Odd for someone who had just stopped in from downstairs. He shrugged, settled into the rocking chair, took out his copy of *To Dance No More* and began to read aloud to Elmo.

NICKI OPENED THE DOOR of her apartment to see Doug hurriedly putting a book in his briefcase. She fought back a rush of pleasure and tried to sound displeased. "What are you doing here? How did you get in?"

"Hello to you, too. Waiting to take you to dinner. Sarah was here when I dropped by to pick you up."

"Did we have a date?"

"No."

"I didn't think so."

"I just decided on the spur of the moment to kidnap you, take you to my place and cook you dinner."

"I could have you put in jail for that." Feigning lack of interest, Nicki pretended to flip through her mail as she watched him out of the corner of her eye. He looked as handsome as ever in a deep orange crew neck sweater and gray pleated corduroys.

"Why don't you wait until you taste my cooking—spinach salad with homemade dressing, warm croissants, succulent prime fillets, an impeccable béarnaise sauce, a nice Bordeaux..."

"And..."

"And?"

"Think hard. What's missing?"

He looked puzzled for a moment then raised a finger. "Got it. And a baked potato with a gallon of sour cream."

"Let me feed Elmo and I'll be right with you."

"Just like that? We don't have to fight about it? I don't have to beg?"

"Nope. You said the magic words and I'm starving. Besides, I owe Stephanie a favor."

"Sounds like I do too. I'll send her flowers."

"Good idea. Keep Paul on his toes."

Nicki fed Elmo and changed out of her camel's hair suit and into dark brown wool slacks, a pale yellow cashmere turtleneck and tan leather blazer.

When she walked back into the living room, Doug whistled. "That's what I like. A woman in leather."

"I thought it might be your style." As much as she hated to admit it, that was exactly what she'd been thinking when she'd bought the blazer.

They maintained their jovial mood on the drive to Doug's house. Nicki again experienced the familiar feeling of contentment that came so often when she was with him. She enjoyed the sound of his voice, especially when he laughed, and the way he cocked his head when he was teasing her or being teased. She liked the easy way he rested his hand on her knee when he was trying to make a point, or against the small of her back as he guided her to the car or through a doorway. She had certainly dated men who had touched her more possessively, even more intimately, but no one had ever touched her with more affection. When she was with Doug, she felt secure, protected and loved. All things she'd never experienced before and all things she was afraid to rely on now. When they got to his house, Doug presented her with a glass of sherry and ushered her into the solarium. "I turned the heat up, how does it feel to you?"

"Delightful." She stepped over to the glass wall to look out. "I love weather like this, and being in this room when it's snowing is just as enchanting as I thought it would be."

"I take it I was correct in assuming you'd want to eat out here?" Doug nodded toward a table already set with white linen, crystal and candles. "Do you want to stay and daydream or accompany me to the kitchen to witness the cooking process?"

"It's a tough choice, but I guess I'll come along. I love a spectacle."

As soon as Nicki realized that Doug intended to make his béarnaise sauce from scratch, she was perfectly happy to settle back and let him handle the meal preparation. After an hour of watching his slapstick version of a television cooking show, she was as weak from laughter as she was from hunger. How he had managed to put on such a show of being inept while producing such a marvelous meal she would never know.

But when they sat down to eat, everything was delicious. Pushing her chair back from the table slightly, Nicki sighed. "That was truly outstanding. I'm impressed." She swirled the remaining wine in her glass and studied the way it caught the light from the candles.

"I'm glad you enjoyed it."

"I enjoy you, Doug. And don't ask me why I needed to say that, I just did." Feeling herself flush with embarrassment, she leaned back and turned to look out the window. The gentle winter snow had become a blizzard, and as she watched the flakes swirl by, she acknowledged another storm beginning within her. "I guess I wanted you to know that all your efforts to teach me how to have fun aren't being wasted."

He smiled softly. "Having fun with you is effortless, curly-top. I'm not teaching you anything. I'm just doing what I want to do." He got up and went into the living room. A slow, rhythmic, popular tune replaced the classical music that had been playing, and he came back to stand behind her chair. "What I'd like to do right now is dance with you."

"I don't dance."

"Why not?"

"Isn't that fairly obvious?"

"Not to me. I'd like you to explain."

"Why are you forcing me to say it?"

"Because I want to know if you will trust me with the truth."

Nicki bent her head and massaged her temples with her thumbs but said nothing. She heard Doug leave the room again. When he came back, he leaned against the door frame and held out a copy of *To Dance No More*.

Nicki walked over and took the book from him. "If you've read this, you already know the answer. I have nothing more to tell you."

"I'd like to hear it from you."

"I can't say it any better."

"Then say it that way, but say it."

She watched him through narrowed eyes, unable to decipher his purpose, but unwilling to run from his challenge. She turned the pages and began to read.

Anyone who has ever stood at the start of a major competition will tell you that just before the starter gives the sign, there is an almost eerie feeling of calm in the air. The athlete is poised and ready, the crowd is leaning forward in anticipation, and yet, for an extra heartbeat or two, nothing happens. It is in that final moment that every competitor must do whatever it takes to conquer the fear.

Some say a prayer. Some swear. Those who want calm conjure up the image of a loved one; those who need the anger visualize an enemy. Whatever the technique, it becomes a ritual, a good-luck charm, an almost sacred rite. And they know that if they ever forsake it, they will fail.

I needed to maintain my sense of rhythm and flow, to move smoothly through all the patterns that had become instinctive after the long years of training. I had always loved to dance, to close my eyes, listen to the music and let my body respond. It all seemed so effortless, so familiar, so safe. When I danced I felt totally relaxed. And in the final seconds before every race, I found my strength and my peace by closing my eyes, taking a deep breath and telling myself, "It's just like dancing."

Every race except one. That day I was upset—wallowing in self-pity over what I felt had been a terrible wrong, yet afraid that the mistake might, in fact, have been mine. I got into position against the starting wand, glanced at the starter and waited. I knew I didn't want to ski. I knew I was in no condition to ski, but I heard the starting signal and pushed off, catapulting through the wishbone. Taking the fear with me.

Nicki closed the book, fixed her eyes on Doug's and finished the passage from memory. "As soon as I realized what I had done and felt the sickening sensation of moving without rhythm or control, I knew that this would be my last race. I knew that I would dance no more." She took a deep breath and released it slowly.

Doug put his hand under her chin. "Sarah was right. You don't cry for yourself do you?"

"Is that what you wanted? To see me cry?"

"I don't think so, but I'll admit that if you'd been with me when I read that the first time you would have seen a tear or two in my eyes."

"That's no test. You've confessed to liking sappy movies."

He shrugged. "Nicki, if you could tell that story to the complete strangers who bought the book, why couldn't you tell it to me?"

"Because the complete strangers had to be satisfied with that. Are you?"

"No."

"So what have we gained?"

"Not much yet, but maybe if you let yourself talk about it, you'll be able to put it behind you. How many people know exactly what happened that day?" She didn't respond and he sighed heavily. "All right, besides your stepfather and your boyfriend, who knows?"

She called on her experience in the courtroom to keep from showing her surprise. "No one else knows, although I'd imagine a lot of people, including you apparently, can venture a pretty good guess."

"Given the way those men abandoned you after the accident, why do you feel the need to protect them?"

"Who's protecting them? I'm protecting myself. Do you think I want the whole world to know how gullible I was?"

"Gullible, or vulnerable?"

"Both, either—sometimes I think they're the same."

"They aren't the same at all."

"You wouldn't say that so easily if you'd known that you put yourself in a position to be betrayed."

"What makes you think you're the only one to have ever made a mistake?" He held out his hand. "Let's sit. I want to tell you something."

She followed him to the wicker love seat and sat down. He went to the table to pour them each a cup of coffee, then joined her.

"I've had my gullible moments too. During the entire time I was in training to be a doctor, I never had a spare moment for a social life. I was either at the hospital or working at another job for extra money. Just as I was finishing up my residency, I met Clarissa. She was beautiful, rich, charming and, I thought, crazy about me. What she was really crazy about was the idea of marrying a doctor. We dated. I fell in love. We got engaged. Through it all

Clarissa made it very clear that she liked the idea of my career, but she didn't want me to spend any more time at it than was absolutely necessary. She had a heavy social schedule and had cast me in the role of desirable escort."

Doug blew on the hot coffee, took a tentative sip and set it aside. "Her parents threw us an elaborate engagement party, and after I'd already been there for several hours, I got a call from the hospital. One of the doctors was out of town, and the man who was supposed to be covering for him had food poisoning. They asked me if I could come in, and I didn't think I could say no. Clarissa was furious. I was still riding high on the idea of being important and irreplaceable, so I went off to do my duty, figuring I'd make it up to her later."

He leaned forward and massaged the back of his neck. "Well, there was no later. She said she wouldn't live her life with someone who put his career before his obligations to her. Maybe I should have been happy to get out of a relationship with someone who felt that way about my work, but I was crushed. I really did think I loved her."

Nicki rested her hand on his thigh. "Doug, I'm sorry."

"You haven't heard the best part. The patient I left my own engagement party to see was the one who sued me for malpractice."

"Oh no!"

"And as the final blow, when the case went to trial, my beloved fiancée got on the stand and testified that I had had several drinks that night, was angry about having to leave our party, and since we had had an argument, was probably very anxious to just get the delivery over with and rush back to her side. She did a good job of making it look as if I had any number of reasons to be careless or negligent."

"It sounds like she was just a bitter and vindictive woman. You can't blame yourself for what happened."

"Yes, I can. I wanted to believe that I could have an attractive woman interested in me. I felt like I'd lost touch with everything except medicine, and I was so grateful to have a chance to prove that I could fit into the right social circles that I didn't open my eyes to the warning signs. Fortunately, I didn't have to pay quite as high a price for my foolishness as you did."

"There are all kinds of scars, Doug, each equally significant to the bearer."

"I guess. Would you like to tell me about yours?"

Nicki arched an eyebrow. "Quid pro quo?"

"No." He took her hand and held it between both of his. "I wanted you to know about Clarissa. You don't owe anything in return."

"The surprising thing is, I think you actually mean that."

"I do. I'm interested in the woman you are today. But I also care about what's hurt you. Not knowing that makes me feel like I'm walking a tightrope blindfolded. One misstep and I'll fall off."

Nicki couldn't help grinning. "Especially tricky since you generally operate with one foot in your mouth." She paused to consider his sheepish look. For the first time since her accident, she really felt that she did want someone else to know what had happened. She wanted to lean against Doug and explain everything to him.

As if reading her mind, he put his arm around her shoulders and pulled her toward him. "Come here, Nicki. Whether you tell me anything or not, come here."

She settled into the curve of his arm. "There isn't that much to tell. I thought my stepfather stayed so involved in my career because he cared about my family and me. I thought Chris wanted to be with me all the time because he loved me. As it turned out, both of them saw me as nothing more than a valuable asset. What I believed to be the love of my life turned out to be a publicity angle."

"How old were you when you met Chris?"

"Seventeen. I know that sounds pretty young to make that kind of commitment, but I was too inexperienced to know any better. No matter what I did, I was always taught to give it my all, so that's what I gave him, my all."

"And you were with him on the day of your last race?"

She nodded. "My stepfather walked in on us. We had a terrible fight and I was an emotional wreck. I wanted to go to my coach and pull out of the race, but Max wouldn't hear of it. He said he was afraid it would ruin my image with the press and my standing on the team. I didn't want to disappoint him any more than I already had, so I tried to ski."

Doug tightened his arm around Nicki and pulled her closer. "After what he did to you, you were worrying about disappointing him. Why?"

"Because I didn't learn about any of that until after the accident. I believed he had a right to be upset. Most fathers would be if they discovered their daughter and her lover together. He was furious with Chris, and I thought he was just being protective over his little girl. I had no idea that he was so angry because he felt Chris was damaging the merchandise. I think Max was afraid that Chris was going to romance me for his own benefit and cut him out of the deal entirely."

"I don't get it."

"I'm not surprised. I had never done as many endorsements as Max would have wanted. He saw Chris as an angle. 'Romance between two Olympians.' It worked, and Chris benefited too. He was slipping as a skier and knew he didn't have too long to make money if it became known that he might not make it to the Olympics. But Chris and I got all the endorsement money and mine was going into my trust fund. Max got nothing. So he needed to keep a hold on me until after the Olympics if he wanted me to invest in the ski school he wanted to start. Marriage to Chris, or anyone, would not have fit his plans." She gave a short laugh. "Or Chris's either, for that matter."

"Did you love the guy?"

"Which one?"

"Either."

"I didn't love Max. I was twelve when my father died, old enough to remember what he was like. No one could have replaced him. But I respected Max. He was an excellent coach and, in spite of everything, I have to admit that I might not have been as good a skier without him. I loved Chris in the desperate way that all young girls love their first crushes. I certainly don't pine for him now, but he taught me to be careful. I regret that I was so naive and that I let so many other people take control of my life."

"So that's why you're so defensive about making your own decisions."

"Not defensive, just insistent."

"And are you standing firm by your decision not to dance again?"

Nicki twisted angrily out of his arms and walked over to the window. "You don't have to make it sound like I'm being a stubborn little girl, Doug. I'd love—" Seeing his startled expression at the intensity in her voice, she stopped herself and took a calming breath. "Sorry, that was uncalled for."

"Was it?"

She nodded and raked her hand through her hair while she debated whether to continue. She'd gone this far; there was no point in leaving this last bit unsettled between them. But she knew it was unlikely he would understand. She didn't really understand it herself.

"The decision not to dance was not a conscious one. I just can't do it. The rhythm and motion of both dancing and skiing were one and the same to me. I never separated them." She listened to the music coming from the stereo. "It's strange. I can ski now without tightening up, but I still can't dance. Every time I try, I can't fight the sensation that something about the way I'm moving isn't right, yet I know I'm helpless to do anything to fix it. I get dizzy—lose my sense of balance. Then the fear takes over, and I experience the same horrible feeling of being on skis and racing out of control. I can't stand to relive that." Her heart beat faster at the memory and the room seemed unbearably warm. "It was bad enough to know I was falling, but it was terrifying to realize that I wasn't even doing that right. I felt like I rolled forever, and with each turn, I expected the pain. I waited for it—I needed something familiar to remind me of what was happening. But it never came. Instead, the sensation of the fall was endless. I kept begging for someone to stop me, but there was no one there." She clutched her stomach against a wave of nausea, amazed that she could still remember it so vividly after all these years.

Doug stepped behind her and slipped his arms under hers, forcing her to relax her grip. She let herself lean back against him and closed her eyes. "Dancing's not like skiing, Nicki. You don't have to dance alone. I'd always be right there to catch you, right there to hold on to. I'll stop the fall before it even starts to happen."

She felt herself go limp. It was nice to have someone else support her for a change. Someone she trusted not to walk away or let go. As he gently kissed the top of her head and the ticklish spots behind her ears, she realized that it was that trust that made her relationship with Doug so special. She'd tried to fight it, to tell herself that he had lied to her, that he was trying to manipulate her, but she'd known all along that she didn't believe it. It wasn't his dishonesty that she'd feared, but his honesty.

From the first day, when he'd taken her off guard by being bold enough to tease her about the way she played with her hair, she'd known that he had the ability to see things about her that she didn't like to show. She'd tried harder to hide, harder to conceal her emotions, not only from him but from herself, but he'd always known where to look. So there was no point in hiding anymore. She turned and put her arms around his neck, pressing her body to his, resting her head against his chest.

Doug gave her a tight hug, then eased his hold on her and began to guide her through the first steps of a waltz. She tried to stay relaxed and to follow his lead, but her muscles began to tense. The more she concentrated, the more she began to panic. She couldn't keep her eyes open, but when she closed them she felt dizzy. Doug stopped. Lifting her chin slightly with his hand he dipped his head and kissed her—a tender and reassuring kiss. Then, before she had a chance to respond, he scooped her up and began to dance for both of them.

By the time the song was finished, Nicki was breathless from the exhilaration of being in his arms as he whirled her around the room.

He was still holding her when he stopped and leaned against the door frame. His eyes sparkled brightly as he looked down at her. "How can you be out of breath when I did all the work?"

"I thought having fun with me was effortless."

"Were you having fun or was that hard for you?"

"It was wonderful." She tightened her grip around his neck. "I feel so safe when you hold me."

"Would you still feel safe if I told you that when I hold you I want to make love to you?"

"Not safe, but happy and excited."

"If we had made love that night at the ski lodge, would you have regretted it?"

"No."

"If we make love tonight will you regret it?"

"No."

"Do you want . . . ?"

Nicki stopped him by putting her finger to his lips. "No more questions, Doug. I've admitted as much as I'm going to admit. Love me."

He closed his eyes and hugged her close. Then he carried her upstairs.

CHAPTER THIRTEEN

As soon as Doug put her down in the middle of his king-size bed, Nicki felt a twinge of panic. Ever since the back rub that had brought them so close once before, she had been anticipating this moment. But she still had no real idea what to expect. What kind of lover would Doug be? What kind of lover would he want her to be?

He sat on the edge of the bed beside her and reached over to turn on the lamp. She caught his hand. "I'd rather have the lights out, if you don't mind," she whispered.

"I mind very much. I want to be able to see you like I did the other night."

"I would have asked you to turn them out then, too. Believe me, my body is nothing to look at." She felt herself blush. "I mean, there are some pretty nasty scars."

"I don't care about your scars, Nicki. At least not the ones on the surface. And as I recall, there are no scars on your positively perfect breasts. May I enjoy that view of you again before I plunge us into darkness?"

She nodded, and as he clicked on the light, she started to sit up to remove her sweater. Doug put a restraining hand on her shoulder.

"No need to rush, love. I've always been one to savor the important moments in my life. I think this one qualifies. Don't you?"

Again she just nodded. Already she'd misread what it was that he wanted her to do.

"Nicole Devlin speechless? That makes this more special yet. Will you mind if I talk while I make love to you?"

"No."

"Do you mind if I get undressed with the light on?"

"No."

She watched silently as he slipped off his shoes, dropping each to the floor with a thud, stood up, wiggled out of his sweater and unbuckled his belt, pulling it out of the belt loops with a flourish. Then he put his hands on his hips, cocked his head to one side and treated her to his magnificent crooked grin. "Do you have any last requests?"

She blinked in confusion. "What?"

"Nicki, you are obviously scared to death and, although I have to admit I find your innocence and your vulnerability extremely tempting, I feel like I'm about to become your executioner instead of your lover. I'm a little uncomfortable with the role."

"I'm not afraid. At least not in the way you mean. I want to make love with you. It's just that I know most woman my age have had more experience than I have. I'm not sure I know what to do."

"Oh, well then, you've come to the right place. I do a birds and bees lecture at the junior high every year, and I'm sure I could dig out my notes."

"You're a terrible man, Doug MacNair." She grabbed the pillow from behind her head and launched it at him.

He snatched it out of midair. "Terrible man, but a great catch. Pun intended." He flipped the pillow back at her. "Why is it so terrible to try to put someone who's nervous at ease?"

She pulled herself into a sitting position and smiled at him. "It isn't. And you are being very good about all this. You're right that I'm nervous. I'm also embarrassed that

I'm nervous, which makes me more nervous. And what's behind it all is that basically I have no idea how to act."

"Ah-ha. A faulty premise. Don't act at all. Just be yourself and react, then everything will be fine. I promise."

"And if I'm not responsive enough?"

"Then I'll have to improve my technique, won't I?" In one graceful motion, he moved from standing beside the bed to lying next to her. He slipped his forearm under her neck, propped his weight on his elbow and rested one of his thighs lightly across both of hers. Then he studied her for a moment as if deciding whether to speak. "Look at my eyes, Nicki. It's not just the color that makes them so much like yours. It's that they reveal all our other similarities as well— the same ambition and sense of duty, the same vulnerabilities, the same fears. Most people don't see us as we see each other because we'd never allow that. To the rest of the world we are strong and clever and always in control. No matter what, we're expected to be the best. We are the people who shouldn't need to be touched."

She could feel the tremor of his muscles tensing and hers followed suit.

"Well, I want something more than that now," he whispered. "I'm still willing to meet my obligations—to keep from disappointing anyone—but I want something for me. I want there to be one special person who knows and understands all my weaknesses and fears. I want to be able to relax and laugh and be crazy sometimes and without anyone judging me for it. I want to be able to confess to someone that I do need to be touched." He stroked her cheek lightly. "I'm not sure yet if you want to be that special person, but I am sure that I'm different when I'm with you than I am with anyone else—happier, more willing to open up, less afraid. That's enough for me to want to take a chance. I do need to be touched, Nicki, and I need to touch you."

She couldn't even try to answer. Instead, she buried her fingers in his hair and urged him to kiss her. He complied, but not in the manner that she'd expected. He brushed his lips gently over her eyelids, across her temples and along the sides of her neck to the base of her throat. Only after he had her tingling did he caress her mouth with a soft, lingering kiss—the kind of kiss she'd always thought of when she heard the word tender. She let herself go weak, totally at ease in his arms. But when he teased the corners of her smile, and she parted her lips to entwine her tongue with his, a very basic need began to grow within her.

As Doug kissed the sensitive skin beneath her chin, she felt him slip his hand under her sweater and rest it against her stomach. But he made no attempt to move farther.

"This, too, is just like dancing," Doug whispered softly as his fingers gently brushed the tip of her breast.

How well he knew her. How well she'd let him know her. She arched against his palm. She was ready to reclaim everything she'd thought she lost.

Doug clasped his arms around her and pulled her closer, running his hands up and down her in a seemingly desperate attempt to melt their bodies together with the sheer heat of his passion. Their clothing became an unnecessary and unwelcome barrier between them.

Nicki pushed against his shoulders, and when he backed away, she reached for the buttons of his shirt. As she released each one, she parted the material and trailed her fingers through the soft, curling hair that she'd exposed. He tried to stop her, but she evaded him, determined to discover the magnificence of Doug beneath the garment. When the last button was opened, he shrugged out of the shirt and cast it aside. Nicki, grateful now for the lamplight, could only stare. His physique was nothing short of perfection. The only thing she wanted at that moment was to lay her head against that welcoming, muscular chest and have Doug stroke her hair.

As if reading her mind, he cupped her head in his hand and held her to him, then eased her back and guided her sweater over her head. She felt a quick chill at being exposed to the air and an equally quick hot flash at being exposed to Doug, both of which fused into excitement as he lowered her onto the pillows and bent to kiss her breasts. He flicked his tongue over first one nipple, then the other, hardening each in turn to an inflamed peak. When he finally ceased his agonizing caress, it was to stroke the length of her half-clothed body, molding his hands to her every curve, until she clutched at his hands to stop him.

"You have no idea how lovely you are." His husky voice echoed all around her, and before she could regain sufficient control of her senses to respond, he'd dipped his head to begin anew the tantalizing process of arousing her.

She arched herself more insistently toward him, but still he ignored her unspoken pleas. "Doug, I can't stand this anymore. If you want to make love to me, you'd better stop your teasing and do it now."

"But that's exactly what I am doing." He grinned innocently. "Making love to you the slowest, sweetest way I know."

She rolled away from him, got to her feet, and stood beside the bed. "You seem to have forgotten something. Downhill racers don't know the meaning of slow." She reached over to turn out the light.

Surprised, Doug blinked against the darkness. His sight was useless to him now, but his other senses became sharply attuned. The unmistakable rasp of her zipper being lowered and the swish of satin slack lining and silken underwear brushing against her skin tantalized him. The edge of the bed sank beneath her weight, and the scent of her perfume enveloped him. Her warm, smooth hands explored the contours of his torso before coming to rest on the snap of his trousers. He assumed she would be intimidated by the task of undressing a very aroused man and reached to help her. But he assumed wrong. She dispensed with his clothing quickly and efficiently, with very little assistance from him.

"Tell me about your lack of experience again," he murmured.

"I used to volunteer at a nursing home."

"Indeed? Terrific training, a nursing home. What else did you learn there?"

"That was it. From now on I improvise. Let me know how I'm doing."

She stretched out full length on top of him, clasped her hands behind his neck and began with a kiss that took his breath away. Just the idea that she was willing to take control was more exciting to him than he would have thought possible. She began to slide down his body, leaving a trail of kisses as she moved. He grabbed her shoulders to stop her. "If you fulfill all of my fantasies the first time, I won't have anything to look forward to."

"Sure you will. You can look forward to when I'll do it again."

She evaded his grip and continued to torture him until he begged her to stop. When she came to her knees beside him, he reached over to put his hand on her breast and felt the unevenness of her breathing. He responded with another rush of arousal at the realization that touching him had excited her. "Can't I turn the light on, Nicki? I want to see how you look when you're like this."

She caught his hand. "No lights, Doug. But I'll tell you what you'd see. My hair is a rumpled mess and keeps flopping in my eyes. My cheeks are flushed. My lips are slightly swollen, moist and ready to be kissed again. My chest is heaving with every breath I take, and I still can't get enough air, which means I'm just on the verge of dizzy. And every muscle in my body is wound as tight as a spring. Does that give you a complete picture?''

"The eyes. What about your eyes?''

"Well, I can't be sure, of course, but I think smoldering with desire would be a safe bet. Oh, and crinkled at the corners a bit, because I'm smiling.''

Doug smiled, too. "From everything you've said, I can only assume that you are beautiful beyond belief.''

"Perhaps, but it appears that I've failed at the task I set for myself.''

"Which was?''

"To assure you that I'm not afraid anymore and to show you just how ready I am to have you make love to me.''

"Lie down, Nicki, and let me prove how successful you've been.''

As Nicki felt Doug's hand urging her to part her thighs she had one more twinge of concern. "I don't know how much weight my back can take, and I won't be able to move much.''

"Hush. You leave your back to me. I promise I won't hurt you.''

"A rash promise. It's been a very long time.''

"Which is exactly why I intend to take it slow and easy. You'll just have to put the downhill racer on hold.''

She opened herself to him, but rather than entering her, he chose to tease her first with his fingers, then with his tongue. Her already tense muscles tightened further still, until she was afraid she would snap in two. She clenched her fists and set her shoulders and thighs, hoping to reach for her own release, but knowing it wouldn't come until he chose to give it to her. The pounding echo of her heart was the only sound she was aware of until she heard Doug's whispered, "Lift a little, love, just a little." She arched to him slightly and he put one arm under her to support her back, then slowly—ever so slowly—slipped inside of her.

"Are you okay, Nicki?"

She nodded.

"May I move for us both?"

"Please." She closed her eyes and gasped at the searing pressure of his first thrust. He hesitated, and she cupped her hands over the taut muscles of his buttocks to reassure him.

He adjusted his weight and rocked against her again. Each time it felt as though he moved more deeply into her, and each time she instinctively tightened herself around him. Her body was numb everywhere except where they were joined. The ache became more and more intense, the pleasure more and more unbearable. She had only one reason for being, only one thing to strive for—to attain the peak that lay just beyond her reach and to do it with Doug.

The dizzying pulse began from so far within that she didn't appreciate the speed or magnitude with which it was building until it engulfed her, and then she was incapable of controlling it. "Doug, I can't stop."

"That's good, love. Take it and I'll be right with you."

She could tell by the shudder that racked them both that he'd meant what he said, and she fell back to ride the waves that crested over her. Nothing she had ever experienced before had consumed so much of her. She didn't think it possible that she could emerge whole but, at this moment, she didn't care—whatever she'd lost was worth it.

It may have been minutes, hours or days later when she opened her eyes and peered out from under her curls to find Doug watching her. His smile flashed in the darkness. "Didn't I say I wouldn't hurt you?"

"Oh, but you did, you brute. Hasn't anyone ever told you there's a narrow threshold between pleasure and pain? The pleasure of you fringed on agony."

He brushed her hair back from her face. "Poor baby. Should I promise never to do it again?"

"That isn't the promise I was hoping to hear."

"Good. It isn't one I wanted to make." He pulled her into the curve of his arm, and from the sound of his breathing, she could tell that he had dozed off.

She considered the enormous step she had just taken and that she'd let it happen. But in reality, she'd known from the very first day that she had no choice. She had promised herself that she would never again lose control of her life, never give her trust to anyone, but she hadn't counted on Doug MacNair or what he could teach her about herself. And now she had no intention of giving him up.

WHEN NICKI WOKE UP the next morning, she knew exactly where she was and sighed with contentment. Doug's arm draped over her waist felt familiar and right. She trailed her hand along his forearm and was rewarded with a muffled grumble. She opened one eye to peek at him and burst out laughing. Sometime since they'd last made love in the early hours of the morning he had pulled the blanket, comforter and pillow over his head. With the exception of his big toe, no part of the man was visible.

"This is not at all unlike waking up next to Elmo."

"Who said anything about waking up." He snuggled closer and rested his cheek against her shoulder. "What time is it?"

"Seven. And I've got a full day ahead of me."

"You sure do. Should we get started?"

She caught his hand before it got to her inner thigh. "Behave yourself, Doug. I've got a meeting this afternoon with a medical expert for Ian's case, and I have a lot of research to do before that.''

"I'm a medical expert and I've got some research I need to do, too.''

"Stop it.'' She grabbed his head to keep him from licking her breast and pulled the covers off them to further distract him.

He let go of her to try to retrieve the blanket and she took the opportunity to escape from the bed, remembering too late that that left her standing naked before him in broad daylight. She looked down self-consciously at the scars on her legs and abdomen and then at Doug. His face reflected no shock, no distaste, only desire.

"You cheated me all last night, love. Now come back to bed and let me look at you while I make love to you.''

She felt herself go weak at the thought. "I can't, Doug, really. I would like to see you tonight, if possible, but I have to work today.''

"Okay, okay. I know when I'm fighting a losing battle. Can you shower here? I have big fluffy towels and I'll make coffee.''

"Sounds great.'' She bent over to kiss him and almost forgot her resolve when her lips touched his.

He kissed her firmly and completely then turned her to face the bathroom. "If you're going, go on before I lose what little self-control I have left.''

When Nicki stepped into the shower, she was still glowing with satisfaction at the idea that she could have such an effect on him. He knew all of her weaknesses, both physical and emotional, and he still found her attractive.

She heard him enter the bathroom and had just put her head under the water to rinse the shampoo out of her hair when she felt his hands slip around her to close over her breasts. "Hello again, love. I couldn't resist the chance to join you." He pulled her back against him.

"You tricked me." She sighed as his thumbs stroked her nipples.

"I intended to be good. Honest. I brought you coffee. I saw your silhouette through the shower door. I lost my mind. May I stay?"

"Sure. Why not? What girl wouldn't want to shower with the mad Dr. MacNair?"

"You won't regret that decision." He reached for the bar of soap and began to lather her shoulders, her breasts, her abdomen. She gasped as he moved lower still, and he switched his attention to her back and thighs. Turning her under the water to rinse, he gently stroked her, following the paths of her scars. She put her hand over his to stop him, but he pulled it away. "These do nothing to detract from your beauty, Nicki. They're a part of you, who you are and what you've been through, and I love everything that's a part of you."

She focused on the word *love*, then let it slip away as nothing more than a term of endearment. "That's sweet, Doug. But you know you'd prefer it if my skin were smooth and silky and delicate like a woman's body should be."

"Your body is exactly what a woman's body should be. And if you'll give up this ridiculous notion of going to work this morning and come back to bed, I'll show you just how perfect your body is with mine." He moved his fingers over her, exploring her in ways he must have known would make her powerless to refuse him whatever he asked.

She turned off the water and handed him a towel. "Begin by drying me off."

"My pleasure."

He toweled them both down, then settled Nicki in the bed and went to get the champagne and orange juice cocktails he had prepared.

"Pretty sure of yourself, weren't you?" She smiled as she accepted the drink.

"Pretty sure of us." He raised his glass. "That wasn't a bad toast."

Nicki started to clink her glass to his when the phone rang. Doug groaned as he pushed off the bed and went to answer it. When he came back a few minutes later, his sheepish expression told her all she needed to know. "Am I to assume that one of us has to go work this morning, after all?" She took a sip of her cocktail and peeked at him over the rim of the glass. "Are you in a hurry?"

He nodded his head and sighed. "Probably just another case of hurry up and wait, but the expectant mothers do feel better once they know I'm at the hospital if they need me."

"So let's get dressed. I've got a suit in my office. You can drop me at the law school on your way, and I'll come by your office this afternoon for a lift home."

He opened the most enormous closet she'd ever seen and began to pull clothes off of hangers. "Do I get to take you to dinner?"

"Yes."

"And spend the night?"

"Yes."

"And all day Sunday?"

"Do you watch football?"

He considered his answer. "Never."

"Then yes."

He stopped buttoning his shirt long enough to kiss her on the nose.

"Hot dog."

NICKI REREAD THE FOOTNOTE. "Steroid diabetes may be a complication if the patient is taking steroids." She looked up from the medical journal and tapped her pen against her teeth thoughtfully. She certainly couldn't dismiss the idea. After all, Ian had indicated that he was very interested in weight lifting before his accident. If he had juvenile diabetes and also took steroids, he might have aggravated his condition. She knew from her own time as an athlete that steroids affected the liver, as did diabetes, and that they could cause cardiovascular problems. Could that be what had led to Ian's cardiac arrest? Maybe that was the secret that Ian's family did not want discovered.

There was a knock on her office door. "Come on in," she called and stood up to greet the distinguished-looking, silver-haired gentleman who entered. "Dr. Fitzhugh, good to see you again. I was disappointed when I learned that my favorite medical expert had left Chicago to take a teaching position at a downstate medical school. Now it seems that was fortuitous."

He shook her hand and smiled. "For both of us. You know I always enjoy working with you, Nicole." Without waiting for an invitation to do so, he took off his hat, coat and muffler, dragged a chair around the desk so it was next to hers, and sat down. "So?" He hooked his thumbs on the pockets of his tweed vest. "What medical mystery are we unraveling today?"

"Diabetic coma."

"Hyperglycemia? Not much of a mystery. If the body doesn't have enough insulin, it can't break down glucose for absorption into the system, which results in there being too much sugar in the blood."

"Anything tricky about the treatment?"

"Any medical emergency can be tricky, depending on the facts, but on the face of it, no. Obviously the patient needs insulin. He'll be dehydrated so he'll need a saline I.V. and probably supplementary potassium added to the intravenous solution."

Nicki checked her legal pad, adding the I.V. and potassium under insulin. "My notes indicate that the symptoms usually start with drowsiness, headache, blurred vision and progress to rapid breathing, nausea and eventually loss of consciousness."

"In severe cases, yes. Hopefully the diabetic is aware of the symptoms and has enough time to get more insulin before the point of passing out."

"What if the patient is a sixteen-year-old swimmer participating in an important competition?"

"Normally exercise like swimming would be no problem for a diabetic. Even intense physical activity is allowed if it's kept at a uniform level so his dosage could be adjusted to compensate for it. But stress of any type can increase the body's need for insulin. The high-pressure atmosphere of a competition might require additional medication."

"So it would not be the best time for him to have forgotten to take even his regular dosage?"

"No, certainly not. The symptoms might have progressed very quickly under those circumstances."

"And what if he were also taking steroids?"

"Steroids for a diabetic could cause any number of complications. Why would a swimmer use steroids? They tend to slow down reflexes."

"Well, I hope he wasn't. I just have the feeling he's trying to hide something and I thought that might be it."

Dr. Fitzhugh took a sheaf of papers off her desk and flipped through it. "There should have been a routine blood scan done when he went into the E.R. so the staff would know what drugs were on board." He pulled out a page. "Here are the blood test results." He studied them for a moment then looked up. "According to this, he wasn't taking any drugs or steroids at all. His blood sugar was quite high, but that's to be expected. The only thing even fringing on unusual is that his potassium level is very, very low."

Nicki checked her notes again. "That's odd. Didn't you just say that potassium in the I.V. is part of the usual treatment?"

He nodded. "It almost always is, yes. And it certainly would have been in this case."

"Well, I'm looking at the order for the intravenous, and potassium isn't mentioned."

He took the paper from her. "No. It certainly isn't. But I find it impossible to believe that anyone could have seen his potassium reading and not have tried to bring it up."

"If Ian was supposed to get potassium and didn't, would that have led to cardiac arrest?"

"No, at least not as a usual result. Now, if he had gotten too much potassium, that would be a different story. That would cause arrest. Potassium is the drug that is used to execute prisoners by lethal injection."

"Could that be what happened? You said his potassium level was very low. Could someone have overcompensated?"

"It's a little more complicated than just overcompensating. When we administer drugs that are used to control or correct conditions like this we generally use an I.V.—drip them into the system slowly through the tubes. If something unusual occurs and it is necessary to step up the dosage, we do what is called pushing the drug. We inject it directly into the vein at the point where the I.V. enters the body." He shook his head. "But it is never appropriate to push potassium."

"Could it have happened?"

"I suppose it could have. If someone who knew that drugs were often pushed, but was unaware of the danger of doing that with potassium, saw the abnormally low reading and felt it was urgent to bring the potassium level up, he or she may have panicked and decided to push the drug."

"And that would be improper treatment?"

"Yes, clearly improper. As I said, in large doses, potassium is a killer."

"Is there anything on this chart to indicate that it may have happened in this case?"

"No. The only thing odd about this chart is that, although there had to have been some potassium administered, there is no mention of it. Everything else is here in detailed entries, complete with times and amounts."

"Doctor, since cardiac arrest is not a normal or expected outcome from a diabetic coma of this duration, how do you suppose the hospital explains the fact that it occurred?"

He studied the pages again. "Well, here, after all the detailed records, there's a notation that the patient had a seizure and then began to arrest."

"Is that normal?"

"Arrest with seizure? Yes, it's not uncommon."

"I mean a seizure with diabetic coma."

"No. Those two don't go together."

"So why would Ian have had a seizure?"

"According to this scribbled note here there's something about the swimming pool. Apparently the E.R. staff assumed the boy had hit his head when he collapsed."

She stood up to read over his shoulder. "But there isn't anything that tells us there was any sign of a head injury."

"No, but there wouldn't have had to have been any visible sign for there to have been a seizure."

"So you think that is a plausible explanation?"

"It is if the boy hit his head." He looked at her over the top of his glasses. "Did he?"

"I don't know, Dr. Fitzhugh, and unless Ian remembers, I don't know how I'm going to find out." She brushed her fingers through her hair. "Do you think the charts may have been altered?"

"Nicole, I'm disappointed in you. You know I don't engage in idle speculation." He winked. "That unsavory task is best left to those of you in the legal community."

He gathered up his belongings and gave her a bit of a bow before leaving. Nicki chuckled to herself, then turned back to her notes. Ian and his family had taken a short vacation, so she wouldn't be able to talk to him until the middle of next week. She was relieved that, whatever Ian's secret was, it apparently didn't involve steroids. And she was also grateful that her suspicions on that front had led her to take a closer look at the blood tests than she otherwise would have. Now if she could just find out what happened to the missing potassium.

She wished she could talk to Doug about it but rejected the thought even as it occurred. Their relationship created the potential for conflict of interest, even though Doug had nothing to do with the emergency room staff. She could not involve him in Ian's case.

"NICE PLACE you've got here, Doctor."

Doug raised his eyes from his ledger as Nicki strolled in. Her cheeks were rosy from being out in the cold and her eyes sparkled. "Hi, gorgeous. I take it you had no trouble finding the office."

"None, but it was a longer walk than I expected. I thought you were closer to the hospital." She leaned across his desk and kissed him hello in such a relaxed and easy manner that he felt as though they'd been lovers forever.

She put her hand under his chin and studied him. "I kind of like your accountant look. How long did you intend to keep the spectacles a secret?"

He pulled off his reading glasses and examined them as though he'd never seen them before. "Oh, these. Would you believe they're clear glass and I just wear them to appear intelligent?"

"Not for a minute."

"Okay, so I'm getting old and falling apart. Do you still love me?"

After tossing her briefcase carelessly on the sofa and removing her coat, she turned back to him. "I don't remember ever saying that I loved you."

He wasn't sure whether she was toying with him or not, but knowing Nicki, it was certainly possible. "Oh, really? And just what were you saying to me last night?"

"Doug, you're operating in the wrong generation again. Sleeping with someone does not necessarily mean that you are in love with them." She combed her hair with her fingers and watched him.

"Not necessarily, but it does for you."

"Indeed. And if I admit to that, may I assume the same applies to you?"

"Sure. But you women know how it is for guys. We just love the one we're with." He grinned at her and waited expectantly for her witty comeback.

"Yes, I guess a grown woman should know how it is." She walked over to the window and stared out at the grade school across the street, fixated on the scene of the school children going home for the day. "You see that little boy leaning against the fence over there?"

Doug stepped beside her and looked where she was pointing. "The little guy in the long gray wool coat and cap?

Cute kid. Doesn't quite fit in among all the bright ski jackets and designer jeans, does he?"

"Look how focused he is on that game. He can't join in until he learns the rules. It would be so much easier for him if someone would just show him what to do. But they won't because rule number one is that the misfits have to look out for themselves."

"So what are you telling me? Did you feel like a misfit when you were a kid?" Doug tried to slip his arm around her but she ducked away.

"Of course, I did. I suppose most people thought I was lucky because everything I was doing was exciting—traveling, racing, winning. But I didn't get to do any of the things that other children my age did. I knew all the rules for competing on the slopes, but I never learned the ones that applied to ordinary life. Not then, and I guess not now."

He could sense that she was trying to put some distance between them, but he didn't understand why. "Nicki, two minutes ago you waltzed in here in great spirits. I can't believe you've lapsed into total melancholia just because you saw a lonely child on the playground. What's the matter, love?"

"My, that seems to be an easy word for you to toss around. Well, love, I'm happy to try to play the game your way, but I'm going to have to insist that you tell me the rules. I'm much too busy to take the time to figure them out for myself."

He caught her shoulders so she couldn't evade him again. "And so am I. You're the one who's playing now, aren't you?" As soon as he saw the tears glistening on her eyelashes, he regretted his harsh tone. "Nicki, I'm sorry, but I don't know what's going on. Please tell me what's wrong."

She shook her head slightly. "Don't worry about it. It's not your fault. I was taking things too seriously again, that's all."

"Not good enough. What things?"

"It's almost too embarrassing to tell you." She sighed. "When you said that I'd proved my love for you last night, I thought you meant it. I just reacted badly when I realized you were goofing around. You're going to have to be patient with me. I have unrealistic expectations, but I'm learning." She stretched up to kiss his cheek.

A hard lump lodged in Doug's chest as he pulled her close and wiped the tears from beneath her eyes with his thumb. "Damn it all, I'm always so anxious to score a point on you in the game of banter that I keep stepping out of bounds." He took a deep breath. "Look at me, Nicki." She complied. "I love you. I don't use the word lightly. In fact, I happen to take lovemaking very seriously, and for some crazy reason, I thought you knew that." She wrapped her arms around his waist, and he kissed the top of her head. "Now, promise me you won't cry, and I'll promise you never to joke about my feelings for you again."

"I won't cry. But you don't have to make any promises. Just tell me what you expect. I don't want to be too distant or too possessive. I want to be intimate, but I don't want you to feel trapped."

"You keep asking for guidelines and there aren't any to give. You can't learn how to be in love. You just are. We just are—together—not in competition. All I expect is for you to act exactly the way you want to when you're with me." He cupped her chin in his palm and kissed first her eyelids, then her nose, then the corners of her mouth. Finally, he pressed his lips to hers, urging her to receive his tongue between her parted teeth.

She pulled her head back and grinned mischievously. "You really just want me to act however I want to?"

"Um-hm." He dipped his head to nuzzle her neck. "Really."

"Well, right now, I think I'd like to try acting like a vamp."

He set her free and walked over to lock the office door. "Then, by all means, let me encourage you to follow your instincts."

CHAPTER FOURTEEN

IT WAS ALMOST TWO WEEKS later before Nicki finally managed to connect up with Ian at the gym.

As she changed from her business clothes to her sweat suit, she contemplated how enjoyable the last several days had been. Ron had continued to send her work, as usual, and she had been busy reviewing Ian's files and preparing for classes. But the added element of having Doug in her life had made everything more pleasant.

He had been extremely busy, too, which meant he no longer gave her a hard time about the hours she put in. But he often called just to say he loved her, stopped by for a quick kiss, or brought over food for a late-night dinner. And she had slept every night blissfully wrapped in his arms. Their time together had become more important to her than anything else she was doing, and although she would have expected that to frighten her, it didn't at all.

She looked at the clock on the wall and tried to calculate how much time she should allot to Ian in order to get to her place to pick up a change of clothes for tomorrow and out to Doug's house by eight for dinner. Two weeks ago she would have felt guilty for trying to fit Ian into her schedule rather than just making herself available to him for as long as he needed, but now she was getting a little selfish. She had needs, too, and one of them was time to spend with Doug.

When Nicki walked into the weight room, Ian was already working out. She waited for him to finish one set of lifting, then asked him if they could talk.

He grinned at her. "Sure, coach. I could use a break. What do we need to talk about?"

She was relieved to see that he seemed to be in a cheerful mood. "I'd like you to tell me what happened on the day of the swimming meet."

"Okay. What do you want to know?" He still seemed relaxed as he sat down on a bench and swabbed the back of his neck with a towel.

"Well, first of all, do you remember whether or not you hit your head when you fell into the pool?"

"I remember and I didn't. I also didn't exactly fall into the pool. I was on the board and I felt dizzy, but I tried to dive anyway. I blew the dive completely and hit the water with a sort of belly flop, but was able to swim to the edge of the pool where one of the guys helped me crawl out."

"No chance you hit your head at any time before you got out of the pool?"

"None. I knew everything that was going on and I made the decision to dive even though I was dizzy."

"What happened after you were helped out."

"I was pretty woozy and sick to my stomach. The coach practically ran over. I thought he was going to make a big deal about my screwing up the dive, but instead he just looked real worried and asked how I was. I told him I was pretty sick and probably needed to go to the hospital."

"So you were aware enough of what was happening to ask to go to the hospital?"

"Oh, yeah. I knew I needed insulin and fast." He reached over for his sweatshirt and pulled it on. "Anyway, the coach was in panic mode. He took my arm, dragged me over to the side and told me to lie down while he called an ambulance.

Of course, I was pretty embarrassed. I mean, the whole meet was at a standstill, and everyone was gaping over at our team wondering what was going on with me. It was easier to just lie down and pretend like I wasn't there."

"Did you fall asleep?"

"Nah. One of the guys who was on the camping trip was sitting next to me talking the whole time."

"Ian, when you arrived at the emergency room you were unconscious. When did you actually pass out?"

"I remember being carried to the ambulance on a stretcher, even though I kept arguing that I could walk. I heard one of the ambulance guys ask the coach if my parents had been called. The coach said they were on their way to the meet and he'd send them right to the hospital. I know I thought about how ticked off they were going to be, and that's it. So I must have faded out in the ambulance."

"Was there any point between the time you got out of the pool and when you passed out that you fell or otherwise hit your head?"

"No way. I was flat on my back the whole time."

"What about on the camping trip? Did you hit your head then?"

"Hey, believe it or not, I'm not a clumsy guy. I don't generally go around banging my head, and if I did, I'd remember."

"One more question about this, then I'll drop it. I promise. Is there any reason that anyone at the hospital would have been told that you might have hit your head? Any reason for them to have written that on your chart?"

He shrugged. "People might be told most anything, and who knows what they write on their stupid charts. But there wouldn't be a reason for it. There were plenty of witnesses. I was dizzy and sick, but I never fell."

Nicki hesitated before asking the next question, but decided she needed to see his reaction. "Ian, I was an athlete too, so I know how these things go. Has anyone ever talked to you about steroids?"

"Talked about?" He nodded. "Sure. Some of the older guys at the gym where I used to lift, but I knew I was too young to get much out of them and, as a swimmer and diver, I needed speed and coordination more than bulky biceps. Besides, steroids and diabetes don't mix."

"I'm glad to hear you're so well informed. I'd hate to think you would do anything to hurt yourself."

He narrowed his eyes and the muscles around his jawline tightened in a way that Nicki knew signaled a change of mood. "What do you mean 'hurt myself'? Like how? Like by not taking my insulin?"

"I didn't say that, Ian. Skipping the insulin was a mistake. We all make mistakes. I just don't want you doing anything that might damage your body, either because you don't realize the dangers or because someone else convinces you it's the thing to do, that's all."

He stood up and glared at her. "That's all, huh?"

"Why are you acting like this? Have I ever given you any reason not to trust me?"

"No, not yet."

"Ian?"

"No. You have never given me any reason not to trust you, but sometimes I get mixed up about whether you're my friend or my parent's attorney."

"Well, I can clear that up easily. Sometimes I am your attorney, Ian—not your parent's attorney but yours—and I'm always your friend. No matter what happened before your accident, no matter what happened at the hospital, no matter what happens next, for as long as you'll let me, I'll be your friend." She put her hand on his shoulder. "Now let's get back to those weights."

DOUG LOOKED DOWN at Nicki's rumpled curls resting against his shoulder and listened to the peaceful sound of her steady, deep breathing. Usually he loved waking up in the night to find her next to him. He would kiss her and pull her closer and fall back to sleep. But tonight he was too restless. He slipped his arm out from under her, kissed her gently on the cheek, then took his robe and went down to his study.

He poured a glass of port and reviewed his notes on the day's Risk Management Committee meeting. He was not going to be able to keep his involvement a secret from Nicki for too much longer. He had just been asked to contact the law school, and Nicki in particular, about staging a mock malpractice trial to educate the hospital staff.

A month ago he had been the one to propose the idea. Now he wished it had not been so well received. As soon as he talked to Nicki about it, she would become curious about his involvement. Although she knew he was taking her class because he was interested in medical risk management programs, she was under the impression that that was a general interest related to his student liaison work for the medical and law schools. It would be reasonable for him to want to sit in on a course that might prove relevant to young doctors who were preparing to establish new practices. She had no idea that he was even a member, let alone the future director, of a committee that would soon be making case-by-case risk decisions for the hospital. Given her conduct this evening, he could tell that she was already beginning to worry about possible conflicts, and over much less serious issues than that.

She had been preoccupied all during dinner, and when he'd asked her what was wrong, she had shrugged it off by saying that she was just worried about Ian. Doug had asked if she would like to talk about it or if there was anything he could do to help, and she had told him that, since it involved Ian's case, she really couldn't discuss it with anyone.

Without thinking, Doug had asked if she thought she would file a suit, and she had sounded angry when she told him that was confidential information. Eventually she had come over to kiss him and explained that she had to be particularly careful not to make references to the case in front of him because their relationship put her in a sensitive position. Since he had privileges at the hospital, someone could argue that because of her involvement with Doug she was unwilling to take as hard a stand as she otherwise would have.

That statement had hit Doug with all the force of an explosion. He had been trying to convince himself that as long as he didn't take part in any of the decisions the hospital made involving Ian, everything would probably be okay, but he couldn't keep playing that game.

He massaged his forehead as if he hoped he could make the problem go away. If Nicki was concerned about talking to him merely because he had the right to admit patients to a hospital she was investigating, she was certainly going to be upset to learn just how closely he might be involved in litigation against that hospital in the future. And, quite frankly, he was getting a little upset himself. He really didn't understand the complexities behind what was and wasn't conflict of interest for attorneys. Maybe he had already put Nicki in an untenable position.

He downed the rest of his port, turned off the light and left his study. His only hope was that Nicki's investigation would turn up no basis for a lawsuit. She would still be furious when she learned the truth, but at least then, none of this would matter very much professionally. Unfortunately, given how absorbed she had been in her thoughts about Ian and his case tonight, Doug had the feeling that she was already planning her strategy.

He paused on the bottom stair. He wanted to hold Nicki in his arms again, but he felt as though he didn't deserve to. He was the one who had started this, so it was up him to determine just how much was at stake for her and to make some decisions about what steps to take to protect her from any false accusations. The best way to begin doing that was to take a look at Ian's records for himself.

He dressed quietly and left Nicki a note saying he'd had to go to the hospital. He took one more look at her sleeping—trustingly—in his bed. He'd been so caught up in the magic of loving her and convincing her to love him that he'd lost track of the real world in which they had to live their lives. Doug MacNair was a man who made his own chances all right. Only this time, when he'd decided to take a chance with his stupid charade, Nicki was the one he'd put at risk.

He stepped out into the cold winter night. He would quit the committee and turn down the directorship without a moment's hesitation if it would do any good—that was what he had been counting on when he'd forged his plans. It had all worked beautifully so far. He had certainly gotten a chance to know Nicki Devlin better, but now that he knew her, he also knew he'd set himself up to lose her.

Two hours later, as he slipped the medical charts back into the file drawer, he had to admit that things were even worse than he'd thought. There was no logical explanation for what had happened to Ian in the E.R. There had been nothing unusual about his diabetic condition. He had been an extremely fit young man who should have recovered completely when he received insulin. The only possible clue to the cause of the cardiac arrest was a scribbled reference to a head injury and seizure, and Doug found the existence of that note to be more harmful than helpful to the hospital. There were no other entries in Ian's records that referred to a head injury, and given that the emergency room notation was in a different handwriting than the rest of the chart and certainly appeared to have been added after the fact, it looked suspiciously like an attempt to cover up.

Doug knew that at this point Nicki was likely to have copies of the hospital records but would not have seen the originals. She probably had not noticed, as he had, that there were several white-outs and fill-ins that also looked suspicious. Doug had worked with Margaret Orb a couple of times, and he knew how meticulous her record-keeping was. Changes like these were atypical for her. Reminding himself to tell Nicki to be sure to come in and take a look at the original file, he started to close the file drawer, then stopped himself midmotion.

In a wave of nausea, the reality behind the conflict issue came clear to him. He couldn't tell her anything right now. He still represented the hospital, and she was the attorney for the enemy. If her photocopied records led her to believe that she had no reason to investigate further, he was supposed to stand by and let that happen. He was supposed to be glad that the hospital had been able to avoid paying damages to someone who might have been entitled to them. He pushed the drawer closed with a slam. How could he do that? How could he both love her and make love to her, allowing her to trust him, while he knew that he'd stood by and let her make a mistake? Even before he completed the thought, he knew that would be impossible.

He leaned against a nearby desk and listened to his heart thumping in the otherwise silent room. He was trapped. He took several deep breaths and tried to make himself think. Just because the charts looked suspicious to him didn't mean there had to be a problem, did it? Maybe there really was a head injury. At this point, he might as well be sure that he had as much information as possible before he had to face the hospital administration—and Nicki. He needed to talk to Norman Gregory and Margaret Orb.

"RON, IF YOU EVER GET to the point where you figure you can do anything for yourself, do be sure to let me know, won't you?" Nicki slammed down the receiver and stared absently out the window of her office. Doug was going to be furious when he learned that she had to go to Chicago tonight for an early Saturday morning meeting, but not as furious as she was with Ron for having scheduled it. He had just assumed that she would be more than willing to drive up there to consult with another one of the clients whom she had thought he was going to be handling on his own. His timing couldn't have been worse. She had wanted to spend the weekend working on the Dorchester suit. Oh well, she could probably still have the complaint ready to file on Monday morning, but it would use up all her spare time.

She spun around in her chair and started at the sight of Doug's muscular form lounging against the door frame watching her with a rather circumspect expression on his face. "Doug, you surprised me. How long have you been lurking there?"

"Not long." He looked almost startled himself. "I was just enjoying the view."

"Oh? Has my office been declared a scenic overlook?"

"That wouldn't be a bad idea, but it would only qualify when you were in the room. Too bad this is one spectacular sight you'll never get to see."

She winked at him. "Not so sad. I get my own thrills from watching handsome devils like you." She noted his weak attempt at a grin with increasing concern. "Is there something wrong?"

"Not really. I just have some troublesome things to think about so I'm a little preoccupied."

"Anything we can talk about?"

"We will." He leaned over and gave her a kiss. "But not right now. Maybe later."

"Oh-oh. I won't be here to discuss anything later. Ron called and, as usual, he's left a client in complete confusion and needs me in the city for a breakfast meeting. I'll have to leave tonight." She braced herself for an angry tirade but Doug looked almost relieved, which both surprised and disappointed her. "Boy, it's nice to know I'll be missed."

"Of course you'll be missed. I miss you when you leave the room for a minute, but it just so happens that this is going to be a really busy weekend for me, too, so if you've got to be away, now is a good choice."

"Believe me, I'd feel a lot better about it if it were a choice. Ron has never been much of a trial attorney, but he does bring in a lot of business, and I always thought he was holding his own on the work front. It's only since I've been away that I've realized how much of his work finds its way to my desk."

"Yeah. I'd imagine that having to send things express mail makes it a little more obvious."

"That's the truth." She sighed. "I guess Ron and I are going to have to have a serious talk. Right now the extent of his contribution to the partnership is ordering stationery with his name over mine on the letterhead."

"Foley before Devlin?"

"Don't ask. He claims the printer made a mistake. Would you buy that?"

Doug didn't seem to be listening. He paced the length of the room then turned. "How soon will you be leaving?"

"Must you sound so anxious? I was planning on taking you out for dinner first, unless you have other plans."

"No."

She waited for him to say something further but he didn't. "No you don't want dinner?"

"No. I have no other plans." Again he lapsed into silence.

Nicki shrugged. "I've asked you what's wrong, you've said you don't want to talk about it, so that's all I can do. In light of your present mood, let's forgo Alouette, which was going to be my suggestion for an intimate evening, and try the Hamburger Corral." She stood and picked up her coat. "We should be able to eat quickly and I can be on my way and out of yours."

He merely nodded, the last remark seeming not to have registered.

Her stomach tightened nervously. She'd felt closer to Doug the first time she saw him in her office than she did at this moment, and she had no idea what she'd done to bring this about so was at a loss how to fix it. Ever since she'd awakened this morning to find him gone, she'd been concerned. She knew that he had gotten up during the night and gone downstairs, so he must have been worried about something then. And his trip to the hospital had probably not been to see a patient, because she would have heard the phone ring if he'd been called. She could only hope that the problem was not with her.

Belatedly sensing her concern, Doug came over and rested his hands on her shoulders. "Nicki, don't let this worry you and don't be angry with me. I'm sorry I'm so distant. It won't last. Let's go to Alouette and have a nice dinner. Then you go take care of your job and I'll take care of mine, and by the time you get back, everything will be back to normal."

"Promise?"

He wrapped his arms around her and pulled her close in what felt like a desperate hug. "Yes, I promise. No matter what it takes, I'll see that everything is okay."

"All right. Then let's get going. I don't want any problems between us, especially mysterious ones, so the sooner you can deal with what's bothering you, the better I'll feel."

DEALING WITH his mysterious problem was exactly what he intended to do. Doug walked into the hospital cafeteria the next morning looking for Norman Gregory.

He found him exactly where he expected him to be—sitting at a table with three nurses, flirting. "Dr. Gregory, do you suppose I could tear you away from your business here for a few minutes?"

The young man looked a little surprised but seemed willing enough. "Excuse me, ladies. Apparently duty calls." He picked up his coffee, followed Doug to an isolated table in the far corner of the room and flashed a smile that Doug imagined was what the women referred to as his "lady-killer smile." "What can I do for you?"

"A lot I hope. I want you to tell me everything you remember about Ian Dorchester."

The smile faded and Norman's pleasant expression was replaced with one of suspicion. "Should I know who that is?"

"A young E.R. patient. Came in in diabetic coma and went into arrest."

"Sorry. Doesn't ring a bell."

"Doesn't ring a bell?" Doug raised his voice in disbelief. "Something went that drastically wrong and it doesn't ring a bell?"

Norman blanched noticeably. "Who said anything went wrong? No one has proven that."

"Ah. So you do remember?"

"Yeah, okay, I remember. But back when the case was being investigated, I was told not to talk about it. I assumed that meant to anyone, including nosy fellow physicians who weren't there when it happened."

"Are you aware that the case is being investigated again?"

"I know there was some hotshot lady lawyer snooping around, but you risk management honchos don't seem all that anxious to keep the victims informed."

"Is that how you see yourself, as a victim?"

"Of course it is and if, as rumor has it, you're going to be the Director of Risk Management for this hospital, I'd hope that would be how you saw me too. But then again, there are a lot of rumors going around right now, aren't there?"

"Norman, I don't know what you're referring to, but I get the feeling you haven't been playing straight here. First you say you don't remember the case at all. Then you pretend you think I'm just being nosy, and now you admit that you've heard I'm one of the people being considered for the directorship. You'd better pick which story you're going to go with, and then you'd better tell me what happened the afternoon that Ian Dorchester was brought into the emergency room."

"Okay, okay, so I knew about the committee and about the new investigation. But I think I have a right to be careful who I talk to, don't you? I need to protect myself."

"I agree. But as a resident in the emergency room, you are a hospital employee, so it's the hospital's interests that are really at stake and the hospital administration needs to know what happened."

"I don't know what happened. The kid came in, we did what we were supposed to do, given what we knew about his condition, and like you said earlier, something went wrong."

"What exactly did you do?"

"I couldn't tell you right now. There's no way I can be expected to remember that far back, but it's all on the charts."

"That brings up my next question. I looked at those charts, and it appears to me as though information has been altered and added after the fact."

"Well, that's none of my business is it? I don't keep the charts, the nurse on duty does. You'll have to talk to Margaret Orb about any changes she made and why."

"Sorry, Norman, but that won't wash with me. I know how detailed and accurate Margaret's charts are and I know her handwriting. Someone else made those changes."

"I wouldn't know a thing about it." Norman pushed back his chair and stood. "Now if you'll excuse me, I have to start my rounds."

As Doug watched him walk away, he knew that his casual manner was a ruse. Norman Gregory was frightened, and he probably had good cause to be. Doug had no doubt that the young resident was trying to cover something. He'd been much too cavalier about saying he didn't remember what had happened that day. Norman had had plenty of time to review the records, and if he were anything at all like Doug had been when his case was being investigated, he had probably memorized every word on those charts and relived every minute that he had spent with Ian a hundred times over. If he'd known that he'd done nothing wrong, he would have been only too ready to sit down and give a detailed explanation of everything that had happened to anyone who would listen and sympathize. Yet from the moment

Doug had mentioned Ian, Norman had been defensive. Rather than trying to explain his innocence, he had wanted to avoid the subject. To Doug, that was extremely suspicious.

When Doug returned to his office and reviewed the records again, he felt slightly sick. Anyone at the hospital who had looked at those charts would have had to have questions, yet there was no indication that any had been asked—not even by the attending physician who should have been supervising and checking on Norman. Doug had assumed that any attempt to hide the facts had been the work of Norman or one of the other E.R. staff. He still hoped that was true. Bad as it was, it was still better than the thought that the hospital administration might be behind a cover-up. He would be a staunch advocate of the hospital's right to defend itself in the event of a lawsuit, but tampering with records or ignoring that someone else had was beyond the realm of defense. For the first time he was beginning to understand Nicki's argument that sometimes injured patients had to turn to attorneys and the courts to prove what had happened to them and be compensated for bad treatment.

Doug spent the balance of the day conducting his own investigation. The hospital staff seemed willing to accept the contention that Ian had hit his head, even though there was no evidence of a blow and no indication that anyone had asked him. He could find nothing on Ian's chart that would explain why no potassium was administered even though his reading was very low. And he couldn't make contact with Margaret Orb, either at the hospital or at her home, even though he'd left numerous messages for her to call him.

He felt as though he'd reached a dead end until he remembered Nicki's lecture on the use of records and going beyond the obvious. He checked the pharmacy records and noted that potassium had been ordered for Ian. He checked the Dorchester's bill and found they had been charged for it. Yet there had been no reference to it on the E.R. charts. That could have been an oversight, or it could account for one of the unexplained white-outs.

Of course. That had to be it. Too little potassium wouldn't lead to cardiac arrest, too much most certainly would. Someone trying to cover up that Ian had received too much might have removed all references to potassium, then added the note about the head injury to provide some other possible explanation for what had happened. Doug certainly couldn't prove it, unless he got Norman or Margaret to admit to something, but he was fairly confident of his scenario.

Now his problem was what to do about it. As a member of the Risk Management Committee, he would like to encourage the hospital to conduct a more thorough investigation and to take appropriate action based on their findings. But because of his relationship with Nicki, who would stand to benefit from any settlement made with her client, the committee would hardly view his suggestion as impartial. Even he had to admit that he might have a different approach if he were dealing with another attorney, someone whom he had no reason to trust. Since he knew Nicki and appreciated her unique brand of fairness, he wanted to be fair in return. It really didn't have anything to do with his love for her, but no one else would believe that. Clearly, as long as Nicki was Ian's attorney, Doug would be more a hindrance than a help to committee negotiations. He couldn't put it off any longer. He had known from the start that if a problem like this arose he would have to resign from the committee and give up any chance for the directorship. Now it was time for him to find Bailey and do just that.

CHAPTER FIFTEEN

WHEN NICKI WALKED into her apartment, she expected to see Doug there reading the Sunday paper, but he was nowhere in sight. "Doug?"

The only answer was an enthusiastic meow from Elmo.

"Hi, guy." She scratched the cat's ears. "Do you suppose we should give your buddy a call and find out what he's up to?" Elmo seemed unconcerned but Nicki was worried. It wasn't like Doug not to call or leave a note, and she hadn't heard a word from him since she'd left on Friday. She reached for the phone just as it began to ring. "Hello."

"Ms Devlin?" The timid voice on the line sounded vaguely familiar. "This is Margaret Orb. I work at the hospital."

"Yes, Margaret. How are you?"

"Can we meet someplace, privately?"

Nicki tried to keep the excitement out of her voice. This could be the breakthrough she'd been hoping for. "How about the coffee shop near the law school in half an hour?"

"Okay, and please don't tell anyone."

"Of course not." She let the receiver fall back in its cradle. Margaret's timing couldn't have been better.

The young woman looked very agitated as she slid across from Nicki in the booth. "I can't take this anymore. Tell me what's happening with Ian Dorchester."

"I can't do that, Margaret. If I file a suit it will become public knowledge. In the meanwhile, you know that I'm conducting an investigation."

"You and everyone else it seems. Doug MacNair hasn't let those files out of his sight all weekend."

Fortunately the waitress came to take Margaret's order, so Nicki had time to cover her reaction at learning of Doug's interest. "Why does this investigation have you so upset?" she asked when the waitress left.

"Because I did something really stupid."

"Something as stupid as pushing potassium directly into the vein?"

Margaret looked surprised for a moment, then shook her head. "No. That wasn't me, but I'm probably going to get blamed for it."

"But that is what happened?"

"Yes."

"And you altered the charts to cover it up."

"No. But I allowed someone else to and I didn't report it."

"Why?"

The woman said nothing while she took a sip of her chocolate then stared down at her cup. "Why else? I was in love." She raised her eyes to look at Nicki. "I even suspected that he was cheating on me and I still tried to protect him."

"So why are you telling me?"

"Because now that Norman's afraid the whole thing is going to blow up on him, he's reminding everyone that it's the nurse's job to administer the drugs and keep the records, not his." Her eyes flashed with anger. "The bastard. I'm not going to sit back and allow him to frame me."

Nicki winced. Margaret would be a better witness if she sounded less bitter. A jury might well choose not to believe a woman scorned. "Would you be willing to testify in court as to what happened?"

"Wow, I don't know. Isn't it enough that I told you?"

"I'm afraid the legal system doesn't work that way. The judge and jury need to hear it from the witness."

Margaret shrugged. "I don't like it, but I guess I'll do it."

"Thank you." Nicki stood and extended her hand. "Hopefully the hospital will offer to settle and I'll be able to keep you out of it, but it's good to know I can count on you if I have to." As she left the coffee shop, Nicki was very much aware that Margaret's attitude might well change once she'd had time to think through the consequences of testifying against the hospital. It was also possible that Margaret was lying to protect herself, but Nicki didn't think so. Everything fit together too well. She was confident that she now had the answer to what had happened to Ian, and that was enough to reconfirm her decision to file the suit.

She couldn't help but wonder why Doug would be checking on the medical records, but refused to let it alarm her. He was probably just interested in learning something about the client who had been taking so much of her time lately, and she couldn't blame him for being curious. Since she had already warned him about her concerns with regard to confidentiality and conflict of interest, she would just have to trust him not to do anything to jeopardize her work.

Nicki went back to her apartment, ate a bag of pretzels for dinner, and settled down to do the final rewrite on Ian's complaint while she waited for Doug to call. He never did. She left a message on both his home and office machines, then phoned the hospital. The receptionist reported he was with a patient and not answering his message page.

At midnight, after telling herself that he would undoubtedly be in touch as soon as he could, Nicki finally decided to go to bed, but sleep wouldn't come.

Although she knew Doug had no right to be told anything about her plans for the Dorchester case, now that she was only hours away from filing the complaint, she would have liked an opportunity to tell him what she was going to do. It made her uncomfortable to think of his hearing about it through the hospital's rumor mill, but she certainly couldn't put Ian's interests on hold while she waited to touch bases with Doug.

Monday morning she tried twice to reach him but failed. Then, on her way to the law school, she stopped by the courthouse and filed the Dorchester suit. She was in her office when Doug finally called at nine-thirty. He apologized for not getting in touch sooner and explained that he had had two difficult deliveries the day before and another patient in labor that morning. In addition, he still had to run down the chief of staff on an important administrative matter.

Nicki saw no need to make his already trying day more so by telling him about Ian over the phone. They chatted about her Chicago trip for a few minutes, and he assured her that, in his mind, he had his problem from Friday under control and was anxious to see her. They exchanged "I love you's" and long-distance kisses before hanging up.

The conversation had been much less intimate than most of the calls she'd had from Doug over the past couple of weeks, but she could tell that he really was busy. And since he had made a point of reassuring her that the problem, whatever it was, had been resolved, she decided not to let herself be concerned about it.

All of her good intentions not to worry had faded by ten that night when, once again, Doug hadn't called. No matter how busy he was, he had always managed to phone two or three times a day just to say hi. She called his home, then the hospital, where she was told that one of the other obstetricians was ill and Doug was covering for him with a patient. Nicki felt guilty for her selfish expectations. Poor Doug was obviously running himself ragged at the hospital, and here she was pouting because he hadn't checked in with her as often as she would have liked. She made a cup of hot chocolate, flicked on the television and settled back to wait.

The phone rang a little after one and she snatched it up.

"Ms Devlin? Is your lover there with you or is he still lurking around the hospital?"

Her heart began to race but she tried not panic. Maybe someone was just teasing her. "Paul, is that you? Doug's not here." She regretted it as soon as she said it.

"No, I'll bet he's not. He already got what he wanted from you. You probably thought you were being clever, getting him to do your snooping on Dorchester."

Nicki could tell by the way the man slurred his words that he was drunk, and by now she was fairly confident that her anonymous caller was Norman Gregory. Hoping he'd reveal something useful, she decided to let him talk.

"Well, he's the one who's been using you, you know." The caller's voice had become more strident. "He's going to take everything you told him about your case and run to the Risk Management Committee with it so he can lock in that directorship he's been campaigning for."

"I don't know what you're talking about."

"Of course not, because lover boy never told you. Why don't you ask him about his beloved committee and why he's taking that trial class of yours, and why he's been chasing you since the day you hit town? Maybe he'll tell you the truth now. He's already set you up for a beautiful conflict of interest rap so he's got nothing to lose. The hospital is going to owe him a big favor for this one."

Nicki felt herself getting sick. Norman might be drunk but he also sounded as though he knew exactly what he was talking about.

"You can talk to Margaret all you want, lady, but you can't hurt me or the hospital with what you know, because MacNair played you just right. You're going to have to dump this case."

She heard the click of the phone being hung up, but she listened to the dial tone for a long time afterward. She didn't want to believe that she had been nothing more to Doug than a pawn in his political strategy. But if he really was involved in risk management at the hospital, it would be hard to think anything else. He must have known that ethically they couldn't be on opposite sides of the same case.

She called the hospital again and was told that he had just left. Without hesitating, she changed out of her nightgown and into jeans and a sweatshirt, then practically ran out of the apartment to her car.

When Doug opened his front door, she didn't even pause to say hello before brushing past him and going into the living room. "Doug, sorry to bother you so late, but I've had a rather strange phone call."

"Nicki, I—"

"Now," she interrupted. "I know this will sound like I don't trust you, and I do, but I need to know the answer."

"The answer is yes."

"Yes, what?"

He crossed in front of her, sat on the sofa, and put his head in his hands. "I had a phone call, too. Yes, I am on the Risk Management Committee right now. Yes, I kept my involvement a secret from you." He looked up. "I made a terrible mistake, but you have to believe me, I never intended to hurt you."

Even though she'd prepared herself for it, the sudden flash of anger stunned her. "Oh, I have to believe you, do I?" She threw her purse and gloves onto a chair and turned to glare at him. "Just what do you expect me to be gullible enough to believe this time? That you had no idea what you were doing? That you didn't know you had thrown me into such an impossible conflict situation that I would have to resign from this case? That you didn't use me to further your position at the hospital? That—"

"Now just a minute!" Doug came to his feet. "You have every right to be angry, but I don't even know what you're referring to with that last slam!"

"Don't you dare yell at me. Just because I finally figured out your angle doesn't give you the right to act like the wronged party. Do you mean to tell me that it didn't occur to you that you would earn the never-ending gratitude of your committee by getting information from me about Ian's case?"

"I didn't get a damn bit of information from you."

"Only because I wasn't stupid enough to give it. But you sure tried everything. When you couldn't discourage me from taking the case because it meant working too hard, you had to make yourself sleep with me so I'd be forced to resign. I suppose you're hoping Ian's family will give up and not get another attorney. Well, it's too late for that. I've already filed a suit. My replacement will just take over where I left off."

"Nicki, you can't really think that little of me and my feelings for you." He shook his head slowly. "Hell. Never mind that. Forget my feelings. What about yours? You would never have let yourself fall in love with someone who would use you that way. You're much too smart for that."

"Am I? I don't think you've listened to all the soul-searching confidences I've shared with you. This all sounds to me like a prime example of history repeating itself."

"Aren't you even going to give me a chance to explain?"

"Hmm. I probably should. I'd love to see which side of your innocent little-boy's grin you'd choose to tell the story out of this time, but I'd better be going. It's late and I'm going to have a long day tomorrow breaking my commitments to the people who were counting on me."

"Don't do that. I promised you I'd take care of everything and I will. I'm quitting the committee."

"Wonderful. That should make a terrific impression on everyone who will be looking for proof that we were trying to cover up your involvement. Sorry, but you closed out that option the minute you started investigating the case on your own. I have no intention of dealing with accusations that I found my most valuable evidence in the bedroom."

Nicki walked to the front door. "This is one game I just want to get behind me. I not only lost, but I can't even console myself with assurances that I played well, because I played stupidly." She slammed the door behind her, and as she turned up her collar against the wind, she thought that even that icy blast couldn't rival the cold she felt within her.

NICKI WAITED UNTIL TUESDAY afternoon to call the Dorchesters. She wanted to be sure that she wasn't overreacting and giving up on the case without sufficient reason. But after thinking about nothing else for hours, she was certain that, regardless of whether Doug quit the committee or not, she still had no choice but to resign. Even if she were confident that she could be far enough removed from her feelings for him to be impartial, no one else would see it that way. If settlement offers were made, and she advised her client to accept them, it might appear that she was being too

easy on the hospital and settling for too little because of
Doug's connection. If she rejected the offers, she might be
accused of turning down good money because she wanted
to get back at the hospital her ex-lover was affiliated with by
dragging it into court. Either way she would be accused of
bias. She had to get off the case.

Mr. and Mrs. Dorchester were furious. She didn't even try
to defend herself when Mr. Dorchester accused her of having acted irresponsibly, because she agreed that was exactly
what she had done. And when Mrs. Dorchester pointed out
that their having to start over again with a new attorney
would put a terrible strain on Ian, Nicki admitted that would
undoubtedly be true.

She had wanted to talk to Ian and to remind him that
whether or not she was involved in his case she was still his
friend, but when she asked to see him, Mr. Dorchester
wouldn't allow it.

Nicki recommended several other attorneys and promised to get the files in order and to send them as quickly as
possible. Then she left and went directly to the gym, hoping she would be able to catch Ian there. But he never
showed up.

Regular checks with her answering machine at home told
her that Doug had been trying to get in touch with her all
day. But she didn't return his calls. She was in no mood to
listen to any more of his excuses.

It didn't matter to her what his reasons were for what he'd
done. The result had been devastating and had served as a
painful reminder that every time she let her emotions go and
began to depend on someone else she lost all perspective on
what she should be doing for herself. It had been a mistake
to get involved with someone affiliated with a hospital she
was investigating, and she should have known that.

In order to avoid Doug, she didn't go back to her apartment until very late on Tuesday night, and on Wednesday, just in case he came to the school to look for her, Nicki took her lecture notes and went to work in the law library. She had only been there a short time when the dean of the law school pulled up a chair next to her.

"Ms Devlin, it looks as though we might be working you too hard."

She smiled. "Not really. I enjoy doing the class preparation. The students are so enthusiastic it's well worth the effort."

"I think your effort might be what makes them enthusiastic. I've heard nothing but praise for you from the people in your classes. But how about your own enthusiasm? Do you find the classroom to be too tame compared to the courtroom?"

"Well, it's very different, of course, but I like it. It's nice to just be able to discuss ideas for a change. The constant competition of trial law can be exhausting."

"I don't suppose you'd consider staying on here?"

"In what capacity?"

"In your present capacity. That is, teaching the same courses but as a regular part of the faculty."

"What courses would Blake teach if I did that?"

"Apparently, Mr. Windham has succumbed to the lure of sunny California. He's given his notice."

Nicki hoped she didn't show her surprise. If Blake was leaving, chances were good that Sarah was too. Her baby sister was moving away and she didn't even know about it because she had been too busy with Doug and her own ill-fated romance. She turned her attention back to what the dean was saying.

"I've touched bases with some members of the hiring committee already, and everyone is quite impressed with you. I'd imagine you could have the job if you wanted it."

"I'm flattered, certainly, but this all comes as a bit of a surprise. As you know, I have an established personal injury practice in Chicago. I've been rather dissatisfied with it lately, but I hadn't thought seriously about giving it up."

"No, of course not. Well, there would still be a possibility of maintaining a small practice while teaching here."

Which meant she would be living and working in the same town where Doug was practicing medicine. That could be a problem, but the idea of teaching did interest her. "Can I have some time to think about this?"

"Certainly. In fact, I'm sure the university will want us to go through the formalities of interviewing some other applicants as well. But I can't imagine we would find anyone better qualified than you are."

Nicki was still somewhat taken aback by the unexpected offer. "I assure you I will give it some very serious thought."

The dean got up to leave. "Oh, I almost forgot, has anyone warned you about the faculty auction yet?"

"Since I have no idea what you're talking about, I guess not."

"Once a year, in order to help the Student Bar Association raise money, the faculty contributes goods or services to be auctioned off to the highest bidder."

"Oh, sure, we used to have one of those at college. Is it the type of thing where the professor who has a reputation for ugly ties contributes one and the student who buys it gets to wear it to class?"

"That's about it. But you can do anything you want. Donate tickets to a play, or offer to cook dinner for the buyer and a guest."

"Please, not that. The law school would be sued for attempted murder. Dinner in a nice restaurant at my expense is probably a safer bet."

"That would be fine. And, of course, you don't have to do anything, but I wanted you to have a chance to decide for yourself."

"Thanks. I'm sure I'll do something, but I'm not sure what just yet."

The dean walked away, and Nicki turned back to her lecture notes. Her last class wasn't over until late afternoon, but as soon as it was, she would have to talk to Sarah.

On her way to class she picked up a message from the law school secretary saying that Doug would have to miss the day's session and requesting Nicki to call him. She had no intention of complying, but she was relieved she did not have to face him in public and pretend that nothing was wrong.

She was in a hurry to leave after her lecture but decided she'd better return the call from Ron marked urgent. As soon as she heard his voice she was sorry.

"Great going, Nicki. Just what did you do to muff the Dorchester case?"

She fought back a flash of anger. "Excuse me, but I must have misunderstood you. What are you asking?"

"You know what I'm asking. How could you have let yourself get in such an embarrassing situation? It looks bad for the firm."

"You are asking me to justify my actions?"

"Damn right I am. Dorchester would have been a big one."

"Yes, it would have been. And how much time did you plan to spend on it over the next couple of years?"

"Come on, Nicki. You know I thought of that one as your case."

"So did I. Just like I think of all the cases as my cases. Give me one good reason why I should have to account to you for anything I do."

"Because, we're partners."

"Not anymore we aren't."

"I don't get it."

"Then let me spell it out for you. We're through, Ron. I don't want to be the only functioning member of a partnership anymore. You can keep the office, the law library, which is at the end of the hall in case you've forgotten, and any of the clients who choose to stay with you once they know I'm leaving. But I want out."

"All this because I had the nerve to ask how you happened to screw up a case?"

"Let's just say it was a factor."

"All right, I'm sorry. I didn't realize you were so touchy."

"Well, you made a big mistake then, didn't you? Goodbye, Ron. I wish you the best of luck."

Nicki sat back in her chair and breathed a sigh of relief. She knew it wouldn't be this easy to terminate the partnership. There would still be a pile of paperwork to complete. But just knowing that she would be completely in control of how much work she chose to take on gave her a marvelous sense of freedom. She could hardly wait to tell Doug that she had finally liberated herself from Ron.

She closed her eyes against the dull ache in her chest at the realization there was no Doug. Her time was her own now—truly her own. The sense of loneliness that crept over her reminded her that the only special person she had left in her life was Sarah, who was probably moving away. She regretted that she had not seen more of Sarah since she'd been teaching here. She'd known Sarah must have been lonely without Blake, but Nicki had failed to make time for her sister.

Her thoughts were interrupted by the hurried sound of high heels clicking down the hall.

"Nicki, are you here? Which of these blasted doors is yours?"

She recognized Stephanie's voice and stepped into the hall. "I'm here. Is Doug sending out scouts now?"

Stephanie had obviously been running. She was flushed and breathing heavily. "He knew you weren't answering your phone, so he sent me."

"I still don't want to hear anything he has to say."

"It's not that. It's Ian. He's tried to kill himself. He's at the hospital now."

"No! Oh God, why?" Even as she asked, she was overcome by the sickening realization that she probably knew why. She grabbed up her purse and coat and pulled the door shut behind her. "Is he all right?"

"He was alive when I left. I don't know anything else. Doug grabbed me in the hall and told me to track you down immediately, so I didn't wait for details."

"You have no idea how much it hurts me to have to ask this, Steph, but this isn't one of those harmless little lies Doug tells to get his own way, is it?"

Stephanie came to a complete halt and stared at her. "It's that bad between you two?"

Nicki just nodded.

"Well, believe me, if you'd seen Doug's face, you'd know this is no joke. My car is in front. I can take you over if you want."

"I'd appreciate that. I'm in no shape to drive right now."

As Nicki settled back against the car seat she fought a wave of nausea. In spite of what she'd been telling herself since Monday, she knew she'd been holding on to a weak hope that Doug would find some way to justify his conduct and that everything would be okay between them. Now any prayer for that was useless. For the second time in her life she had taken action without regard for her true priorities, and someone she cared about a great deal, someone who had depended on her, had been damaged.

Yet as upset as she was with Doug for creating the situation that had led to this, and as sure as she was that they had no future together, she couldn't deny that she would feel much stronger now, much more able to cope, if only he were there beside her.

CHAPTER SIXTEEN

IAN'S PARENTS were in the waiting room when Nicki arrived, and Mr. Dorchester wasted no time challenging her. "What are you doing here?"

"I heard about Ian. I was concerned."

"It's a little late for that, isn't it? How do you think it made him feel to find out that you were passing him off to someone else?"

"I never intended to reject him as a friend."

"Oh, really? Well, apparently he didn't believe that." The man turned his back on her and walked away.

Nicki wandered down the hall to the lounge where she could be alone. The confrontation with Mr. Dorchester hadn't been completely unexpected. From the moment she'd talked to Stephanie, she had been afraid that this might be her fault, that Ian had felt abandoned. But she had been hoping that his family could assure her that she was wrong.

She barely glanced up as Doug pulled out the chair next to her and sat down, but his pale, drawn appearance finally registered, and a twinge of panic gripped her. "How is he?"

He shrugged. "They say stable, for now. I was here for an emergency C-section when he came in, and I've been checking on him whenever I can."

"I'm surprised you're so concerned. I'd imagine the hospital considers him to be a liability."

A flash of defensiveness tensed his muscles before lines of deep hurt settled in the corners of his eyes and mouth. He started to get up and she put out a hand to stop him.

"Don't. I'm sorry." He slumped back on the chair. "I'm so raw right now I'm just lashing out." Nicki pulled her fingers through her hair to find it wet from snow and hopelessly tangled by the winter wind. She closed her eyes against the memory of Doug's teasing offer of a comb on the first day they'd met. She never had remembered to get one for her purse. "Thanks for sending for me."

He simply nodded in acknowledgment.

"Do you know what happened?" she asked, studying the bottom of her coffee cup.

"He went into the garage, closed the door and turned on the car. A neighbor ran out of gas for his snowblower and went over to the Dorchesters to borrow some. He heard the engine running, looked through the garage window and kicked the door down." Doug slammed his fist on the table. "Damn it. If only he'd talked to someone first."

Nicki shook her head. "He didn't think he had anyone. He thought I'd deserted him."

Doug regarded her with amazement. "Come on, Nicki. With all Ian's had to deal with the last couple of years, you can't possibly believe he tried to kill himself because he was worried that you weren't going to talk to him anymore."

"You said yourself it might not have happened if he'd felt he had a friend to confide in. Someone has to take responsibility for this."

"Maybe, but I don't see how that can be you. The Fates were at fault for Ian's disease. Ian was at fault for not taking his insulin to begin with and for this last desperate measure, and the hospital was at fault for the negligent treatment that led up to this fiasco, but . . ."

Nicki cocked her head to one side. "Are you saying you're willing to admit that the hospital or one of its staff was negligent?"

"I shouldn't say anything if I want to avoid incurring a lot of hostility from the hospital and other doctors, but yes, that appears to be the case. Unfortunately, it's still all speculation on my part, nothing that would stand up in court. Unless someone comes forward with the truth, I'm going to have a hard time proving it."

Nicki was so amazed by his candid admission that she started to tell him about Margaret, then stopped herself. That conversation had taken place when she was functioning as Ian's attorney, so it was confidential. It would be up to his new attorney to decide when and how Margaret's willingness to testify would be revealed to the hospital.

She leaned back in her chair. "Given what you believe to be true, what is the hospital going to do?"

"I don't know. I have no control over the final decision."

"Oh, really? Isn't that what you've been working so hard for—to become Director of Risk Management and make certain that the hospital never settled another suit?"

Again the hurt expression crossed his face, but she did nothing to ease it. She had been hurt too.

"I haven't decided to take the directorship yet, Nicki." His voice sounded tired and far away.

"Why didn't you tell me about it?"

"At first, because I didn't see any point in sabotaging our relationship before all the facts were known."

"Known by whom? You had all the facts."

"No, not then I didn't. I wasn't sure if I was going to be offered the position, or when. And I had no idea whether you would end up filing a lawsuit or not. But I did know that if I told you I was being considered for the directorship, you would use it as an excuse not to see me without even giving us a chance. It seemed like that would be an awful waste of something potentially beautiful, especially if there ended up being no conflict after all.'' He paused and reached his hand toward her cheek, then caught himself and pulled it back.

She couldn't let herself respond to what she recognized as a plea. He knew her too well. If she said anything, if she even looked at him, he would understand what was in her heart and she would be vulnerable again. ''And how long did you intend to hide the truth from me? Until the ethics board came knocking on my door?''

''Of course not. Once you expressed your concern about the fact that I had privileges at the hospital, I realized that I had seriously underestimated the complexities of the conflict issue, and I was afraid I had unwittingly gotten you into trouble. I checked Ian's records, hoping to reassure myself that there would be no lawsuit. Instead, I found sufficient reason to panic and acknowledged a conflict of my own. When you went away last weekend, I finished my investigation and intended to tell the chief of staff that I was resigning from the committee, but he was out of town. I thought it better to wait until I was officially off the committee before telling you. Then you'd know I was serious about fixing the problem I'd created for you, and you'd be in a position to say that you really never knew the potential conflict had existed until it was over.''

''And you thought everyone would believe that?'' Nicki regarded him incredulously. ''Didn't it ever occur to you that I had a right to know—a right to make my own decisions?''

''I can see that now. I realize I made a mistake. But at the time, I honestly thought that as long as I was the one who was willing to pay the price, as long as I acknowledged that

I might have to turn down the directorship, I was the only one who needed to know, because I was the one who had the situation under control."

"Wonderful. That's just what I need, someone to step in and make my decisions for me, to make my reputation and my identity dependent on their integrity." She pushed her chair back with a clatter and stood up. "Well, thanks but no thanks, Doug. You go ahead and take your hard-earned directorship. Get your kicks out of controlling your special committee. Maybe you can even find it in yourself to encourage them to do the right thing by Ian, but give me back control of my own life."

He stood, too, grasped her shoulders for a moment, then let his hands fall dejectedly to his sides. "Goodbye, Nicki. I'll keep you informed."

She raised a brow. "Oh? How ironic."

"I meant about Ian."

This time the flash of pain in his eyes touched her. "I would really appreciate that."

"You know I never wanted to hurt you."

"I believe that, which, I guess, must be why this hurts so much." She barely managed to keep from crying as she walked through the main exit of the hospital and caught a cab to take her back to her car.

By the time Nicki reached home, it was late. She tried to call Sarah right away but got no answer, so she spent the rest of the evening pacing the apartment until Doug called at a little after midnight to tell her Ian was out of danger. In spite of the tensions between them, she found the sound of his voice reassuring. She thanked him for letting her know. The hesitation on his end of the line made it clear that he wanted to keep talking, but finally he said good-night and hung up.

Without her fear for Ian's survival to keep her from thinking about Doug, she could no longer control the tears.

She pulled back the comforter and crawled into bed next to Elmo, who rubbed against her chin and seemed to try his best to distract her with his most endearing purr. But his efforts gained him only a weak smile and a pat on the head before Nicki cried herself to sleep.

WHEN SHE STILL couldn't reach her sister by noon the following day, Nicki went down and let herself into Sarah's apartment. All of her suspicions were confirmed. The place was in a shambles. Boxes were stacked up in the corners, every shelf was bare and lamps stood without shades. Either Sarah was moving or some very thorough burglars were absconding with her possessions.

Nicki heard laughter in the hall just as Sarah and another young woman burst through the door carrying empty boxes. Sarah stopped midlaugh when she saw Nicki. "Hello, big sister. I was hoping I would be able to avoid you until this was over."

Nicki didn't even try to disguise her hurt. "Why would you have wanted to do that?"

"Because this is my problem, not yours. I got myself into it and I have to prove to myself that I can get out in one piece." She turned to the other woman. "Nicki, this is Roxanne—who is about to go to get us all some burgers and beers."

"Gotcha." The woman gave her the okay sign.

When Roxanne was gone, Nicki sat down on one of the few empty chairs. She felt too tired to make cheerful conversation. "So what happens with your graduate program? You're not going to give it up entirely are you?"

"Of course not. Why would I do that? I've worked hard on that program and you've worked hard to pay for it. Which is going to stop, by the way."

Nicki felt empty at the idea that she was being so completely replaced in Sarah's life. "I think it's a mistake to move now, Sarah. I'd be happy to continue to help you out until the end of the semester, then you can transfer the credits and make a fresh start in the fall."

"Transfer?"

"Sure. Why just give up all the courses you've worked on since January? Most of the schools out there will probably recognize the hours."

"Out where? Nicki, what in blazes are you talking about?"

"I thought we were discussing the details of the move to California."

Sarah shrugged. "We could if you'd like to, but since neither of us is moving to California, it would be sort of a waste of time."

Nicki stared at her sibling for a moment. "Sarah, the dean of the law school just offered me Blake's job because Blake is staying in California."

"Is he? How nice for him."

"When I walked in and saw this mess I assumed you were moving there to be with him."

"Afraid not. It would be a little too crowded for my taste."

"Listen, little sister, I have just had a series of very bad days. Show me some mercy and just tell me what is going on here."

Sarah pulled up a crate and sat facing her. "Okay, quick recap. A few weeks ago I had both of my Thursday classes canceled so I decided to take a long weekend and surprise lover boy. I got on a plane to L.A., rented a car, drove to his address and found an enormous tudor style home, two cars, three kids and a dog. The lady of the house was beautiful, intelligent, gracious, and introduced herself as Mrs. Blake

Windham. She identified me immediately as another one of Blake's young research assistants, invited me in for a drink and explained that dear Blake, although the perfect husband in many ways, had one little tiny weakness that involved attractive, vulnerable young women.''

"Oh Sarah, I'm so sorry. It must have been awful.''

"I suppose it was, but Elnora, Mrs. Windham, was really very nice. Apparently, Blake has been like this forever, but she couldn't prove it until a few years ago. She's not dumping him until she can be sure she can maintain herself and her children in the style to which they have become accustomed.''

"Sounds pretty ruthless.''

"You wouldn't think so if you met her. It's sad, and she certainly deserves better than that, but until she finds it, he owes her something.''

"And no one around here knew he was married?''

"How would they? He didn't tell a soul and she didn't care as long as she had the house and bank accounts in California. She hadn't even seen him in over a year, but he decided to return for a visit and moved into the guest house. She'll be crushed when she finds out he's coming back permanently.''

"Speaking of which, if you are not moving, why are you packing?''

"Simple. Blake owns this building. He let me live here rent free so he could have me close at hand, so to speak.''

Nicki couldn't ignore the bitterness in her sister's voice. "And now the jerk is kicking you out?''

"Oh no, he's always the gentleman. I may stay as long as I wish. I don't wish. Roxanne was looking for a roommate, so I'm going to move in with her.''

"I assume you're no longer working for him, either.''

Sarah shot her a dirty look. "I decided I didn't like the job description."

"Now don't get testy. I just wanted you to know that I'd have no problem giving you money for rent."

"Thanks, I appreciate that, but I've already got another job that should cover it. I'm afraid I'll still need help with tuition for a while though. I'm hoping for a scholarship next year."

"Well, it sounds like my little sister has everything under control."

"I'm trying."

"Good for you." Nicki hesitated, hoping she wouldn't sound as left out as she felt. "Sarah, why didn't you come to me with any of this? I would have been there for you."

"I know that. Which is exactly why I didn't want to drag you into it unless I got desperate. You've done a good job, Nicki. You have taught me how to take care of myself, and it's about time you started getting the benefits of that, don't you think? I'm not going to keep dumping on you forever, especially not when you're already running yourself ragged with all the work you do, all the people you have counting on you, and your relationship with Doug to worry about."

"All past tense."

"What is that supposed to mean?"

As briefly and unemotionally as possible, Nicki explained the events of the past few days. "So between Friday and now, I've lost a client, a partner and a lover."

Sarah shook her head. "And you were giving me a hard time. When were you going to get around to confiding in your kid sister about all of this?"

"It's all happened so fast there really hasn't been time. To tell you the truth, I'm still reeling. I don't know where you found the strength to take control of your situation like you did. And although I admit I'm a little hurt that you don't seem to need me anymore, I'm also really proud of you."

"Well, if you're proud of me, be proud of you, because I just tried to do what I thought you would do. And I'll always need you, Nicki. Knowing that you'll be there to pick me up if I fall is what gives me both the luxury and the courage to take a chance at standing on my own."

"If that's true, I'm glad I've been able to give you something you can count on, because I certainly owe it to you. As you reminded me the other day, you carry your share of scars too and all because of me."

"I never said any such thing. I said I'd been hurt, too. I didn't say it was because of you."

"But we both know it was. If I had done what I was expected to do, instead of losing sight of my goals, I would have gone to the Olympics. Max would have gotten his medal. Mom would have a husband, and you a father. Who knows, maybe then you would have been a lot less susceptible to the charms of a father figure like Blake. As it was, everyone was left with nothing."

Sarah looked dumbfounded. "Believe me, Blake was anything but a father figure, and why in the world would you think I'd be better off if Max had stayed around? He had no interest in Mom or me. Unfortunately, I was too young to realize that he didn't care about you, either. Until your accident, I always thought that he really loved you and I resented that. Then when you couldn't ski anymore, I thought it would be my turn to get some attention and instead he took off, and Mom, who was the one who had always made me feel loved, became a basket case. Of course I was hurt, but by Max and circumstances and my own foolish expectations, not by you."

"And all those years you thought Max loved me—you didn't hate me?"

"No. Never. You always have been and always will be my idol. I thought you were talented and smart and incredibly brave. I used to watch you on the slopes and actually cry with pride because I knew I'd be terrified to do what you were doing and you were so damn good at it. After your accident, I grieved for those moments. I didn't want to face the fact that I'd never be able to experience that vicarious bravery again. Little did I know that I hadn't seen anything yet."

"I don't understand."

"All those months you were in the hospital, the doctors were always calling Mom in to advise her that you wouldn't walk again. Then she'd cry and I'd sit there and be frightened, and meanwhile, you'd be off in physical therapy proving them wrong. For all appearances, you were totally broken, both physically and emotionally, yet you were still stronger than anyone I've ever met."

"There was nothing strong or brave about it. I messed up and I just did what I had to do to try to fix it."

"Why do you keep saying that? You fell, Nicki. You competed for years in a very dangerous sport, and one day you fell and were seriously injured. That is not messing up, making a mistake or failing."

"It is when I should have known better. I've never told you..."

Sarah held up a hand. "If this is when you do a confession scene about how Max found you and Chris together the morning of the race, you can skip it. I've known for years."

"How?"

"Because Mom and Max had a big fight about it right before she kicked him out. He told her the story then made the critical mistake of calling you a slut in front of her."

"Are you saying that Mom is the one who sent Max away?"

"Basically, yes, although without your ability to win for him, he probably would have gone anyway."

"Then why did she have the breakdown after he left?"

"And here I thought you were the expert on guilt. All these years you've been feeling guilty because Max left the family, while Mom's never forgiven herself for not making him leave sooner. She was so desperately lonely after Dad died, she would have married anyone. She realized pretty early on that all Max really wanted was a medal in the name of Bernard, but she chose to let him stick around. When she had to face the fact that his greed almost destroyed you, she couldn't deal with it."

"Why didn't you ever tell me this before?"

"Because Mom asked me not to."

"That's crazy. If I had known what she was feeling, I could have settled it with her—told her that it wasn't her fault."

"And what makes you think she'd have bought that? People have been telling you for years that what happened to you wasn't your fault—that you don't have to spend the rest of your life trying to make up for it. But you've never been able to let yourself believe that, have you?"

Nicki shook her head. "I really don't understand this. I thought Mom and I had a good relationship. Doesn't she know that I love her?"

"Yes. And she loves you. That's her problem. As she sees it, in a time of weakness she allowed herself to trust and depend on someone who wasn't worthy of that trust. Because of her mistake, the people she loved got hurt. Sound familiar?" Sarah paused and leaned forward resting her elbows on her knees. "She reacted to her guilt by having a breakdown. You reacted to yours by getting even stronger. She spent a few years turning to everyone else for help, and you're spending your life convincing everyone you don't need any. You two are so similar in motivation but so different in response. But now she's found Jared, a great guy who wants nothing from her except a chance to laugh and cry and love with her. She's put her past behind her and taken control of her life again by returning his love. And you've found Doug. Do you want me to take the comparison one step further or can you fill in the blanks yourself?''

''I can fill them in but probably not the way you'd want me to. Doug and I have no future.''

''Then I guess I wonder just what your future is. An endless stream of successful cases and satisfied clients—one obligation met and replaced by another—day after day, followed by lonely nights? Back when you were skiing, besides being proud of you, I was enthralled by your determination, your energy and that magic light that glowed in your eyes announcing to the world that you had a dream. So what are your dreams now, Nicki? What do you want for yourself? Or are you so afraid of falling again that you've given up on dreams completely?''

''You are the one who keeps talking about how brave I am. I have no illusions. I am perfectly capable of giving love, but I don't have the necessary courage to trust anyone to love me.''

''I know it's scary to let your guard down enough to believe that someone really cares about you. If it's someone like Blake, you end up feeling like a fool. But you can't let the fear of appearing gullible keep you from ever taking a chance on someone special like Doug.''

''And what is it that makes you think Doug is such a find?''

''Because he's a lot like you. He understands you. He cares about you. And of all the people you know, even those of us who love you, he's the only one who has never used you.''

"I have no way of knowing that."

"I think you do, Nicki, because I think that's what your heart will tell you as soon as you're willing to give it the chance."

Nicki started to respond but was interrupted when Roxanne burst through the door. "Okay you guys, heart-to-heart is over. Lunchtime."

Sarah gave Nicki a wink. "As I recall, intense emotional upset never had any effect on your appetite."

"You recall correctly, and that's especially true when we're dealing with junk food." She took the bottle Roxanne handed her and thought about how disappointed Elmo would be if he knew she was having a beer without him. Nicki smiled at the mental picture of the normally sluggish, big orange tabby dashing to his bowl as Doug poured a splash of beer in it. In such a short time, Doug had managed to leave his touch and his laughter on so many of the important things in her life. He had made her happy.

CHAPTER SEVENTEEN

DURING THE FOLLOWING WEEK, Nicki had tried daily to see Ian, but his parents hadn't allowed it. So she was both surprised and relieved when Mrs. Dorchester called on Monday to say they would appreciate it if Nicki could find the time to visit Ian that afternoon.

As she drove to the hospital, Nicki was hopeful that this conversation, besides allowing her to apologize to Ian, would establish whether he still considered her a friend and wanted her help in the future. Ian's expectations would be an important factor when she made her final decision about staying in Riverdale to teach.

The dean had had several more discussions with her on the subject and had been only half joking when he'd said he was launching a full-fledged campaign to keep her. Since they had talked that day in the library, the law school had been requested to explore the possibilities of becoming part of a new instructional program on risk management and malpractice, which would be offered through the medical school to area hospitals and medical practitioners. The dean was very anxious to participate in the program and, of course, Nicki was uniquely qualified to serve as the instructor for the relevant classes.

It had sounded like a terrific opportunity for her. Staying at the law school would enable her to combine teaching and consulting and to cut back on her trial load to take only those specialized personal injury cases that most interested her.

She probably would have agreed immediately if it weren't for Doug. They seemed to be getting along fine, but their contact had been limited over the last week to his presence in her class and an occasional hello in the hall. Even at that, she would be kidding herself if she tried to deny the sadness that washed over her every time she saw him. If she participated in the medical school risk management program, she would undoubtedly have to work closely with Doug, and she wasn't at all sure she could handle that.

If she had other reasons for staying in Riverdale, such as being near Ian, she might be better able to put her personal concerns over Doug aside and take the job.

When Nicki reached Ian's room, his parents were sitting outside waiting for her.

"Ms Devlin." Mr. Dorchester rose and extended his hand. "Thank you for coming. I'm afraid we all owe you an apology."

Nicki returned the handshake. "The only apology owed is mine to Ian."

"I think he'll convince you otherwise. He—"

"Let Ian tell her, dear," Mrs. Dorchester interrupted. She turned to Nicki. "We've been having some family counseling sessions with Dr. Henderson, and after listening to what Ian has had to say about how much you've done for him, we couldn't help but conclude that we had been very unfair to you. I only hope he can learn to trust and respect us as much as he does you."

"What does Dr. Henderson say?"

The woman sighed. "Only that these things take time."

Mr. Dorchester slipped an arm around his wife's waist. "And we almost ran out of time. We're extremely grateful that we're getting another chance. I guess we're both sorry we didn't tell you the truth in the first place. You may have been able to help him even more than you already have."

"It doesn't seem to me I helped him much if he tried to take his life."

"Go talk to him. You might feel differently."

Ian's face lit up with a big smile when Nicki entered the room and she gave him a hug. "Oh, Ian, I'm so sorry. Did you really think I would just pass your case off to another attorney and not see you again?"

"Of course not. Mom and Dad told me that they came down real hard on you, but I don't know why. They knew that none of this had anything to do with you."

"But if you had been able to talk to me first you wouldn't have done what you did."

"I never felt I couldn't talk to you. I knew if I called you you'd come." He shrugged. "Maybe I didn't want anyone to stop me."

Nicki was taken aback by Ian's matter-of-fact attitude, but what he'd said was true. She hadn't abandoned him. Nothing about her relationship with Doug had interfered with the friendship she had offered Ian.

"So why, Ian? What happened?"

"Jerry Phillips got his driver's license."

"I'm afraid I don't understand."

Ian blushed. "Ycah I know. I don't really understand it myself. Of the four guys that went camping together last spring, I'm the oldest and Jerry is the youngest. I should have been the first one to get my driver's license, but because of the epilepsy, I can't apply until I can prove that the medication has everything under control, which means I have to go six months without a seizure. Well, I had just had a minor seizure, so I had to start the waiting period all over again, which was depressing enough, then Jerry came by grinning from ear to ear and waving his license under my nose, and I couldn't deal with it. Dumb, I know, but that was the reason."

"I can't believe something like that gave you the idea to kill yourself."

"But it's not exactly such a new idea for me. This wasn't the first time."

"Oh, Ian, no!" She took a deep breath to calm herself. "Why didn't you ever tell me?"

"Because my parents wouldn't allow it. It was right after I found out about the diabetes. That's why my family moved to a new town and put me in a new school, so no one would know my history. When the last attorney found out, he told us I wouldn't be a sympathetic plaintiff. He thought the hospital's attorneys would make it look like I had deliberately not taken my insulin because I was suicidal or something. Dad was furious and he fired the guy. To be honest with you, I think my parents actually were afraid that I had skipped the medication deliberately."

"Did you?"

"No. I just forgot to bring it, and since there had been other times that I'd missed injections, I really did think I'd be okay until I got home."

"How is it that your last attorney found about that first attempt and I didn't?"

"That's easy. I told him. Dad had taken some pretty elaborate steps to cover it up when we moved here, but I thought you were supposed to tell your lawyer everything. My folks were pretty upset, which is why they never wanted me to talk to you alone. But now they're willing to tell anyone who might help me. As Dad put it, they finally recognize that I have a very serious problem."

"Is that how you feel about it?"

"Yes. But I think I'm going to overcome it. Thanks to Stephanie . . . uh, Dr. Henderson, I'm finally starting to believe that my folks will love me whether I win any medals or not. They aren't like your stepfather was."

Nicki squeezed his hand. "Good for you, Ian. That's an important step."

He nodded then grinned. "Hey, that reminds me. Dr. MacNair hasn't been by in the last couple of days. He's probably avoiding me because he owes me five on the basketball game. So when you see him, tell him I want to thank him for getting my parents to agree to talk to Dr. Henderson with me."

"I'll do that, Ian, but I'm confused. How do you know Dr. MacNair?"

"I thought you sent him. He usually comes in to say hi two or three times a day. He's a pretty neat guy."

"Has he asked you anything about your accident or what happened in the emergency room?"

"Nope. Wait—once he did ask if I'd hit my head, but that was it. Most of the time we talk about sports and school-work. He's giving me all sorts of hints on chemistry."

"Speaking of schoolwork, when are you getting out of here and back to the grind?"

"Day after tomorrow. I've felt great for days, but I guess they wanted to be sure I had my head on straight."

"Do you?"

"Yeah, finally."

"Good. I'll be back before you leave, and you take care."

"From now on I intend to."

As soon as Nicki stepped outside of Ian's room, she sat in the nearest chair and forced herself to focus on the things he had just told her. After all the hours she'd spent agonizing over just how much of the blame had been hers, she found it almost impossible to believe that the answer was none. It surprised her and, in some ways, confused her, but it also gave her a sense of freedom that she wouldn't have believed possible.

As she got up to leave, she saw Stephanie coming down the hall.

"Steph. Hi. You sure seem to be making progress with Ian."

She nodded. "I think I am. Now that the whole family is committed to working on the process, we have a pretty good chance for success."

"Ian tells me Doug set it up. How did he manage that miracle?"

"You know Doug. He can be pretty persuasive when he wants to be. Unfortunately, he's not doing nearly as well with the Risk Management Committee. I hope Ian isn't going to have to go through an ugly trial."

"Are you just trying to pique my curiosity or is there some more devious motive?"

"Nothing new on the curiosity front. I know that Doug already told you he was pretty sure he had figured out what happened to Ian in the E.R."

"Yes, he did."

"And as far as a devious motive goes, I guess I have one. I think you two make a great couple and I want to see you back together. Doug told me what he did, and I can certainly see why you are angry with him, but I can't just stand by and let him hurt like this. In spite of his kidding around, *you* know, probably better than I do, that it's not necessary to look too far beneath the surface to find the vulnerability. And it's the vulnerability that really tells the kind of man he is. It's what gives him the compassion and the integrity to strive so hard to be fair and to do the right thing no matter what the cost. Which is why he is currently putting his career on the line to take on the hospital board and convince them to offer a settlement to the Dorchesters."

"Doug is advocating settlement? I can't believe it."

"Well you'd better believe it, and it's much more than just advocating settlement. He's demanding it. In fact, he's taken such a hard line on this that if the hospital doesn't accept his position he's going to have to leave because he will have accused them of being unethical."

"What do you think will happen, Steph?"

"At this point, I think he'll lose. Doug is confident that his scenario of what happened in the emergency room is the correct one, but it's all conjecture on his part. If he wants the board to agree to a settlement, he's going to have to find some way to prove to them that he is right."

"And that might only be the first step." Nicki speculated. "Even if the hospital administration knows that malpractice did occur, they still might not want to settle unless they think that Ian's attorney can prove his case in court."

"Do you really think that's possible? They wouldn't make him take it to court if they knew the hospital was guilty, would they?"

"There was a time when Doug told me that was exactly what he'd always choose to do." Nicki lowered her pitch to try to imitate a blustery Doug. "'I'd never agree to an out of court settlement again, no matter what. It's about time we make the attorneys fight for every penny they get.'"

"Come to think of it, I guess I have heard that speech. You sure changed him."

"No. I didn't change him. He changed himself. It's all part of that underlying sense of fairness and integrity you referred to." At that moment Nicki realized that she had trusted and believed in Doug all along. That was why she had always been able to talk with him, to confide in him in a way that she did with no one else. If she had been as honest with herself as he had been with her, she would have admitted that she loved him right from the first kiss. Instead, she had kept running from him because she hadn't wanted to lose her precious sense of control. She had been quick to accuse him of playing games with her, but she was the only one who had been playing a game, and she had cheated herself.

Now when she thought of Doug taking on the hospital and risking his career to do what he felt was right, she knew she had to do whatever she could to help him. She had already begun to think about her next step before she realized that Stephanie was still standing there. "Steph, I'm sorry. I was lost in thought."

"Well, if that half smile and the glint in your eye means your thoughts had anything to do with making up with Doug, don't let me interrupt you. That was my devious motivation, remember?"

"You'll never know how glad I am to have found such a sly friend. Thanks."

"Think nothing of it. Paul and I owed you one, and I wasn't sure the wedding invitation would be enough to pay the debt."

"Wedding invitation? That's great. Congratulations. You do work fast, don't you?"

"Not really. I've been in love with Paul since I was a kid, so it hasn't been quite the whirlwind romance it seems."

"No, I suppose it hasn't, but as someone who's lived through Hurricane Doug, I have to say some whirlwinds have a lot to recommend them."

BY THE TIME Nicki got back to the office, she knew she had to call Margaret Orb, even though it meant endangering her own career. She could lose her license if the hospital still refused to offer a reasonable settlement and if Ian's attorney accused Nicki of interfering with his case by revealing information she had acquired while acting as Ian's attorney.

But it was a risk she was willing to take. She had enough faith in Doug to believe that if he just had some concrete evidence to work with, his argument for the equitable outcome would prevail.

The phone rang eight times and Nicki was just about to hang up when Margaret answered.

"Hi, Margaret, Nicki Devlin here."

"Who?"

"Nicki. You remember. You called me the other day and we discussed Ian Dorchester."

"I have no idea what you're talking about."

"Margaret, are you alone?"

"I'm alone, but I still don't remember you, and I'm sure I never had a conversation with you."

"Okay, fine. Then just let me talk for a minute. I know that you're regretting having confided in me about Ian. And I understand why you might be unwilling to testify against the hospital. But I can't really believe that you don't want to do the right thing now and get this lie behind you."

"That's what Doug MacNair keeps saying. He even dragged me in to see Ian, then asked me if I wanted to be the one responsible for the fact that he might not get a fair deal."

"And do you?"

"I have no control over what's fair. That's up to a jury to decide."

"Of course, but there are a lot of different factors that enter into the jury's deliberations," Nicki said.

"I know. Doug told me that, too. He says the jury might determine that Ian's two suicide attempts mean that he places no value on his own life so he shouldn't receive much compensation."

"That is exactly what might happen."

Margaret hesitated. "But he's such a nice young man, certainly the jury will feel sorry for him."

"Maybe. We never know what a jury might do. Which is why, in situations like this one, we always hope to get a fair settlement offer before we have to take the case to the jury."

"So what do you want from me?"

"Go to Doug and tell him what you told me. Then he can inform the committee that there is a witness who can testify to what really happened."

"And how can I be sure they won't fire me or make my life miserable for testifying against them?"

"I don't think it will come to that. If you talk to Doug first, he should be able to prove to the board that his theory about the potassium was right. If the hospital administration is ethical, the knowledge that there was actual malpractice should lead them to settle."

"Do we know if Ian's family will even take a settlement?"

"No, but I'd like to think that if the offer is a fair one, they will accept it and save Ian the agony of a trial."

"And what if all of this is a trick? What if Dr. MacNair has no interest in Ian and, as a member of the Risk Management Committee, he's just trying to determine how good a case the other side has?"

"Then I will probably lose my license for interfering in another attorney's case, and the hospital will start applying all sorts of subtle pressures on you to convince you not to testify. But Doug wouldn't do that."

"You're sure?"

"Absolutely."

"Okay, but I really can't believe I let myself get into this situation. Why is it that we're always so gullible when we're in love?"

"Because trusting is what makes love so special."

"Sure, sure. Tell that to Norman."

"I don't think Norman has it in him to understand, and that's sad."

"Yes, I guess it is. What do you think will happen to him when all this comes out?"

"Not much, I'm afraid. At the worst, he might be asked to transfer his residency to a different hospital. Who knows, he might even be frightened enough to become a decent doctor someday. If not, he'll move from state to state, hospital to hospital, leaving a string of lawsuits behind him, and no one will ever be the wiser."

"He ought to be familiar with that technique. It's the same one he uses with women."

"And it hasn't worked all that well for him, has it? He let a pretty special lady get away."

"I suppose." Margaret sighed. "Now I guess I should go find Doug. Keep your fingers crossed that he's all you think he is."

"He is, and I don't need any good-luck rituals this time."

ON HER WAY HOME from the law school, Nicki stopped to see her sister's new apartment and shared some popcorn with Sarah and Roxanne, who both professed to be on a study break. From any evidence that Nicki could find, the only things that had been studied so far that evening were fashion magazines and the cable television guide. She smiled to herself as she listened to the two young women planning the St. Patrick's Day party they intended to throw. Sarah had certainly managed to bounce back quickly from the fiasco with Blake.

Maybe if Nicki's own ill-fated romance with Chris hadn't been so intertwined with her accident, she would have been better able to dismiss it as an unfortunate mistake that had caused her some embarrassment but left no lasting scars. As it was, she had carried her hurt with her for years and had almost let it ruin her relationship with Doug. She closed her eyes against the painful catch in her chest that served to remind her she had no way of knowing whether Doug would accept her apology. She did not even know yet how she was going to go about making it.

As Nicki was leaving, Sarah told her that Carol Stuart had called to be absolutely certain that Nicki and Sarah would be at the wedding a week from Saturday.

"That's odd. I already told her we were coming, and why would she call you instead of me?"

Sarah shifted her eyes to the floor as if she were embarrassed. "I don't know. I guess she just wanted to do some girl talk and figured you'd be too busy."

"Oh?" Nicki narrowed her eyes, certain that her sister was holding out on her. But after staring at Sarah for a moment, she gave up. Whatever was going on here, she was probably better off not knowing about it.

By the time she'd stopped for groceries and beer and filled her car with gas, it was already long past time for Elmo's evening snack, and he let her know about it as soon as she came in the door. After tripping over him on three separate occasions, she found herself longing for the days when he had been happy to live his life as a lump under the comforter.

"Mind your p's and q's, fuzz-face, or you just might become my donation to the Student Bar Association auction, and you'd better hope your buddy, Doug, will be there to buy you back."

Elmo sat down, blinked at her a couple of times, then began to wash his face, making it quite clear that he wasn't concerned in the least.

Nicki laughed. Of course she would never part with her precious feline but she began to wonder whether Doug would attend the auction and felt a little rush of excitement at the thought that she might see him there.

She had intended to spend the evening reading a mystery, but she couldn't concentrate on it. Her thoughts kept wandering to Doug and his challenge to the hospital administration. She wondered if he was frightened or concerned for his future, and if he would feel stronger or better able to cope if he knew that she supported him.

She was just about to give in to her desire to phone him and tell him she loved him, when Margaret called to report that she had finally made contact with Doug and had told him everything she knew about Ian Dorchester. He'd thanked her for the information, promised to do everything he could to protect her position at the hospital and asked if she would be willing to tell her story to the full committee.

Margaret was quite proud that she had managed to handle the whole thing without bringing up Nicki's name. Although Nicki was grateful for whatever protection that might afford her, she was also a little disappointed that Doug had no way of knowing that she approved of what he was doing and had been willing to take a chance along with him.

Again she considered calling him and then thought better of it. He was engaged in some very delicate negotiations right now and her involvement might only complicate matters. She would just have to wait until the hospital had completed its internal investigation.

The waiting seemed interminable. Nicki was certain that Tuesday alone lasted for at least a week, and by Wednesday afternoon she had put a note on her office door warning away anyone who came to see her about a matter less critical than life or death, all of which apparently had no effect. She was still besieged by a steady stream of visitors, each of whom was certain that their problem met the criteria. She was just about to leave, when the dean stuck his head in the door.

He pointed to the sign. "Is it reasonable to assume that you are harried, frustrated, distraught and in an otherwise weakened state?"

She smiled. "It is."

"Good." He walked in and sat down. "Then let me pressure you for a while about taking the teaching position."

"I accept."

"Honestly, I think it could work well for you if you'd—"

"I said I accept."

"But I thought you were kidding."

"I rarely kid about life-altering decisions."

"Nicole, are you all right?"

"No, but if you're asking whether I'm going to try to get out of this later by pleading insanity, don't worry. I've given it a lot of thought and if you hadn't ambushed me today, I would have talked to you by Friday anyway."

"Wonderful. With your participation this program has the chance to become a prototype for others like it."

"I hope so. Cooperative efforts between law schools and medical schools might go a long way toward easing some of the hostility between doctors and lawyers when it comes to malpractice."

"Well, of course, that's part of what we want to accomplish and that's why I'm so glad you've agreed to join us. Doug MacNair has been the med school contact on this and he seems confident that, in spite of your malpractice litigation background, you will have no difficulty winning the respect of the medical community. He claims you have a unique ability to see both sides of the issue and sufficient empathy for the doctor's position to be fair."

Nicki tried to hide her pleasure at the compliment Doug had paid her. The dean got to his feet and Nicki walked him to the door. "I think you've made a good decision, Nicole. I hope you'll be happy here."

She shook the dean's hand. "I know I've made a good decision, and I'm sure I'll be happy." But just how happy she would be depended on Doug.

NICKI DROVE UP in front of her apartment building just in time to see Paul walking away. She honked the horn and signaled him to wait while she parked.

"Hi Paul. What's up?"

"I'm here on a mission of mercy. You'd better get to the hospital right away and talk some sense into Doug."

"That's more like mission impossible. No one can talk sense into Doug. What's he doing?"

"The Risk Management Committee adjourned about an hour ago, after making a very generous offer to the Dorchesters, which the boy's attorney accepted on the spot."

"Oh, Paul, that's wonderful. Doug must be thrilled."

"To put it mildly. That's the problem. He practically ran out of the meeting, charged down to the E.R., picked up Margaret Orb and started dancing around the halls with her. Poor woman was totally humiliated." Paul shook his head sadly. "And to make it worse, the guy is such a lousy dancer. I couldn't help myself, I had to cut in."

Nicki burst out laughing. "Sounds like just the thing to reestablish the reputation of the E.R. after a malpractice suit—send in the clowns."

"That's just about what Steph said when she saw us. How was I supposed to know the little old lady she was with was Mrs. Bellamy, the head of the foundation that's funding her research project? They can't pull back your funds just because your fiancé makes you do a dip in a hospital hallway, can they?"

"I don't think so."

"Not even if he sort of drops you, right?"

Nicki raised an eyebrow. "Sort of?"

"You will go talk to her for me, won't you? I mean, the engagement party is in two weeks, and we'll need to be speaking to each other by then."

She shook her head, then realized she might be able to take advantage of the situation. "Look, I never get involved in lovers' spats, but this time I'll make an exception. You be sure that both you and Doug are at the Student Bar Association auction on Friday, and I'll get Stephanie to come with me. Then I'll see if I can patch things up."

"No good. Doug was going to be there anyway, but I'm on call that night."

"Paul?"

"Like I said, I'll just have to find someone to take call Friday night. See you at the auction."

As Nicki rode the elevator up to her apartment, she tried to imagine Doug's victory dance and the ensuing scene. Life around Doug certainly never was dull. Margaret was normally so shy she must have been mortified when he'd picked her up. Nicki smiled to herself as she remembered the last time he'd swept her into his arms and whirled her around the room. She knew now exactly what her auction donation would be.

CHAPTER EIGHTEEN

Doug had arrived at the auction a full hour early so he could guarantee everything would go exactly as he intended. He handed a small package wrapped in tissue to the young woman who was assigning numbers to donations. "Now let me be sure I have this right," he asked as he signed the slip of paper she handed him. "I'm expecting someone special to be here to see this. If she doesn't come, there is nothing to keep me from bidding on my own donation?"

She smiled at him. "That's right. It's a pretty common ploy. One of our professors donates her fur coat every year and then buys it back. It's really just a fun way for her to make a cash gift in the form of a bid. But I should warn you, if the students figure out you are committed to redeeming this yourself, they will run the bids way up."

"That's fine. I'll take the chance." He started to walk away then turned back. "You do have my special instructions?"

"Yes, sir. I have a note right here for the auctioneer."

Doug went into the auditorium, put his topcoat and sport jacket on two seats in the front row for himself and Paul and began to pace the aisles.

What if Nicki didn't come? What if she came and didn't bid on his donation? What if she bought it then threw it away? He rolled his eyes heavenward. "Sorry, Grandma. I know it was travesty enough to have it engraved."

As soon as Paul walked into the room, Doug was at his elbow. "You are positive that she's coming?"

"For the thousandth time. I'm positive. She's the one who required my attendance, remember? She's driving with Steph."

"Are you two speaking yet?"

"Not technically, but I think she's weakening. It's amazing how much I miss her."

"I know what you mean, but at least you're pretty certain you'll get her back. What am I going to do if Nicki walks out tonight?"

"She won't."

"How can you sound so positive?"

"I am. Look what she's done for you already. She put her career on the line to get Margaret to go to the board for you."

"Why are you so sure she was the one behind that?"

"Use your head, Doug. You tried everything you could to get Margaret to talk and nothing worked, right? So who is it who can consistently beat you in a debate? Who do you think could be just smart enough, just charming enough, just honest enough to persuade a frightened young nurse to take on a hospital? Who achieved the minor miracle of finally getting Doug MacNair to admit that he made a mistake?"

"You're right. It had to be Nicki's doing."

Paul took Doug by the arm and led him down the aisle to his seat. "Sit down before you get run over. You're in everyone's way."

Doug glanced toward the door and noted the steady stream of people arriving. "How can you expect me to sit still? The place is filling up. Where the heck is she?"

When Nicki and Stephanie walked into the auditorium after circling the parking lot for what felt like ages, most of the seats were taken. They found two together in the middle of the next to last row and had to climb over several people to get to them. By the time they were settled, Nicki felt hot and harried, which was particularly frustrating since she had planned on cool, calm and collected as her image for the evening.

She arranged her coat on the seat, plopped down and began to scan the crowd for Doug. She finally located him, looking handsome as ever, in the front row. Unconsciously she began to straighten her hair with her fingers. Of course, he picked that minute to turn around. Other than a slight grin, he did nothing to acknowledge either her or the familiar gesture but simply turned back to face the stage. He must have said something to Paul, though, because a moment later Paul turned around and waved at Stephanie, who much to Nicki's surprise, waved back.

"I thought you guys were fighting?"

Stephanie blushed. "Oh, we were. I mean we are, but there's no reason not to be cordial."

Nicki raised an eyebrow. "My how civilized." She put her purse on the floor and settled more comfortably into her seat. "And I thought I was going to have a long, hard evening trying to get you two back together."

Stephanie grinned. "Well, I was still mad at him when I walked in here, but now I see him sitting up there, so far away, and I'm beginning to mellow. I miss him. Besides, it's probably best if we're back together before the big engagement party that Doug is throwing for us."

"Doug is throwing your engagement party?"

"Yep. It was all his idea. Personally, I can't really understand the need for it."

Nicki smiled to herself. "I bet I can. And here I was just noticing that he hadn't done anything devious in over a week. Glad to have him back."

Stephanie looked confused. "I have no idea what you're talking about, but I hope you're serious about having him back. When I talked to you outside Ian's room at the beginning of the week, I thought you were going to take some steps in that direction, but I've seen no signs so far."

"The best laid plans take time. Just be patient." She nodded toward the stage. "Looks as though they're going to start."

The auctioneer held up the most atrocious sport jacket that Nicki had ever seen. He announced the name of the professor who had contributed it and asked him to stand and take a bow. Nicki realized that he was actually wearing the most atrocious sport jacket she'd ever seen and that the one being auctioned off was only a close second. The bidding began and Nicki was daydreaming when she noticed Stephanie put her hand over her eyes and groan. "Oh, no, he wouldn't!"

Nicki glanced back at the stage just in time to see the auctioneer point to Paul and yell, "Sold! To the tastefully dressed man in the front row. You may claim your purchase backstage at your convenience, but it's probably not going to fit you, sir. It is quite small."

Paul stood up. "Oh, it's not for me. It's for my fiancée."

Stephanie groaned louder and Nicki chuckled. "Strange peace offering."

Paul turned to the audience. "As soon as we move into that house we saw last week, the one with the big yard and room for a garden, she'll want to be ready to outfit the scarecrow."

"Nice peace offering," Nicki just managed to whisper before the professor who had donated the jacket made a mock attack on Paul only to be restrained by Doug and a woman Nicki assumed to be the man's wife.

The rest of the evening passed in much the same way. Some of the items were serious and some were frivolous. The faculty seemed to exert a real effort to step out of their classroom demeanor and show their human side to the students.

Since Nicki had waited so long to decide to participate in the auction, her donation would not come up for bid until the end of the program. As the long process of auctioning contributions went on, people started to leave. By the time she and Stephanie were the only ones left in their row, she began to worry that Doug might not stick around long enough to learn what she had donated. Rather than listening to the proceedings, she watched the clock and worked herself into a frenzy.

She heard the announcer say, "The next donation for this evening is from Dr. Doug MacNair," but she didn't focus on it until Stephanie nudged her and pointed toward the stage. Her heart skipped a beat when she saw the auctioneer hold up a silver comb. "Dr. MacNair has asked to make a few comments before this lovely antique goes on the block."

Doug stepped up to the microphone and nervously cleared his throat. "This silver and amber comb is part of an antique dresser set that has been in my family for generations. The entire set has always passed from mother to eldest son to be given to his wife on their wedding day. I have had it and cherished it for eighteen years. Now, after all that time, I have broken the family tradition. I've had the comb engraved with a personal message, and before I offer it up for auction, I have another message to deliver." He scanned the crowd, then looked in the general direction of Nicki's seat. "In the short time that we've known each other, I've asked you on many occasions in many different circumstances to trust me. You've always professed to be afraid to do that, and yet, you've given of yourself as only someone who trusts can give and taken chances that only someone who trusts would risk. So now it is my turn. Only a few people in this auditorium know who I'm talking to. You may still walk away with your anonymity intact and allow my precious family heirloom to be purchased by the type of person who wears a horse blanket for a sport coat. I, on the other hand, am willing to risk public rejection of what you have probably guessed by now is a proposal. I'm willing to take the chance that you are going to bid on the first piece of the set I'd like to give you as we start our future together. But whether you choose to buy this symbol of my trust or not, whether you choose to accept the whole set or not, I hope you'll always do what the inscription requests." He pushed his fingers through the hair above his right temple. "Think of me."

The auctioneer smiled broadly as he held the comb aloft again. "Okay, ladies and gentlemen, and I do hope the special lady is out there, what am I bid for this antique silver comb?"

For several moments there was absolute silence in the auditorium, until Nicki regained her composure. Finally she rose slowly to her feet and fixed her eyes on Doug's. "Since I don't intend to let the man or the comb get away, I'd like to open the bidding at one thousand dollars." The students in her trial practice class began to cheer and the rest of the audience soon joined in.

Doug came down the aisle to her seat, gave her a hug and a discreet kiss for the benefit of the crowd, then tried to usher her out the auditorium door.

"Doug, wait—stop—ho. I have to pick up the comb."

"Don't worry. I've arranged for Paul to take care of it."

"They haven't auctioned my gift yet."

"So? You don't have to be here for that."

"Yes. I do."

Fortunately they didn't have long to wait. The auctioneer's voice came over the microphone. "Ms Devlin donates an all-expense-paid evening of dinner and dancing for two at any location you wish. The high bidder should see her afterward to make arrangements. What am I bid?"

Doug squeezed her hand and smiled, then waved his arm toward the podium. "I'll match my lady's bid at one thousand dollars."

The auctioneer looked stunned. "Dr. MacNair, you are bidding one thousand dollars for dinner for two?"

"Forget the dinner." He wrapped his arm around Nicki's waist and pulled her close. "The dancing is the important part. And as high bidder, I'm in a bit of a hurry to meet with Ms Devlin and make those arrangements."

This time Nicki conceded and followed his lead to the door of the auditorium, but when they got to the hallway she stopped. "The Student Bar Association is having a party for contributors afterward."

"We'll skip it. They'll understand."

"I know they'll understand—that's why I don't want to skip it. What about my professional image?"

Doug just raised an eyebrow.

"You're right. Who cares about my professional image? My place or yours?"

"Mine. I hope Elmo will understand, but I'd rather have you to myself right now."

As soon as they got to Doug's house, he led her up to the bedroom, where he had already placed champagne to chill in an ice bucket on the dresser. As Nicki walked over to inspect the bottle she noticed that the silver dresser set was laid out beside it. She turned to smile at him. "Pretty sure of yourself I see—as usual."

He popped the cork on the bottle and handed her a glass. "Not sure of myself at all. Just desperate enough to try anything and hope for the best. In fact, you haven't really told me yet. Will you accept the entire set?"

"Of course I will." She winked. "After all, I've already invested a small fortune in the first piece."

He poured champagne into her glass and his own. "I hope you're going to want to secure your investment in the not-too-distant future. You have no idea how miserable I've been—how much I've missed you."

"Oh I think I have an inkling. How soon can you get away for a short honeymoon?" She walked over to sit on the edge of the bed.

Doug sat next to her. "Ah, well—" he began to blush "—we can get away during the week, but the next few weekends are kind of full."

"Oh? Really? With what?"

"Come on, Nicki. I had to prepare for the possibility that you wouldn't be there tonight."

"And what would you have done in that case?"

"Well, first, since you wouldn't even have had a chance to buy the comb, I would have had to buy it back myself. Then I have a date planned for us every weekend for the next month."

"I might have refused."

"You couldn't have. I had Sarah confirm with Carol that you were going to the wedding next weekend, and then I begged an invitation. The weekend after that is Paul and Stephanie's engagement party, which is costing me a fortune, but I knew you'd consider it a command appearance."

Nicki grinned. "I thought that might be the reason you were being so generous."

Doug simply nodded in acknowledgment. "Then there's the cocktail party at my house for the combined law and medical faculty of the risk management program, another must for you, and finally a St. Patrick's Day party hosted by Sarah and Roxanne but funded by me. By that time I figured I'd have worn you down enough to wrangle a real date but, as a safety precaution, I talked Ian into trading weight training lessons for chemistry tutoring so whenever you met him at the gym, I'd be there too."

"You do think of everything."

"Like I've always said. I'm a man who makes my own chances."

"You certainly do, and that includes the one you made for me." She touched the rim of her glass to his in a toast. "Thank you for giving me another chance to dream."

He took a sip of champagne then put his glass aside and wrapped his arms around her tightly. "I can't take credit for that, curly-top. That's one chance we made together for one dream that we'll always share."

Nicki breathed a contented sigh as she took her next taste of champagne from his lips.

HARLEQUIN SIGNATURE EDITION

VIOLET WINSPEAR

HOUSE OF STORMS

Editorial secretary Debra Hartway travels to the Salvador family's rugged Cornish island home to work on Jack Salvador's latest book. Disturbing questions hang in the troubled air over Lovelis Island. What or who had caused the tragic death of Jack's young wife? Why did Jack stay away from the home and, more especially, the baby son he loved so well? And—why should Rodare, Jack's brother, who had proved himself a man of the highest integrity, constantly invade Debra's thoughts with such passionate, dark desires...?

Violet Winspear, who has written more than 65 romance novels translated worldwide into 18 languages, is one of Harlequin's best-loved and bestselling authors. HOUSE OF STORMS, her second title in the Harlequin Signature Edition program, is a full-length novel rich in romantic tradition and intriguingly spiced with an atmosphere of danger and mystery.

Watch for HOUSE OF STORMS—coming in October!

HOFS-1

Temptation™

TEMPTATION WILL BE EVEN HARDER TO RESIST...

In September, Temptation is presenting a sophisticated new face to the world. A fresh look that truly brings Harlequin's most intimate romances into focus.

What's more, all-time favorite authors Barbara Delinsky, Rita Clay Estrada, Jayne Ann Krentz and Vicki Lewis Thompson will join forces to help us celebrate. The result? A very special quartet of Temptations...

- **Four striking covers**
- **Four stellar authors**
- **Four sensual love stories**
- **Four variations on one spellbinding theme**

All in one great month! Give in to Temptation in September.